Allan McFadden trained as a secondary school music teacher. He has worked as a teacher, composer, arranger and actor. With fellow Australian Peter Fleming he has written many musicals: *Airheart; Noli me Tangere and Madame De*. His first published novel was *Big Gig in Rock 'n Roll Heaven* and he is the author of the 'Dougay Roberre' series. All books are published by Austin Macauley.

For Bill Conn

Allan McFadden

SUMBAR ON SUMBEACH

AUSTIN MACAULEY PUBLISHERS™

LONDON * CAMBRIDGE * NEW YORK * SHARJAH

A CIP catalogue record for this title is available from the British Library.

ISBN 9781035862290 (Paperback)
ISBN 9781035862306 (ePub e-book)

www.austinmacauley.com

First Published 2024
Austin Macauley Publishers Ltd®
1 Canada Square
Canary Wharf
London
E14 5AA

Introduction

Sumbeach on the Gulf of Thailand is home to fishermen, tradesmen, labourers, businessmen, policemen, service providers, expats and tourists all going about their lives in measured tranquillity under the heat of the oriental sun—its bars, restaurants and golf courses overlooked by the towering *L'Hotel Majestique.*

Sumbar, a short walk along the beach, offers upstairs rooms with a sea view, a swimming pool and cold beers in the noon-day sun.

For Australian tourist, Jack Featherstone, *Sumbeach* is a locale to relax in, on a stopover to Paris.

For wealthy Texan businessman, Donald Randalson Jnr, *Sumbeach* offers a week of golf.

For Australian librarians, Beatrice Young and Eugene Parry, *Sumbeach* is a place for unexpected love and the exposure of dark secrets.

For English policewoman, Amelia Sanderson, *Sumbeach* is where she'll search among the expats for a murderer.

Overseeing all is Police Captain Choniburshakanari. He knows everything about the activities in his sleepy town, particularly among the expats. Or does he?

Sumbeach is an idyllic paradise, though that may be a façade, particularly when the disparate guests celebrate a fortieth birthday at *Sumbar on Sumbeach.*

Notes

Sawadee means hello / welcome.

Thank you in Thai is said differently for a man and a woman—*Khob Khun Khrup* (male) and *Khap Khun Kha* (Female).

Pord means please.

The village of *Sumbeckarnawan* is fictitious though the towns of *Cha-Am* and *Hua Hin* exist.

Chapter 1

The large white tourist coach, sides emblazoned with *Wild Orchid Vacations* in purple and pink, eased its way out of the semi-circular driveway of the towering *L'Hotel Majestique*. Bouncing over the kerbside drain with an audible *thump!,* the mix of middle-aged and elderly Western package tourists exclaimed *ughh* as it hit and then bounced from side to side. By the time their self-conscious laughter had settled, the bus had come to a complete halt. Horns blasted. A tuk-tuk, spewing blue smoke, gyrated noisily by and braked suddenly, stopping in the path of an oncoming elephant.

Chaos—though no one seems to mind, thought Sally Baker. *If this had occurred back home, there'd be foul language leading to fisticuffs in the street.* Here, in the Asian heat, no one had the desire to become overly excited about a small inconvenience such as an elephant blocking traffic.

By contrast, inside the coach, the tourists scrambled for their phone cameras and began clicking—pushing and straining forward to gain a clear view through the large front window and then through the side windows as the elephant passed. Sally watched on in delight as people on the footpath, without breaking step, eased to one side allowing the lumbering beast through. *Perhaps elephants walk down this street every day,* she thought.

After taking several hastily shot photos, Sally fell back in her seat, placing her phone carefully back into her handbag. She commented to the woman next to her, "I've never seen an elephant! Well, maybe as a child—no, I can honestly say I never have. What a magnificent animal. And it was perfectly happy to be led along by that man in front."

"Didn't you see he had leaves in his hand?" questioned Sally's neighbour. "He was teasing the elephant, leading it on with temptation. He'll stop down at that market we visited last night and charge people to take photos of their children with it."

Sally considered that. "Still, I guess he has to pay for its up-keep and survival, some way. It was huge."

"The Asian elephant is not as big as the African," said the woman, dismissively.

Sally leant into her. "Have you been to Africa?"

"Of course."

"Oh, I never have. This is my first time in an exotic land."

"Exotic? Thailand is actually quite civilised."

The coach seemed to be crawling forward, though it was hard to tell, as the people strolling by were moving at the same pace.

Sally had enjoyed her twelve days in Thailand. She'd saved for two years for this fourteen day package from the UK with flights, accommodation and all internal transport included in the price. On arrival she'd been confronted by the Asian heat and seemingly disorganised bustle, though in a short time she had come to appreciate the many differences to home. For her the elephant lumbering by the coach topped off everything perfectly, ready now to return, happy she'd taken the chance offered her in that newspaper advertisement.

"It's very different here," she said.

"Yes, it's not England," said the woman in a North American accent with a slightly sneering tone.

Sally was not to be put off. "Last week I took a tour—the bus and boat were much smaller than this—from Bangkok up to the River Kwai. It was so beautiful on the river. Hard to imagine all that war tragedy. I mean, I've seen the film on the tele back in the old days, but it really is placed into perspective when you actually visit it. And the horror of that prisoner camp as well." Sally couldn't resist adding, "You've been, of course?"

"Of course."

Sally quietly enjoyed her unregistered dig at her neighbour's pomposity. *Opinionated people are so difficult to engage in conversation*, she thought.

Seated by the window, Sally turned her gaze outwards onto the street, as the bus started creeping forward, picking up a little speed. She noticed the mix of Thais, expats and tourists stepping onto the footpath to let the bus squeeze by.

"My god!"

Her head turned quickly to get a better look. She snatched for the phone inside her handbag, looked at its face and searched for the camera icon, cursing her eye sight. *Where are my reading glasses?* She touched the top of her head.

She pulled the glasses down and tapped the icon. Lifting the phone to her eyes she searched through the window and onto the street beside her.

"He's gone," she said out loud and then under her breath, "Oh no!"

The woman beside Sally looked at her unconcerned, her gaze returning down the aisle of the bus and onto the road ahead.

"Come on, where'd you go?" Sally began searching the footpath out of her window, pressing her face to the glass to see as far forward as she could.

Then she saw him up ahead. He was talking with another man. As the bus pulled alongside him, she clicked. The coach braked suddenly and she lurched forward.

Moving on, the bus caught up with the man. He had a baby in his arms. He stepped up onto the footpath and then the front step of a restaurant to get a little further from the huge vehicle. It was then, as he turned slightly towards her, that she clicked once more. The coach lurched forward as the road ahead suddenly cleared and became wider, accelerating towards Bangkok.

Sally looked behind her, desperately trying to see through the advertisement for *Fabulous Thailand* which covered the large rear window.

She sat back, unable to settle. Had she really seen what she thought she had? Had she really seen *him*? Her hands shook as she picked up her phone and checked the snap she'd taken. It was a man in profile and from above she noted his hair was thinning. The baby he carried looked Thai. *Is it him?* Sally questioned again as memories from over thirty years flooded back—Doreen as a baby, Doreen's first day at school, Doreen's first day as a hairdresser and of course Doreen's wedding.

Fifteen minutes later, still muddling things over in her mind, and slightly shaking, she excused herself, pushing past her neighbour. She swayed down the aisle to the front of the coach and stopped by the Thai guide.

"Excuse me, sir?"

"Yes, Madam?"

"That town we just left—where we stayed last night—what is its name again?"

The guide looked at her and stated as clearly as he could: "*Sumbeckarnawan.* For you, *Sumbeach.*"

*

Sally's flight landed at Heathrow on time, a little after 7am. She took the tube to Kings Cross station and from there a train to Newcastle upon Tyne. She was home by dinner, though she didn't stop to eat. Dropping her bags by the front door, she immediately rang the mobile of her twin sister. "Wendy, are you home?"

"Yes."

"I'm on my way over."

"Did you meet a gentleman in Thailand?" asked Wendy, ever hopeful.

"Better than that."

"What can be better than a …?"

Sally had hung up. Wendy put the kettle on.

*

"Have you eaten?"

"No, that can wait." Sally pushed by her twin and headed to the living room. "You'd better sit down."

Bemused, Wendy knew there was no stopping Sally once she had her mind made up. She did as she was asked.

Sally patted her hands on her knees, waiting a moment. "I saw him. I saw him in Thailand."

"Who?"

"Harry Brown."

Mere mention of the name gripped Wendy as if in a vice. Sally waited. Then she rose from her arm chair and joined her sister on the lounge, holding her hand for comfort.

Wendy took a deep breath and asked quietly, "Are you sure?"

Sally took out her phone and showed her the photograph she'd snapped on the coach.

Wendy studied it. "Dear Lord, you may be right."

*

Next morning Sally walked into her local police station and stood in front of the desk sergeant.

"Can I help you, Madam?"

Taking out a sheet of paper from her handbag, Sally nervously cleared her throat. "I've written down the pertinent details for you." She passed it over. "About twenty years ago, my niece Doreen Brown was found strangled in her bath, here in Newcastle. Her husband disappeared immediately afterwards. Three days ago I saw him—Harry Brown—alive as you and me, walking down a street in Thailand."

Chapter 2

Port Macquarie sits on the east coast of Australia, between Sydney and Brisbane. Always a popular holiday destination, enough people have settled there to constitute it as a city.

Jack Featherstone had done that. Holidaying as a young man, he'd fallen for local beach girl, Jenny, married her and stayed on. Using his carpentry skills to build houses for the growing population, he'd studied architecture at night and began designing them. And then he'd bought a timber yard—all because somewhere in his past he had grown tired of climbing ladders.

Now he sat in his soon-to-be-no-longer office watching Morgan Cook, solicitor, check through the contract of sale.

Morgan looked up and satisfied, turned to his client. "Everything is in order, Mr Ferndale. You can transfer the money now."

Simon Ferndale studied his laptop, opened his bank account and clicked 'Pay'. The solicitor first offered Jack his embossed pen and then witnessed both signatures. Simon reached forward and shook Jack by the hand.

"Simon, *Featherstone Timbers* is all yours. Thank you, you have just made me filthy rich."

"If I'd known that, I'd have dealt a harder bargain," joked Simon.

They'd known each other for many years. Jack had supplied architectural plans for many of the apartments and town houses Simon had constructed in and around the area. When Jack and Jenny had invested their life savings in the timber mill, Simon was the first builder through the door, placing a larger than necessary order.

"Simon, this is a growth area. You know that! Retirees from Sydney and Melbourne everywhere! You'll have your money back in a couple of years. See that timber going out the gate on the back of that truck? That's *your* sale. It's no longer mine. Enjoy."

"A celebratory drink at the hotel on the corner?" asked Simon, closing his laptop.

"Sounds good. First I have to visit my travel agent. I'm taking a long awaited holiday."

"Somewhere special, I hope," commented Morgan.

"Thailand, France and then—who knows. Your contract of sale stipulates that I can't set up a business in the area for at least three years, so—I just might never come back."

*

Perth, on the opposite side of the Australian continent, is a bright, brash city, trying to match Sydney in every aspect. It has grown thanks to the discovery of iron ore to its north and the subsequent mining boom.

Beatrice Young, as she did every workday morning, sat on the passenger ferry crossing the Swan River from South Perth to the pier on the city side. From there she walked a few blocks north to the State Library of Western Australia. She loved her workplace with its lack of pandemonium, its stillness and its silence. The first six years of her working life had been spent teaching first grade. Sitting at her desk in the library she'd often wonder how any child could possibly learn in the hub-bub of a classroom.

She'd lost her husband in a motorbike accident early in their marriage. Now the quiet, the aloofness inherent in her job, made her less interested in organised social activities. She'd lately offered excuses, such as: *Sorry, Sarah-Jane, I can't. I've got to paint my toenails tonight.*

A shadow fell over her computer screen. Beatrice glanced up and smiled.

Eugene Parry, a grey haired, fastidiously groomed manager returned her smile. He made a drinking motion with his right hand, little finger elegantly extended. Beatrice glanced at her watch and held up her ten fingers. Eugene nodded and left.

Sarah-Jane seated at her desk behind, leant forward and whispered, "How many times have I told you? He's gay."

Beatrice smiled. "Of course, but he does buy me an exceptional cup of coffee."

Sarah-Jane was unconvinced. "Beatrice, you're too young. You can't live the rest of your life as a librarian spinster."

"I'll be fine," replied Beatrice, clicking 'save' on her computer keyboard. "I know I'm Eugene's handbag. That's okay. He's an entertaining, intelligent man."

"My husband wouldn't call you a 'hand bag'. He'd call you a 'fag-hag'!" They both laughed—quietly!

"Listen, Beatrice, my brother-in-law is a good looking guy. Okay, he's going through a sticky divorce at the moment, his wife's trying to bleed him dry, and he has the three kids every second weekend, but he's rather appealing."

"Do you do stand-up comedy, Sarah-Jane?"

"Okay, okay, go to Thailand with a gay man. But when you're sitting in the sun by the pool, drinking your third Pina Colada, and the guy you're with is *not* interested in you when you undo your bikini top, remember there might be a future for you back here in South Fremantle."

"You *do* do stand-up!"

*

Jack Featherstone stood by the gravestone, held by the stillness in the air.

"I'm going overseas, Jen. Thailand, then France, then who knows where. No matter where, you'll always be with me, you know that."

*

Eugene was seated in their usual coffee shop. Beatrice joined him. The waitress brought the two cups and a slice of carrot cake with two spoons, on cue.

"You are always so organised, Eugene," said Beatrice, smiling, gathering her skirt underneath her as she sat. "And generous—buying my daily coffee."

"You're my project, Beatrice."

"Project?"

"Yes, I don't have a sister, so I've decided that you can be her. A daily cup of coffee is a small price to pay for an adopted sibling." He smiled, blew a long cooling breath over his hot cup and sipped. He placed it carefully on the saucer. "Now, everything's still okay? No last minute hold up or spanner in the works?"

"No, everything's fine. Don't panic," reassured Beatrice. "Coffee's good. Then again it always is."

"It's not that I'm panicking, it's just that I'll be away for the next two days. I have to visit an aunt in Kalgoorlie of all places. Heat and all those beefy miners—how will I ever cope?"

"I'm sure you'll find a way," smiled Beatrice.

"I'm afraid you'll have to find your own way to the airport as I'll be coming directly from out there. Probably won't even have time to wash off all that gold dust."

"I'm a big girl now, Eugene, I'll manage."

"And I apologise in advance—I couldn't get the honeymoon suite. However, the room will be neat and clean, though basic."

"You're paying for the room, so I'm not complaining. What's the town called again?"

Eugene sipped his coffee. "*Sumbeckarnawan*—very quiet."

"Sounds like a perfect spot to tan, swim and read. You've obviously been there before?"

"Oh, yes. Your poolside reading won't be interrupted. Nothing exciting ever happens there."

*

"Everything I was waiting for has fallen into place," confessed Jack, "so don't cancel my flight please."

"It's all still in your name, Mister Featherstone. Your flight is safe," reassured Ms Gorridge, the local travel agent. "And for accommodation?"

"All covered. I was there five, six years ago with my wife, and since then the owner of this beach-side bar keeps sending emails about the refurbishments and extensions he's managed to do during that time. Some new rooms have been added above the original restaurant and he's put in a pool out the back. Obviously, we were paying far too much for his drinks," Jack joked. "It's a great spot—right at the beach, on the Gulf of Thailand."

"So you'd recommend it? I have clients always asking me for safe, not too expensive, out of the way places. Where is it exactly?"

"About three to four hours south of Bangkok, on the Malay peninsula side. Lots of expats live there, so there are several good restaurants in town. *Sumbeckarnawan*—*Sumbeach* for short. His bar and rooms are right on the sand. Rather obviously, he's called it *Sumbar on Sumbeach*."

The travel agent escorted Jack to the front door. "Jack, you have my business card. When you finally decide it's time to come home, send me an email and I'll book you a flight out of wherever in the world you are."

"That's a deal." He shook her hand and thanked her. As the door was closing, Jack stopped it with his foot. "Oh, sorry, I forgot, Ms Gorridge. Can you arrange a car transfer from Bangkok Airport for me, please?"

"Of course—what was that beach town called again?"

Chapter 3

On television, the spinning sign outside New Scotland Yard appears much larger than it actually is, being framed to carry gravitas.

DCS Amelia Sanderson sat on a bench in a corridor in one of the floors above street level. She wondered why her long-time friend and then fellow graduate, Assistant Chief Constable David McPherson, had summoned her to Scotland Yard and not to his home. *If there's anything he needs to tell me, he can simply ask Cathy to call me,* she thought.

She sat and waited. Male officers walked by, pretending to ignore her. Even conservatively dressed, her blonde hair and striking facial features made her a head turner. She was relieved none of them stopped to offer her a cup of the regulation plastic flavoured coffee, as an introduction to obtaining her telephone number, which she knew she'd never give out.

"DCS Sanderson?"

Amelia surfaced from her reverie. "Yes." She stood.

"I'm Detective Sergeant Houghton." A tall dark haired man stood over her. "Please come this way, ma'am."

Amelia picked up her small overnight case and followed him down the corridor to the end room. DS Houghton opened the door for her and she entered past him and took a seat. "ACC McPherson will be here shortly". He sat in the room with her.

After a pause Houghton asked, "Pleasant train trip?"

Before she could reply, the door burst open and McPherson entered. "Amelia! So good to see you!"

Amelia stood and they put their arms around each other, genuinely hugging.

"Sergeant, you didn't see that," stated McPherson. "No sexual harassment took place here. There's no way you can possibly say that DCS Sanderson threw herself upon me. It simply won't hold up in court."

"No, sir. I …"

McPherson dropped his voice and smiled. "Roger, get yourself a coffee."

Good luck, thought Amelia.

"The DCS and I are going to talk about old times for a while. I'll let you know when I need you."

"Yes, sir." Houghton gently closed the door behind him, turning the handle so as not to slam it.

"Amelia, you're looking terrific."

"So are you. A bit grey around the temples. Probably brought on by all that promotion you've never knocked back."

"Definitely. Now, you'll be staying the night with us." And before she could object, he added, "No, no. I insist. Actually, Cathy insisted. When she heard you were coming she said she wanted to prepare something special. She's been experimenting lately with sauces. I'm hoping tonight she's going to add chicken to one of them. So, Amelia, I should be home by seven."

Amelia asked quietly, "Davey, what's this all about?"

He sat. She sat opposite him, an interview table between them. Amelia tapped it. "I've never sat on this side before," she admitted, humour in her voice.

McPherson cleared his throat. "Three weeks ago a sixty-two year old woman from Newcastle holidayed in Thailand. From a tourist coach she recognised a man." He touched his folder, though didn't open it. "A Harold Keith Brown— name ring a bell?"

Amelia considered that. "No."

"About twenty years ago we believe he strangled his wife in a bath and fled the country. This Newcastle woman is the dead wife's aunt. The dead woman's mother is her twin sister, so the identification carries a lot more weight than one from say your 'run-of-the-mill crank'. Do you feel like a holiday in Thailand?"

"Thailand?" Amelia asked, taken aback. "A holiday, Davey?"

"Sort of. I'd like the identification verified." Davey studied his old friend a moment. "You seem wary, Amelia. You won't be out of pocket. As usual there's not much money to fling at this but I've managed to get enough to cover air fare, accommodation and per diems, though the pound exchange rate is pretty good over there, so you shouldn't go without. From the outset I need to say you'll have no power of arrest. We just want to know if you think it's him or not."

"You want me to go out there and … Thailand is a large country. It would be 'needle in a haystack' stuff."

"I can narrow it down for you. He was spotted in a beach town called," Davey opened the folder and consulted his notes, "*Sumbeach*. That's not its Thai name—it's what all the expats call it. And he had a baby in his arms." He read from the file, "A Thai-looking baby, jet black hair."

He looked up to Amelia, "So he's probably shacked up with some innocent, unsuspecting Thai woman who idolises him, not knowing his violent history."

He glanced at his notes again. "Walking casually, out strolling, looking like a local." He closed the folder. "That's what this witness says. She goes on to say that he stopped to chat to another expat. So, I think he definitely lives there. All we want to know is if it's him or not. If it is him, we'll go about the formalities of extradition later—Foreign Office, Embassies, lawyers, Thai policemen—all that stuff will not concern you. I just thought you might like a break, somewhere away from our superb English weather."

Amelia eased back in the chair though to McPherson she didn't seem to settle comfortably.

"Is there something bothering you, Amelia?"

"No. It's just … Asia, wow! No, for you, for the job, I'll go."

"Good. I know there are a million and one questions still to be answered; however, you won't be alone. I want you to go with another female officer. I thought maybe as stepmother and stepdaughter, so as not to raise any undue alarm among the local expats. Don't be concerned," he smiled, "you will out rank her."

"And knowing you Davey, she's waiting outside, right?"

He looked at his watch. "Not yet—in fifteen minutes."

"Davey, Davey, Davey," she began with confidence, over riding her initial concerns, "of course I'll go—anything to help you. The worst that can happen is I'll probably fall foul of some Asian crime syndicate."

"Observe, Amelia, not engage."

"I'm joking, Davy, though I will probably end up sun burnt and suffering from chronic alcoholic poisoning."

"Mmm. Sounds good. I might go instead." He consulted his notes. "Your stepdaughter is DS Olivia Toms—very reliable, an up and comer I'm told, with a bright future."

"Well, we all once had a bright future."

He looked at her and asked, "Personally—any interesting men in your life?"

"The only interesting men I stumble across, I tend to arrest." He laughed. She paused and steadied herself. "How's the shoulder?"

"Oh, it itches when it rains. But that's fine because it means I can never forget. The twentieth anniversary is three weeks away."

"Yes—and a day doesn't go by when I don't see his face."

"The same for me. You know if the angle had been different, Mark would have only been wounded and I'd be dead."

"Davey, every time we meet, you manage to tell me that. Don't beat yourself up about it. The four of us were great mates and the three of us will continue to be so."

"Amelia, you're far too smart to be a copper. And far too beautiful. Sorry, am I allowed to say that these days? God, when did telling the truth become a convictable offence?"

They sat staring at each other smiling, reliving their different memories. They'd never been lovers. David was always with Cathy and Amelia had always been with Mark. They'd all gone through training together, met up as often as they could and for a couple of summers the four had holidayed together. However, then there was that shooting and—well, with time people move on, move away, move apart.

He sat there looking at her. Amelia read his eyes. "Go on. There's something you want to say."

"This Brown character—we believe he was a driver and general dog's body—we don't know how high up the food chain—in the Newcastle branch of the 'empire' of Xavier Fingle."

"Oh." Amelia began to recall the criminal reach of Xavier Fingle—the diverse and numerous pies he was suspected of having his fingers in.

"Yes, and we believe Fingle got him out of the country." Amelia sat and waited for McPherson to continue. All concerns had left her and she was now one hundred percent copper.

ACC McPherson went on. "Reading the earlier reports, detectives in Newcastle believed that Brown was in possession of something that really unsettled his wife. She didn't say what it was, though she had hinted to her mother that there was something in the house she was very uncomfortable with. What if the wife finally gets up the nerve to tell him to get rid of it? He of course refuses—he is in deep with Fingle, don't forget—and when he tells her categorically 'no' she ups the ante by telling him she'll go to the police. We know that night a phone call was made from a public phone box in Newcastle to Fingle's 'office', the legitimate front for his criminal business. And later that night Brown gets rid of the problem—his wife."

"If he's no one of much importance, just a driver in Newcastle, why would a London crim furnish him a new identity and a fake passport?"

"He has had to have been taking care of something very, very important for Fingle. Special documents, political bribe material, photos." He paused and looking into her eyes, lowered his voice. "Or a gun that killed a policeman."

"Oh, no, no, Davey. That's drawing a long bow."

"Yes, I know. I'm not saying Brown pulled the trigger. From what I recall that night it appeared to be a larger framed man, but Harry Brown would be doing Fingle a very big favour if he kept the gun away from London. As you know I'm a suspicious old bastard, so I went and checked dates. I'm not saying Harry Brown was hiding the gun that killed Mark, but dates allow it to be. That's all. *It—could—be.* So that's why I'm keen for this little holiday of yours to go ahead. We eventually get Brown back here and apart from charging him with his wife's murder, we ask him a few other questions."

"Why wouldn't Fingle have simply had the gun tossed into a river?"

"Perhaps he kept it to plant on someone who one day would try and double cross him. I don't know."

"You only want me to identify this Harold Keith Brown?"

"Yes, that's all."

"Will Thai police be involved?"

"I've been thinking about that and ..."

There was a knock on the door. McPherson turned and called loudly, "Come!"

Houghton entered. "DS Toms is here, sir."

"Thanks Roger, send her in."

DS Olivia Toms, twenty-eight, dark haired and effervescent, smiled enthusiastically as she stepped through the doorway.

Yes, thought Amelia, *a very keen up and comer!* She stood and extended her hand. "Hello. I think you'll make an excellent stepdaughter." Olivia looked puzzled. She turned to the ACC.

"DCS Sanderson, DS Toms knows nothing yet."

"Sorry, jumping ahead of the game," apologised Amelia. "Then I've always been a bit like that."

"DS Toms, DCS Sanderson and I go back a very long way, which explains her speaking out of turn." He winked at Amelia. "Then again she's always possessed a dose of insubordination."

*

"Here's to the best boss a bloke could ever have wished for!" Barry Vardey, Jack's foreman from day one, stood at the opposite end of the table from him. He raised his glass of beer and waited for the others to get to their feet.

Jack's staff had gathered at their favourite Chinese restaurant to bid him farewell. "Let's hope he comes back from Thailand with a mail order bride and the phone number of her sister for Charlie there!"

Everyone laughed and ribbed Charlie, who'd been married three times and vowed 'never again' a thousand times.

Suzy-Wu, the owner of the restaurant, put a large bowl of rice onto the table. "What Charlie, you no wait for me?" she asked, overly leering at him.

They all laughed again.

"Any time you want, Charlie, you say. For you, I poison husband's Mongolian lamb!"

Barry banged on the table, trying to gather back control.

"No, seriously, *seriously*," he went on, managing to quell the noise, "to the best boss. Jack, have a great trip and stay away forever because no one here wants to see your ugly face ever again!"

Everyone cheered.

"To Jack!" shouted Barry.

"To Jack!" his ex-employees chorused back.

*

True to his word ACC David McPherson opened his front door at precisely 7pm. He immediately heard the friendly chatter of Cathy and Amelia from the kitchen. "How many glasses of wine have you two had already?" he called out as he closed the door behind him.

Cathy called back, "Once a breath-test cop, always a breath-test cop!"

He joined them in the kitchen, after having carefully placed his brief case on the floor of the lounge room. He kissed Cathy, both lingering.

Amelia noticed, "Tut, tut, tut!"

Davey cleared his throat. "Amelia, I'm just testing to see if she's managed to get any better at kissing over the years."

Cathy gave forth a sound of mock-shock. "Oh! What a dead-beat for a husband I have. If I didn't still have the hots for him, I'd have left minutes ago."

"Alright, alright," pleaded Davey, "enough of the underlying problems in our marriage."

Cathy laughed. "He hasn't changed." She patted his stomach. "Well, deep down he hasn't."

"*Now*," stressed Davey getting back to his train of thought, "before I forget and drink the rest of this bottle, Amelia, after dinner remind me we've something important to discuss."

He filled the glass Cathy had put on the bench before him and raised it. "A toast—one word." He shouted, "Mykonos!"

The two women exclaimed gleefully and all three drank.

"Ah, that wine is ten times better than that retsina you girls forced us to drink in Greece!"

"*Forced* you?" laughed Amelia.

"And better than the raw onion we were forced to eat by *you*!" added Cathy.

Davey qualified. "Ah, be fair. It was a Sunday, the banks were closed, we only had a handful of euros between us and it was Mark's idea to buy the two bottles of 'high grade' retsina as he claimed they were on sale—two for the price of one."

Cathy scoffed. "We should have known he was lying. No Greek ever sells anything at half price—not around Palmer's Green, anyway."

"However, he did say you girls could have the apple, after we all ate the onion entree. That was a big concession."

Amelia groaned a little. "I've never been able to drink retsina again."

Cathy raised her glass to the ceiling. "God I miss him."

"Cathy …"

"Sorry, Amy."

"What I miss," began Davey hoping to lighten the moment, "is his naked white bum waddling drunkenly over the rocky beach and tripping into the sea."

Cathy laughed and Amelia conceded, "We all miss that, Davey."

"One wave from him, and we automatically stripped off and followed!" Cathy pointed at her husband, accusingly. "Darling, today you'd have arrested us all."

*

After dinner Cathy began clearing the plates. "Stay there, Amelia, I'll do the dishes. You two talk police business."

"Ever miss it Cathy?" asked Amelia. "Really miss it?"

"Actually—*no*." She gathered up the plates and cutlery and left the room.

Davey stood, found his briefcase and took out the file. He sat back down, pulling his chair under himself. "This is what I'm worried about. What connections has Brown made in his community over the last twenty or so years? I can't say. And out there I don't know who to confide in, whom to trust— Government official, expat or local cop. That's why I want you only to look. Don't get involved in anything. Don't put pressure on anyone. Not too many prying questions. You're a tourist, keep in mind. It's a look and see, not an investigation."

"I understand."

"You are a stepmother and stepdaughter on vacation. On the plane, work out the history between you two. Here's the photo the woman took from the coach."

Amelia looked at it. "Not much of an ID—top of a head, sort of a profile— baby looks cute."

"Even so, the Newcastle woman swears by it. So, this is the old photo we have on file." He handed her an enlarged mug shot from an early arrest. "That's the only one we have. Even his mother-in-law couldn't find anything else, anything more recent, not even an old wedding photo. Apparently, he'd burnt anything with his face on before he bolted."

He leant over and tapped it. "Study it. Memorise him. I don't want you taking it with you. I need to protect you while you're out there, so I'll keep it here. That's an early photograph. Keep in mind he's twenty—twenty-five years older now. He'd have greyed, put on weight, maybe even become respectable."

"Even so, Davey, his eyes won't have changed, nor the end of his ears." Amelia remained studying the photo of the dark haired man in his early to mid-twenties. "How will Olivia recognise him?"

"After you left, I showed it to her. She's studied it."

Amelia returned her gaze to the photo. "Nostrils and nose shape would still be the same, unless he's had plastic surgery over there in Thailand."

"Well, let's hope he hasn't. Amelia, I *do* want you to introduce yourself to the local police, just to be on the safe side, so they don't get all high and mighty and official if they happen to stumble upon what you're doing. It's better to be honest with them upfront."

"If I tell them I'm looking for a fugitive, won't they ask to see a photo?"

"Yes and that's why you show them this." He handed her another similarly sized photo.

"You?"

"Yes. I'm the face you're looking for in Thailand. I actually look like a crim in that shot, don't I? This way the Thai police won't need to tip-off anyone of your presence, because in their eyes you'll be looking for someone they've never seen. I am unable to say whether the local police are corrupt or not; however, as you know, it only takes one bad apple. We don't want some young Thai copper having a word with Harold Keith Brown for the price of a Singha beer."

Chapter 4

The overnight train heading north from Hat Yai in Thailand's south eased into Hua Hin before dawn. Hawkers rushed the carriages offering cooked chicken sticks and brightly coloured drinks in soft plastic bags to the passengers leaning out the windows. A brisk, noisy trade ensued.

From the carriage doorway, Werner Weisman, struggling with his backpack in front of him, stepped carefully down onto the platform. He was immediately set upon by an old woman offering him satay which she'd cooked on her bicycle-kitchen, one of many parked haphazardly outside the railway station's perimeter. He smiled at her, courteously waving her away and carried his pack into the small temple-like station house. He propped it against a wall and searched his wallet for handwritten instructions.

Since leaving school Werner had tried many things, satisfying a need to get his hands dirty in various trades. He'd resisted his natural intelligence and the idea of wearing a clean white collar to work every day. After some years of doing that, he'd satisfied his desire to 'get down and get dirty' and he'd applied for university. Accepted as a mature aged student, he decided on an arts degree as he had no idea what he wanted to do. He was introduced to Goethe and Brecht and enjoyed the political machinations of Bismarck. And he'd enjoyed studying an additional course in English conversation in the evenings, off timetable.

Now he was on a year's break and he'd come to Thailand to visit his father. He didn't fly immediately from Munich to the side of his estranged parent, for at the age of twenty-seven, he wanted to see some of the world outside Germany.

He'd spent the three month visa limit in India where his mother's advice to take out traveller's health insurance before leaving home was appreciated. For three days he thought the diarrhoea would never leave him.

Once he'd recovered, he could have stayed there forever. He loved it. India was not Germany. India was loose and easy going; Germany was rigid and uptight. He'd only ever been outside of Germany once—a school trip to

Strasbourg, over the border in France. The region had been fought over for centuries, so that city felt no different to being back home. India? It was as if a light had been turned on. *Wunderbar*!

From India he took a cheap flight to Singapore, bus into Malaysia and a ferry to Tioman Island. There he found his 'beach holiday'—snorkelling in pristine waters, swimming among brightly coloured fish, climbing to mountain waterfalls, a bungalow on the beach and dining cheaply—cold beer, tasty satays, hot curries and barbecued whole fish. The light had been turned on brighter.

He headed back through Kuala Lumpur before meandering north on buses through to Penang Island, the sense of urgency determined by the hours in the long day behind him.

He finally headed north to his father.

The crumpled note Werner had written for himself told him to get off the train at Hua Hin and to take a tuk-tuk 20 minutes south to *Sumbeckarnawan— Brauhaus Helmut*—the restaurant his father owned.

The light was beginning to streak across the dawn sky. Outside the station building, a line of tuk-tuks and taxi-trucks waited for the train from the south. Several families tossed large brightly striped red and blue bags full of clothing onto the backs of taxi-trucks before climbing up to sit on the benches. His eyes had been well and truly opened since leaving Munich and he now relished everything he was experiencing—the heat, the sights, the smells, the flavours. He now knew why the nineteenth century Westerners had referred to the whole area as the 'mysterious Orient'.

He waved to the driver of the last remaining tuk-tuk and said in his pronounced English, "I go 'Sum-beck-ar-na-wan'."

"Yes, *Sumbeach*!" came the exuberant reply.

He tossed in his backpack, and climbed in after it. The driver revved the handlebar throttle and the 'lawn mower' engine squealed into life. Werner grabbed the metal strut next to his left ear as the tuk-tuk crazily sped off, spewing its mandatory blue smoke.

*

Werner stood in front of *Brauhaus Helmut*, his backpack by his feet. The entranceway was open as there were no doors to lock, even if one wished to.

A man down the back was sweeping. He stopped and leaning his broom against a table came towards the stranger outside his restaurant. "Too early—open later," he said in accented English.

"Papa!"

The man's eyes widened. He threw his arms around Werner, both men hugging. This was not as Werner had imagined. His father did not let him go.

"Papa," pleaded Werner, "I'm no longer six."

They stood at the entrance, taking in the changes in each other. It's a big deal to see your father cry.

Werner realised why he'd taken so long to get to Thailand. Deep down he hadn't wished to face his father, didn't know what to say to him, didn't know how he would react. Now all those fears had been instantly swept away.

Helmut picked up Werner's backpack and beckoned his son to follow, carrying it through the restaurant to a room out the back. There, he placed the bag next to a bed. "Not five star, I know, but the roof keeps the rain out and that net over the bed keeps the bugs out. It's Thailand, you won't get cold." He embraced his son again.

"Papa!"

With his arms around him, Helmut lifted his son, and half singing-shouting, rubbed his stubble across Werner's face, as he'd done all those years ago.

"Papa! Put me down!"

"*Wunderbar!*" shouted Helmut, lowering Werner to the floor. "Tonight I need your help. A group of countrymen are coming to celebrate their final night in town. They've been here for a week playing golf, and tonight they will drink, eat and sing. The money spent will pay my bills for the next three months. You speak to them; have a drink with them; make them feel *Brauhaus Helmut* is a home away from home. I want them to return next year. Come and meet Achara." He stopped. "Ah, no. It's early! Come and have a juice with me—my sweeping can wait. So, what have you been up to? Tell me everything!"

An hour later a Thai woman walked in from upstairs. "Achara!" called Helmut. "Look who is here!"

Achara knew Werner's arrival was imminent though neither she nor Helmut had known what day. She smiled broadly, joyously, cupping her hands under her chin and bowed her head. "*Sawadee.*" Petite, gentle, with a winning smile, she was the epitome of Thai graciousness and hospitality.

"Werner, this is Achara, your stepmother."

Werner was taken aback. He'd never thought of the woman in Thailand as his 'stepmother'. According to his mother, his father had 'shacked up with some Thai whore over there in the god-forsaken east.' To Werner this woman did not look, nor carry herself, like a whore.

Achara bowed again, and went into the kitchen to begin the daily preparations.

Werner whispered to his father, "Papa, you've …"

"Yes, legally. I must be the only expat who's actually married the Thai woman he lives with."

Werner turned. A beautiful teenage girl, with six year old twin girls in either hand, had appeared in the restaurant.

"Werner, these two little girls, Gretel and Hannah, are your half sisters! Girls, say hello to your big brother!"

The dark haired, bright eyed little girls held the teenager tighter and moved in behind her legs, shyly looking at the new arrival.

"Oh, come on," encouraged Helmut, "give your brother a hug!" Still the girls stayed where they were. "No? Maybe later. And this young woman? This is Achara's sister, Busarakham—'Bussy' for short. Her name means 'yellow sapphire' and she is the jewel of our restaurant." Bussy blushed. "Bussy works here with us when not at school."

Werner nodded to the teenager. With hands beneath her chin, Bussy bowed her head in reply. Werner knelt and offered outstretched arms to his newly discovered sisters. They held back at first and then the temptation to study the stranger began to overtake their shyness. Gretel moved followed by Hannah, happily falling into Werner's arms.

Helmut applauded, tears in his eyes. "*Wunderbar!*"

Returning from the kitchen, Achara whispered to Helmut, "Do not forget the floors." She stood by her husband. "Busarkham, breakfast cutlery needs placing on the tables before you take the children to school."

Werner sat and the two girls climbed onto a knee each. Helmut saw him looking at Bussy and whispered, "Don't even think about it. Achara watches her like a hawk. You're going home in three months and my wife has plans for her sister to one day marry well."

"I'm not intending to do anything, Papa."

"Good—because Bussy is your aunt!"

Chapter 5

The flight was three hours out of Heathrow. The meal trays had been cleared and Olivia was on her second whiskey sour. "I've been thinking," she said, leaning into Amelia. "I've been creating a back-story."

"A back-story? About what?"

"About you and I and how we became beautiful stepdaughter and evil stepmother."

Amelia pursed her lips. "I don't know that I wish to hear it."

"Okay," Olivia settled back. She waited a moment then smiled beguilingly at Amelia.

"Oh, alright," conceded Amelia, "you're desperate to tell me."

"And you're not desperate to hear it?"

"No. But tell me anyway. It's a long flight. I may as well get it over and done with sooner than later."

"So, evil Stepmummy, this is what happened. Two years after my father married you, he died, and you had to raise me on your own. I was twelve at the time."

"Were you as annoying then as you are now?"

"Of course, but that's the reason we're so close. We've been together for fifteen years, so this is why we can come away together on a holiday to Thailand."

"Well, I can't fault that thinking. So how did my 'husband' die?"

"*In flagrante.*"

"What, during sex? He was having an affair?"

"No, *in flagrante* with you!"

Amelia laughed. "Now you have me really hooked on your back-story."

"After his usual wild Friday night of drinking with the lads, 'dad' comes home and throws himself onto you to enjoy his conjugal rights. He thrashes about in his drunken stupor, has a heart attack and collapses on top of you. He was so

32

fat, so heavy you couldn't get out from under until our help arrived to clean the flat at nine o'clock on Monday morning." Olivia laughed.

Amelia considered the absurdly comical image, daring not to give into Olivia's wild fanciful humour. "Where were you? Why didn't you drag me out from underneath?"

"I was on a girl guides camp with my friends. What do you think of the back-story, Stepmummy?"

"If your father hadn't have died, I'd have certainly divorced him."

*

An hour out of Bangkok, Olivia's tone became serious. "For a while now I've noticed you've become unsettled."

Amelia looked at her, considering her observation. *Too astute by half,* she thought. "Perhaps you notice too much."

"You don't like landing?"

Amelia thought for a moment, deciding she'd confess—a little. "It's not landing. It's Asia. I don't like Asia."

"A bad experience?"

"Oh, I've never been. It's just those news items, films, you know. Many, many people, overcrowding, crime gangs."

"Perhaps you should have watched different films."

*

Jack's flight from Sydney had been late departing. As his plane began its descent into Bangkok, he instinctively over-tightened his seat belt. Once the plane landed, he filed out across the gangway into the terminal and began the long walk through the airport, making use of the sections of moving footpath. He joined the crowded lines at the immigration desks.

His suitcase was circling the carousel and upon picking it up without knocking over the passengers around him, he headed out to search for his name. The arrivals hall revealed hundreds of milling people. Jack recognised his misspelt name on a piece of white paper, held by a smiling transfer-service representative.

"Featherstone," he said, pointing to the computer printed sign.

"*Sawadee.*" The neatly dressed transfer-representative bowed her welcome. "Mister Featherstone, your flight was delayed?"

"Yes."

"No problem. Your flight was not the first to be delayed into Bangkok." She smiled at him warmly. "Please, I take your bag."

"No, I can do that," he said. The woman was petite, slightly framed and so precisely groomed, so immaculately dressed, that Jack feared the weight of his suitcase may break her.

"Thank you," she said, again smiling radiantly. "Please, you wait over here. Because you delayed, I put you with two others. You all go same place. Please, here you wait." She indicated a people-free spot by the escalator and then returned to her position where she resumed watching the emerging faces for recognition of her sign.

Jack did not have to wait there long. The transfer-representative escorted a couple towards him. He smiled at the two Westerners. The woman smiled back.

"Please, follow me, we go down," said the Thai woman.

Jack followed her and the Western couple down the short escalator, and out into the underground bus parking and car pick-up area. Out of the air-conditioning, the Thai humidity hit Jack like a stage curtain dropping in front of him. "Ah," he exclaimed, "That's what I remember. Welcome to Thailand!"

The female tourist turned and smiled, miming a fan with her hand, indicating she felt the same. Her grey haired companion kept walking, his eyes ahead, searching for their transfer car.

Jack caught the word *Sumbeach* on a passing minibus—*All Sumbeach Golf Tours*. In a rear window seat, a straight backed man, wearing a Stetson, grabbed Jack's eye as the bus moved by. From the air-conditioned interior the cowboy's eyes were firmly fixed on the female tourist.

"Ooh! That's where *we're* going!" the woman said excitedly. "*Sumbeach!*" And then to Jack, "Yes, you're right. It sure is hot! And humid! And—I—*love* it!" she exclaimed, immediately dispelling Jack's belief that she wouldn't enjoy Thailand.

The transfer-representative spoke into her mobile then turned to them, "Driver come."

To their right a dark grey transit van pulled up in front of the waiting tourist coaches parked in their bays. The driver was out immediately, and opening the trunk, apologised. "Many cars." Taking their luggage he placed it into the rear of the vehicle. The passengers climbed in, appreciating the air-conditioning lingering inside the vehicle. The transfer-representative said to the driver, "*Sumbeckarnawan. Sumbar on Sumbeach.*"

The driver nodded, she signed his clip board, and he climbed back in behind the steering wheel. He turned around and greeted his three passengers. "I am Danny. I drive. Please—ice bottle water by seat and I turn air-con for you." A blast of cold air shot out from the slats in the rear of the front seats. "Three half hour. I drive—good." And off the van went over the concrete flyovers that led from the airport towards Bangkok's city centre.

Out here the traffic moved freely. Jack remembered the sharp left hand bend not far from the airport. The van sped along above ground level on flyovers, other roads moving into and others leaving the main one they drove along. Sometimes the three lanes of traffic became four, four lanes became five, with no regard for the painted lane lines.

On the way the driver stopped at several toll booths. Each time motor bikes threaded their way in and out, moving to the head of the queue. The driver manoeuvred into the automatic lane, creeping forward and once out the other side, sped on again.

"It's not Perth," the woman commented.

"It's a lot slower paced in *Sumbeach*," Jack said to the couple.

"Oh, I don't mind. I love it! Fascinating." A little further down she blurted out, "It's all such a rich tapestry!" She turned around to Jack. "Sorry, I sound like a tourist brochure!" She laughed at herself.

Lucky man, Jack thought, appreciating her positive attitude. Then considering their age difference, wondered, *A second marriage for him?*

The van climbed an impressively high bridge crossing the Chao Praya River and drove through endless similar suburbs until finally it left the urban sprawl behind and headed south on the dual carriageway towards *Sumbeach*.

The woman turned around again and extended her hand awkwardly over the back of her seat towards Jack. "I should have introduced myself earlier. I'm Beatrice."

"Oh, Jack—Jack Featherstone."

"We're up from Perth. My first time, though Eugene has been several times." Eugene raised a 'hello' hand in the air, not turning around.

"Me? Sydney, well further north actually, Port Macquarie."

"You've been before, I gather?" she asked, moving to get herself a little more comfortable in her twisted position.

"Several times, though not since the last five, six years."

Jack felt that Eugene had indicated she should refrain from speaking because she glanced quickly at him, then smiled at Jack, and turned forward, looking at the oncoming highway through the Buddhist good luck charm dangling off the driver's rear-view mirror. For the first time she noticed the little shrine the driver had erected on the dash board.

"Eugene, do all the drivers have those shrine things?"

"Yes. If they have an accident it gets them to Heaven quicker."

"An accident? Heaven? Maybe they should slow down and not consider getting to Heaven today."

The transit van whizzed on.

Halfway down the highway, the driver pulled into a petrol station/shopping centre/toilet block. He pointed Beatrice towards the 'Ladies' while Eugene and Jack followed him. Eugene walked into the clearly marked 'Gents'. Jack kept following the driver. To his surprise, behind the amenities block was a long trough against a wall covered by a narrow make-shift awning. In the open air, Jack stood with the driver, urinating, their backs facing the remainder of the highway south.

I've certainly left Australia, Jack thought.

*

The House-Guest Manager, immaculately dressed with make-up perfectly applied, opened the door to room 1014 at *L'Hotel Majestique*. Olivia held a hundred baht note in her hand and thanked her. The manager took it and bowed. Cupping her hands in a prayer position beneath her chin, she gently said, "*Khob Khun Kha.*"

As she closed the door, Amelia whispered, "A hundred!"

"Yes, about two and half pounds."

"That all?"

"Yes! Let's hit the bars." Olivia laughed.

Amelia looked about the room. It was a twin, with single beds. "I thought we might have had separate rooms. Sorry about this. I'll have a word in Davey's ear when we get home."

"It's okay, *mum*."

"I don't like the way you've enthusiastically adopted this ruse."

Olivia laughed again and flung open the heavy drapes covering the large window. "O. M. G." she uttered in disbelief. "Have a look at that."

Amelia joined her and they stood staring over the Gulf of Thailand, the evening sunlight from behind the hotel bouncing off and across the water. They stood like that, mesmerised, until there was a knock at the door and Amelia let in the porter with their bags. He efficiently lifted them up onto the bench by the wardrobe and bowed to them. Olivia gave him a hundred baht.

"*Khob Khun Khrup*," said the man, bowing his head, leaving.

Olivia took a key from her purse and started opening her bag. "I suggest we unpack and then go and make a reconnaissance of the town—the bars in particular."

"Who's supposed to be in charge here?" asked Amelia, hiding her anxiety at Olivia's suggestion.

"You are—evil stepmother!"

*

Darkness had settled as the transit van passed under the overhead lighting bisecting the highway at Cha-am and further down at Hua Hin. Five minutes south of Hua Hin, the van left the highway and slowed into a narrow street. In the darkness outside his van's window Jack could make out the ediface of the high rise building positioned by the water. The red neon sign on top read: *L 'Hotel Majestique.*

The van stopped on an empty block. On getting out Jack heard the gently rolling sea, bringing a smile to his face, for he was back where he had so many happy memories of time spent with Jenny.

The driver lifted their bags from the van. Two, thin, mangy looking dogs eyed them without moving from the shallow hole they'd dug for the night. The driver turned the van around, bumped his way back to the narrow road and out of sight.

Eugene picked up his bag and without a word headed off towards the light at the end of the vacant block.

Beatrice turned to Jack, "It's a bit dark out here."

"You'll be fine. Those two killer guard dogs over there will protect you."

"I'm so pleased the Australian sense of humour still works in Thailand."

"Beatrice," began Jack, "may I carry anything for you?"

"No, thanks. If I put the hand luggage on top of the suitcase I can drag both. A bit bumpy here though. It's so dark!"

Eugene hadn't looked back to help. *Marriage on the rocks?* Jack couldn't help thinking.

With Eugene in front as a kind of beacon, the three, spread out in single file, dragged their bags towards the single exposed light on a pole illuminating a concrete path that led past a swimming pool. Eugene pointed and called back to Beatrice, "That's the new pool I was telling you about!"

We can see that, thought Jack. The rear of the old restaurant had been extended and was now dwarfed by the brick veneer accommodation above it. *If the original foundations haven't been reinforced,* the architect in Jack thought, *I hope I'm up town when the whole thing decides to collapse.*

"What an ugly looking plant!" commented Beatrice. "Or is it a small tree?"

Jack looked again to the pool area. "Yes, very ugly."

Eugene was first to the door and pushed it open. Light from inside spilt out onto them. They walked down past the toilets and the kitchen on the left, to a small open space beneath the new staircase.

Eugene called out, "Garry? We're here!" Into the kitchen he called, "Mai! Hello, Mai!" Then to Beatrice he said, "Leave your bag here." She did and Jack followed suit.

Garry Sutherland looked up from the bar as he carefully placed two glasses he'd been drying by hand onto the shelf behind him.

"Garry, we're finally here and..." a little louder and more pronounced, Eugene added, "...I've managed to find friends along the way."

Garry came from around the bar and shook Eugene's hand. "Good to see you again, Mister Parry. I've given you the end room overlooking the sea." He spoke in an English accent, not unlike Eugene's. Jack wondered if perhaps they'd known each other in the past, back in England. "And this beautiful lady must be ...?"

"Beatrice. Beatrice Young. I'm with Eugene, not with ..."

"No, no, I understood Mister Parry's email."

No, they're not married, Jack finally realised as he noticed Eugene relax for the first time since meeting him.

"And Mister Featherstone, welcome back."

"Thank you, Garry."

Jack turned towards the large open doorway at the front, behind which he could just make out the sea. That black emptiness leading to the water was as he remembered it. The rest—the pool, the upstairs rooms at the back—had all been added since he'd been here, exactly as Garry had said in his promotional emails.

A lone couple sat at a table towards the beach, the Western man looking out to the darkness, the Thai woman facing the visitors. The man had turned when he heard Eugene call out; however, he was now drinking his beer again from the bottle, still aware of everything that was being said. The Thai woman smiled at Jack.

"Sunny!" called out Garry. "Bags upstairs!"

From the kitchen, a handsome thirtyish Thai man came to them, beaming. "Mister Parry, welcome back, sir." He looked at Jack. "And … yes, I remember." He looked beyond him down the corridor. "Your wife is …?"

"No. Sadly she passed away."

"Oh, I am so … er, *sad* for you."

"Thank you, Sunny. At least you remembered us!"

Garry, clapping his hands, broke the air. "Sign in tomorrow. Tomorrow I'll write down the passport numbers and all the boring things the Kingdom of Thailand insists upon. Mister Featherstone, room twelve."

"Jack. Call me Jack."

Garry nodded.

"And you too, Sunny," Jack informed the young man. Sunny nodded, pleased to be included. Jack deliberately looking around said, "Big changes since I was here last."

"Oh yes, we basically knocked out all those little rooms," explained Garry. "And halved their number, doubling their size and adding ensuites. And there are newer rooms out back. I've kept you all closer to the front, closer to the beach, closer to the action of Sumbar." Garry laughed at his own self aggrandisement.

From his bag, Eugene took out three bottles of Australian baby formula and placed them on the bar's counter.

"Oh, Mr Parry!" said Garry, genuinely pleased. "Thank you so much! How much do I owe you?"

"Nothing, my pleasure, Garry," said Eugene, waving away any offer of remuneration.

"You're too kind." Garry turned to the kitchen and holding the bottles in the air called: "Mai! Mai!"

A Thai woman came from the kitchen and bowed in front of Eugene, placing her hands beneath her chin."*Khob Khun Kha. Khob Khun Kha.*" She took possession of the much coveted gift.

Two overly tanned men came down the stairs and without a word eased by Jack and Beatrice. To Eugene, the man in front said, "*Goedeavound.*" Reflexively, Eugene replied with the same greeting. The man gave a curt nod, the second man a half-smile of recognition and both continued through the bar onto the veranda and down into the darkness of the beach.

"Eugene, I didn't know you spoke German," commented Beatrice, impressed.

"Dutch, not German, and I only know the one word—'good evening'."

The new arrivals moved to the stairs. Eugene led the way, following Sunny.

Halfway up, Beatrice turned to Jack. "I was sorry to hear about your wife. I lost my husband a while ago. Anytime you need, or feel you'd like to have a chat about things, I have a very good ear."

"Oh—thanks—I'll be okay."

"I'm not a busy body." She turned to go then changed her mind. "Sorry I said that—that was a strange thing to say—came out of nowhere."

"It's okay, Beatrice," said Jack, understanding. "How long are you here for?"

"Ten days."

"Well, I'm sure we'll bump into each other and maybe over a cold drink we can compare notes—or whatever."

"Thanks—yes, let's do that." She turned and continued up the stairs, following Sunny to the room she was to share with Eugene, two doorways beyond Jack's.

Chapter 6

The foyer of *L'Hotel Majestique* was its usual flow of people criss-crossing each other in an extemporised pattern, which was remarkably collision free. An incoming guest had pushed the revolving door and Olivia jumped in the quarter opposite him and waltzed out into the evening's heat.

Amelia, ever cautious, waited until the door slowed, then took a deliberately deep breath. *Asia can't be that bad. You're a big girl now, Amelia. Back home you solve cases, arrest bad men. You can do this.*

Olivia watched Amelia spin towards her. "You know, your legs aren't that bad. At your age you could get away with wearing shorter skirts. Come on, mum, time's a-wasting!"

On the uneven footpath outside the hotel, Amelia put her arm in Olivia's. "Left or right? Come on, I'll let you be the guide."

*

After Jack had dumped his bag by the bed and inspected the bathroom, he opened his wallet and placed his Australian money at the back, folding two fifty dollar notes. He planned on keeping them there until he needed them one day back in Sydney for the taxi ride from the airport to a hotel room. He took out the Thai Baht from the bank's soft plastic wallet he had purchased back home and taking the room key, left, locking the door.

Downstairs he dropped the key on the end of the counter and walked through the bar, waving to Sunny. The lone couple were still seated at their table.

"Ev'ning Squire," the man said as Jack passed.

"G'day, mate," replied Jack, good naturedly.

"Ah, an Aussie," the man said.

"Afraid so," replied Jack.

41

The stranger pointed his index finger at Jack in the shape of a hand gun. He clicked his tongue, flicking his thumb back and forth, as if shooting him.

"I hope that finger isn't loaded," quipped Jack.

The Englishman laughed. The Thai woman smiled at Jack—again.

The Englishman continued, "No, that's good—being an Aussie, I mean. Maybe tomorrow night we can have a drink, or several. I'll be on my own then. Ah, wife's got to work."

"Sounds good." Jack moved off, noting that the Thai woman was not a young bar-fly although she had the features of someone who may have been in her youth. He could tell that youth had been lived tough.

Jack stood on the veranda leaning forward on the wooden railing, making out the tiny waves of the languid sea easing onto the shore, enjoying the warm breeze. *How different to that time when the waves pounded these steps,* he reminisced.

Sunny came to his side. "It has changed, yes, Mister Jack?"

"Upstairs, yes—not this. This is as I remember it—exactly."

"You like Heineken or Singha?"

"Sunny, when in a foreign land, drink locally. Singha, please."

"You want food?"

"No, I ate too much on the plane. I'm fine, thank you. Only the beer."

Sunny returned to the bar. Jack remained taking in the ambience, recalling walking arm in arm with Jenny many a night along this stretch of beach. Behind him he heard the drunken Englishman wolf-whistle.

Beatrice joined Jack by the railing. "Did you hear that deviant?"

"No," he lied. "What did he say?"

"Nothing—just whistled and leered. And he's with a woman."

"He probably can't speak Thai and she can't speak English."

"A whistle is universal, isn't it?"

"Of course. Perhaps he's missing old fashioned conversation."

"Maybe you're right, though I don't think the conversation would be of a very high standard. What could he possibly talk about past his opening offer of going to bed with him?" Beatrice shuddered. "Perish the thought."

Peering through the light spilling onto the sand from the bar out into the darkness, Beatrice asked, "Is the ocean safe to swim in?"

"It used to be. The sea here is quite shallow, not like Australia. You have to walk out a way to get above your knees. However, I have seen it at high tide, and during a storm, when the water pounded the bottom of these steps."

"Will you hold my towel and dress?"

"The pool out the back might be a better option."

"I'll be fine. I've swum in the Rottnest Channel race. Here." She handed her towel to Jack. "I'll give the dirty old bugger a thrill."

She lifted the dress over her head, shook her hair back in place and before running off down to the water, wiggled her bum for the benefit of the man inside.

Jack watched her go, half disappearing into the darkness and then followed her tracks in the sand. He stood with his toes in the water. Several metres out, Beatrice slid down and called back, "It's so warm! Come on in!"

"Tomorrow!" He called back. She laughed and breast-stroked a few metres further out. Sunny surprised Jack with his beer.

"Sorry, Sunny, I got distracted."

Sunny, standing by Jack as he sipped his beer, studied Beatrice, luxuriating, swimming in slow motion.

"Mister Jack, you going to—you know—*fook* with her?"

"No! She's with a man."

"No worry him. He no like girls." Jack turned to Sunny. "True. He have friend here—live in white house up near mountain. Man from Australia—very rich. He here—three, four years—I cannot really say."

"He retired here?" Jack asked for clarification.

"Yes and no. Come for long time then go, come back. Do same again. One day I hope I have money to quit work. First, I want red motor bike."

"Save your money, Sunny, and one day, hopefully, you shall."

"Aussie Gene—he always here, two, three times a year. He's a good tipper when he's in the bar."

Jack let the conversation die and then pointed his beer towards Beatrice in the dark water. "Sunny, I'm not planning on *fooking* her or anyone else. I'm merely holding her towel."

"Ah, you good man, Mister Jack. You know I would *fook* with her. I'd *fook* so good she buy me new red motor bike—rich lady like that."

"How do you know she's rich?" asked Jack.

"She's Australian and white."

"There are a lot of poor white Australian people, you know, Sunny."

"Yes, but they do not come to Thailand for holiday. They go to Bali."

Beatrice stopped swimming and stood waist deep in the water. She waved. Jack raised his beer and Sunny gave her a full armed friendly wave. Beatrice, imitating Sunny, waved back.

"Maybe she like me more than you, Mister Jack."

"Maybe, Sunny."

"Hello, Sunny—beautiful evening."

Jack turned to see a forty-something English expat carrying a baby in his arms.

"Oh, hi, Mister Michael," said Sunny, smiling.

"Little Mickey couldn't sleep, so I thought I'd bring him out." Without losing momentum, he walked on by. Jack and Sunny watched him disappear into the darkness.

"Short and sweet," commented Jack.

"He always walk with baby—morning and evening. He is good father."

"You stopped watching!" exclaimed Beatrice as she approached. "What if I had drowned?" she asked, squeezing excess water from her hair. She took her towel from Jack.

Sunny said to her, "I no help, Miss. Look or no look—I no swim!"

Beatrice flicked her wet hands at him. Sunny shouted in surprise. The three laughed. She wrapped the towel around herself and took her dress from Jack.

"You like drink, Miss? I have all good spirits. Can make Mai-Tai. Best Mai-Tai you ever try. You try my Mai-Tai?" Sunny burst out laughing at his English language joke.

"Yes, I'd love to try a Mai-Tai," said Beatrice. Sunny beamed and headed back to *Sumbar*. Beatrice adjusted her towel and followed.

Looking out to sea, Jack gave up counting the number of green lights bobbing on the water. The local ad hoc nightly fishing fleet was out in their usual numbers. Looking further up to his left he saw the three Thai Navy vessels, a string of lights suspended above from stern to aft. He uttered to himself, "Ah, the King is in residence at his summer palace."

*

The waitress placed two drinks on the table between the two English women.

Olivia leant into Amelia. "I do love a drink with a colourful umbrella." She raised it in toast. "Welcome to Thailand." Amelia hesitated. "It isn't drugged, mummy."

Amelia smiled at her over-cautiousness and raised her glass. The two women clinked. After sipping, Amelia leant back and said to no one in particular, "How gorgeous is this evening air?"

"This isn't the exception," commented Olivia, pleased Amelia was letting down her guard a little.

"Exception to what?"

"It's often like this, I'm told. This—this warmth and stillness—is normality."

"Yes," nodded Amelia. "I guess I've seen too many news reports of monsoons battering the coast and landslides covering villages."

"Disasters and crises are easily promoted on news networks. They rarely show you the ordinariness of most people's lives."

Amelia studied her companion and smiled at how knowing she seemed. "How old are you again?"

"Sorry. I have my father's tongue. He often couldn't hold it."

"No need to apologise. It's an admirable trait although you're going to have to be guarded when dealing with the hierarchical structures within our police force. Surely you've worked that out."

"Yes. I've already come across that."

"Care to elaborate?"

"Not really. Suffice to say it was minor and more suggestive than critical."

"Someone didn't like your input into an investigation?"

"Let me just say, this detective expected me to hold open the door for him and not to contribute to the investigation."

"All women of lower ranks have experienced that."

Olivia laughed at the memory. "He did get quite a shock when I let the door slip from my fingers and into his face."

"Any name you care to share?"

"No, Amelia," grinned Olivia, cheekily. "That would be unethical."

Amelia laughed, her eyes taken by a white concrete three storey building across the road. All the other buildings in this part of town were wooden and old. "This must be the original quarter," she stated. "That large white building over there is so incongruous and garishly out of place."

The young waitress passed their table.

"Excuse me, Miss," said Amelia. "A question please?" The waitress nodded her head. "See that building over there, the white one, why are all the windows blacked out?"

The waitress blushed. "Oh Madame—that—you know—not nice building—that is—how you say?"

"A whorehouse?" Olivia offered. "A brothel?"

The waitress put her hands to her face and reddening further nodded her head up and down. The three women burst out laughing.

The waitress returned to her other customers.

Amelia and Olivia sipped their drinks in silence, looking out over the ever-changing evening scene. A steady stream of people passed by the brightly lit clothing shops, massage parlours, Indian tailors and restaurants. Out front of all of them, stood a spruiker or hostess trying to entice some baht their way. A lottery ticket man with his numbers on a stick stopped in front of them. Olivia shook her head; he moved on. A woman presented brightly coloured sewn cloth, little children ran up with beads in their extended arms.

The waitress returned. "Madame, no buy. They belong to gang of bad men. Come from North Thailand. If they cannot sell beads they will be sent home, back to their families—so better they no sell."

A motor bike stopped opposite, on the footpath outside the white building. There were thousands of bikes in Sumbeach and they all, when not whizzing by, parked on the footpath. It was the rider who caught Amelia's eye.

The man was Thai. He dismounted with a confidence, an air of unhurried superiority about him. He wore an ironed cream short sleeved collared shirt. Middle-aged, with cropped black hair, he was muscular, solidly built. He stood his bike and strode into the whorehouse.

Amelia, curious, leant over to Olivia. "A man just went into the whorehouse. He's wearing an ironed shirt. He is looked after, cared for. I wonder why he needs to go in there?"

"Maybe he ironed the shirt himself."

"Really? Here, I'd have thought a man grabs a polo shirt and tosses it over his head. Done! No, this man carries himself as if he thinks he's important."

"I'll have a look in thirty minutes time," dismissed Olivia. "Should we have a second umbrella?"

Amelia sat forward as the man reappeared.

Olivia laughed, "He's a premature ejaculator!"

The thick set Thai man carried a white supermarket shopping bag. He quickly rolled the bag around whatever was in the bottom of it, stuffed it beneath the bike's seat, turned the engine over and rode off. The two women watched the bike's tail light disappear down towards the fishing piers.

Olivia whispered, "Drugs? Money?"

"Well, we can be sure it wasn't condoms."

"It *is* a whorehouse," stressed Olivia.

"Yes, but who takes condoms *away* from a brothel?"

"A cleaner?" joked Olivia. The two women laughed.

Contemplating what she'd witnessed, Olivia commented, "Tough looking guy, though. He's not our man, so I suggest we stay away from *him*."

"I agree," said Amelia, nodding.

Olivia indicated to the waitress, "Another two umbrellas, please."

Chapter 7

Amelia lay on her bed, eyes wide, staring at the dark ceiling. Although the drapes were drawn, she sensed there wasn't yet daylight outside. Not wishing to disturb Olivia's regular breathing in the bed beside her, she sat up slowly and peered across to the red light of the bedside clock: 5:23.

Come on, you can do this. Go for your early morning walk.

Sitting on the edge of the bed she tried to recall where she'd unpacked her shorts. In her t-shirt and knickers, she carefully found her way through the dark. Silently opening a drawer, she half stumbled as she pulled on her faded favourite walking shorts and quietly did up the zip. She remembered her sandals being left by the doorway, and taking her room card, picked them up as she silently slid out the door and into the lit corridor.

The four elevators were down the end of the plush carpeted corridor. She pushed the 'down' button and waited. After a while a gentle bell rang—*ping!* A door behind her opened. As she entered she reassured herself that only those wanting exercise would be out this early, so all should be safe out there. She rode the elevator to the ground floor. As she crossed the foyer, the night manager glanced up from his computer screen. "Is everything alright, Madame?"

"Oh yes—jet lag—can't sleep—thought I'd see the sun come up out of the sea."

"Out the door, to your right are the fishing piers. That will be the best place to see the sunrise. But be warned—it can smell down there."

"Thank you, I'll keep that in mind."

The night manager nodded and watched Amelia step cautiously to the spinning doorway.

Walking to the end of the street and keeping the ocean on her right, Amelia headed towards the piers. She passed last night's bar and the white whorehouse. The Indian tailor shops were shut tight, the spruikers long ago home in bed. A mangy dog looked at a cat on a wall and decided it was too high to jump up. He trotted off, having smelt a pile of vomited rice in the gutter up ahead.

Standing on the fishing pier, the forewarned strong smell of fish smacked Amelia's nostrils. Instinctively, she turned her head away. *Oh, that's not too bad.*

Her eyes were taken by the three naval vessels. The first of the green-lit fishing boats was tying up on the water below, the two Thai fishermen on board busily folding their nets, ignoring her. She walked to the end and looked over the sea, past the Navy boats, as the first rays of dawn streaked the horizon.

"Mark, it is so beautiful. I wonder why we never came here?"

Out loud she answered her question. "Me!"

*

To the south, on the other side of town, Jack stood on the veranda of *Sumbar* and watched as the sun turned red, assisted by the mounting haze of Asian heat.

Finding a chair he soon nodded off. When he woke the sky was brighter with locals briskly walking down by the water's edge while some others in a group were doing Tai Chi. The occasional tourist was ambling by, walking in the water, with no particular place to go. An orange robed monk stopped by a woman who put baht into the bowl he carried on his belly. The day had begun and the beach would be alive like this until stopping for the noon-day's heat.

Before dawn, Jack had put on his swimming trunks. Stretching, he left his towel on the railing of the front veranda and walked onto the sand and then into the water, wading out, as Beatrice had done the previous evening. He bent forward and splashed the warm salty water onto his face. Further out he half dived under and recalled the first time he'd been to *Sumbeach*. He didn't swim in the sea at all then as its entirety seemed to be covered in large jellyfish. Jenny had joked that they could have walked over the water to Pattaya.

He did a few strokes, stretching his cramped muscles and then floated on his back taking in the view of the beach back towards *Sumbar,* which was jammed against the sand's edge and engulfed on either side by undeveloped blocks of trees and wild vegetation. Above the bar, on a small balcony, he could see his shirt from last night where he'd left it draped over the chair. *The addition of the new rooms has certainly enhanced Garry's investment,* Jack thought.

On the balcony, two along from his, Beatrice slid open the door and emerged. She stretched. She saw him and waved. He waved back.

Exiting the water, he made his way to the spot by the front veranda of *Sumbar* where someone had constructed a large crude concrete bowl on the edge of the existing concrete path. He stood in the bowl's water sloshing the sand from his feet.

He showered, dressed in his room and then walked along the beach towards town.

*

Jack couldn't remember what had been on the site previously. He'd have sworn it wasn't a German Beer House. *Hadn't this restaurant been down a bit, closer to the piers, further up a side-street?* He recalled it was much smaller then, built into the front carport of a house with only three or four tables in the front garden. It was the same name—*Brauhaus Helmut*—though it was hardly a beer hall—even now relocated to a bigger and better fronted property.

As he stood on the footpath thinking, a Thai girl asked, "Breakfast? You want? German. English. Thai—we have."

"Ah, I'll come back." He looked at his wrist watch. "I want to keep walking a bit. I want to buy the morning newspaper."

He moved off, stopped and called back to her, "I promise! I *will* come back."

*

"Breakfast is included? That's terrific! I'm starving!" Olivia was now awake, showered and seated on her bed, her feet hovering over her sandals.

Amelia sat, her back leaning against the room's writing desk, waiting. "After breakfast we should go to the local police station."

"Amelia, have you been out, already?" asked Olivia, suddenly aware that Amelia was fully dressed.

"I saw the sun come up out of the Gulf," confessed Amelia, pleased she'd made the effort.

"You? You went out by yourself?"

"It was beautiful. I'm going to try to see that every morning."

"You'll be seeing it by yourself. Sun gets up far too early for me." Olivia stepped into her sandals. "No matter where in the world I am."

In the corridor, by the elevators, Amelia confessed, "You know, it's not only films. My Nanna also. Ever since I was young she'd tell me: *You've beautiful long blonde hair, Amelia. It is so loved by the Chinese.* I guess I used to think they'd come in the night and cut it off my head."

*

"See? I came back!"

Bussy smiled and showed Jack to a table. He sat, stretched out his legs beneath the table and opened the *Bangkok Daily.*

"*Morgen!*" A tall young man greeted him.

"*Morgen!*" echoed Jack.

"*Wie geht's?*"

"Sorry—Australian."

In English the young man said, "But you say—to me—in Deutsch."

"It was only *good morning*," Jack explained.

"Yah. Okay. So—I Werner. I will welcome you in *Brauhaus Helmut.* Bussy, step sister, will bring menu." He looked up and waved her over. Jack closed his newspaper. It was then that he noticed two little girls attached to the young man's legs.

"Papa?" Werner called out. "It is time to take Gretel and Hannah to school!" Helmut appeared, nodded his greeting to Jack and walked the two girls out through the restaurant.

While the young man stood on the footpath surveying all the morning action on the street, Bussy handed Jack a menu.

"Could I have an orange juice to begin with, please?" asked Jack.

Bussy bowed and went behind the bar. She returned to the table with his drink; however, Jack was now on the footpath with Werner, both surveying the town waking up.

"I am new here. It very good Papa have restaurant opposite police station—very entertaining for me. I watch people come and go and some who walk past—very quickly."

Across the street a policeman stood on guard duty, his sub-machine gun draped over his shoulder, barrel pointing down, with his finger by the trigger.

I'm not in Port Macquarie now, thought Jack.

A tuk-tuk pulled up spluttering blue smoke. Two women alighted.

"Wow!" Jack exclaimed quietly.

As they handed money to the driver, Werner turned to Jack and commented, "Yah—hot ladies!"

"How beautiful is that woman?" Jack asked, rhetorically.

"Which one?"

"Ah—the blonde, the blonde."

"Ah, the old one."

"She's hardly old." Jack laughed, realising. "You're young—of course she's old."

"No. I like—how you say?—the 'age-ed woman'."

"Older woman."

"Yah."

They watched the two women walk into the police station. From behind Bussy asked, "You want order? Eggs, bacon maybe?"

"Sounds wonderful," said Jack. Bussy gestured for Jack to go before her. She followed him back inside to his table.

*

"You—I help?"

Amelia and Olivia stood at the police station's front desk facing a thin moustachioed policeman.

"Would it be possible please to speak with the officer in charge?" asked Amelia. The policeman stared back at her. He put up his hand indicating 'stop'. He left the desk and walked through a door. Amelia and Olivia glanced at one another, puzzled.

The officer returned with another man, a little older. "I speak English. How may I help?" the man asked.

"Are you the officer in charge?" asked Amelia.

"No, I translate. You will want to speak with Captain Choniburshakanari. He is not here. What is it you want?"

"Simply—we are visiting police—on holiday—from London—and we thought we'd come by and say 'hello'." Amelia had no intention of telling a lackey the real reason for their visit.

The translator studied them for a moment. "Sit there, please." He pointed to a bench behind them next to the door. Then he turned around and went back into an inner office.

Amelia and Olivia sat. The thin moustachioed duty officer studied them.

After a time Amelia began to stir. She did not like his acute inspection, his eyes obviously taking in every detail of her and Olivia. *Is that look sexual?* she wondered.

Olivia leant into her. "That thin moustache makes that officer look like he's an old fashioned card sharp."

"Yes. Pencil-thin. It takes longer to maintain that than to pluck one's eyebrows. Olivia, do you know, he looks exactly like that evil Chinaman my Nanna warned me about."

"He's Thai, not Chinese."

"I know. It's just my Nanna's warnings are hard to shake."

Olivia stretched out her legs. "I guess we have no choice but to sit here and wait and wait."

Inside, the quiet of the police station allowed the noise of the traffic outside to be clearly heard.

The translator returned. "Captain Choniburshakanari is on his way. Please, you wait."

Chapter 8

Donald Ranaldson Jnr adjusted his Stetson, hitched his trousers over his bulging belly and knocked on the door next to his room, high up in *L'Hotel Majestique.* He'd risen, showered and dressed in anticipation of his first day golfing, all without opening the curtains to his room and witnessing the view over the Gulf of Thailand. From inside room 1124 he heard no movement. He knocked again. Finally he heard a muffled, "Yeah?"

"I'm heading out to golf. God damn it, it's too good a day to be wasted inside!" He picked up his bag of clubs leaning on the wall beside his door. He stopped and returned to 1124, raising his voice to the door. "They got breakfast downstairs—a smorgasbord. Not bad, for Asia, I guess. They could do with some Texan beef!" He thumped on the door. "Move your ass!" he shouted over his shoulder as he headed to the elevators.

Inside room 1124, his son Donald Ranaldson III, moaned softly, "Fuck off," rolled over and went back to sleep.

*

Olivia consulted her watch, 'hearing' the silent seconds ticking over and glanced sideways at Amelia, whispering, "We could be shopping."

The entrance door to the police station flew open and a decorated uniformed policeman swept in. The desk officer stood to attention. Without looking at the two women, the superior officer strode by, removing his hat and passing behind the front desk and into the inner office. Once the door was shut the desk officer relaxed.

Amelia squeezed Olivia's knee.

"Yes, I saw," Olivia whispered.

Captain Choniburshakanari had arrived and he was the biker in the ironed cream shirt from last night.

The translator appeared. "Come."

The two women stood and followed him, both catching each other with a warning glance of 'be careful'.

*

Beatrice sat on the small wooden chair by her bed—the bed she shared with Eugene, though he hadn't returned during the night. She wasn't missing him.

"You'll be totally safe sharing a bed with me," he'd told her months ago. "You're my alibi."

"Eugene, it's okay," Beatrice had said. "Everyone has 'come out' these days."

"Sorry—I'm too old fashioned and too private. So I ask you to keep this small secret. All you need do is have the occasional breakfast with me. Maybe lunch, you know. We'll play it by ear."

As Beatrice tightened her sandal strap she thought of last night. After her swim she'd followed Sunny into Sumbar and gone up stairs to shower. Eugene had already disappeared. A note on the pillow read: *I'm at my friend's house.* She'd returned to the bar downstairs thinking she'd have a night cap.

"Sunny," she asked, as she entered the bar from the accommodation end. "Jack not around?"

Sunny looked up with his welcoming smile. "Miss—he go bed."

"*I'm* still here though, darling," commented the wolf-whistling Englishman with the Thai woman.

Beatrice smiled, "Yes; however, and sadly for me, you're spoken for."

"Spoken for?" He began to laugh. "There's no speech in this relationship."

Beatrice heard no bitterness, if anything, a sense of pride.

"What'll you have?" the drunken Englishman asked. "Come join us. Sit. We don't bite."

Beatrice tossed it up. *What the hell, I'm on holiday!* She sat at the end of the small table, the man and woman on either side of her, ready for a quick exit if needed.

"I'm Billy Mackie—this is Boonsri."

"Hello," said Beatrice. The Thai woman nodded curtly recognising the English greeting. Sunny placed a Mai-Tai in front of Beatrice. The Thai woman continued to look at Beatrice, inspecting her, rating her as a possible threat. As

Beatrice sipped, she decided she'd only be having the one, followed by a measured exit.

"So, where are you from in Convict-Land?" Billy laughed.

"Oh, Perth, in the west. There are a lot of Brits living there. They didn't have the stamina to migrate all the way to Sydney." Beatrice smiled to herself.

"You like swimming, huh? I guess all Aussies do," he said, attempting to make small talk.

"Yes. Back home I try to swim once or twice a week and I walk every day."

"That's probably why you look so hot. You been with that guy long?"

Beatrice feared where this was probably leading. "Yes. We met on the plane over and it was love at first sight." She downed the Mai-Tai. "I've gotta go. He's panting upstairs for me as I speak." Then smiling, she said to Boonsri, "Lovely meeting you."

Beatrice smiled at last night's recollection. Rising from the bedroom chair she wondered if she'd wait for Eugene or walk up the beach to town and grab a bite of breakfast alone. She decided Eugene could take care of himself. *I am after all an alibi, not a baby sitter.*

Stamping her foot a couple of times and happy the sandals were snug, Beatrice locked her door, stepped breezily down the stairs and through *Sumbar* to eagerly take on her first morning in Thailand.

The sun was climbing in the sky as she stopped on the sand. She laughed to herself, *Why did I bother?* She removed her sandals and set off carrying them.

Friendly locals walked by nodding their greetings. A man leading a short horse with a bright red and blue flowery saddle approached. "You want ride? Very cheap!"

"No, thanks." Beatrice walked on. *Did Jack say last night that waves pounded those sea walls? It must have been a typhoon for that to have occurred. It's so peaceful here!*

After ten minutes Beatrice came across a crudely painted sign on a wooden arrow pointing left between two shady trees. It read: *Sumbeach Town.*

In the centre of town, opposite the police station, she spotted Jack seated at a restaurant, talking with a young man, while a Thai girl removed Jack's plate from in front of him.

"Jack!" she called. Both men looked up. Jack gave a wave and she entered.

"Werner, this is Beatrice," introduced Jack. "We're staying down the beach at *Sumbar*."

"Happy to meet you," Werner said, smiling. As Beatrice began to settle at the table, Werner whispered to Jack, "Your wife—good looker, my friend." He patted Jack's shoulder in a congratulatory manner as if they'd been friends for years.

"No wife", whispered Jack. "We stay—same hotel—that all—no *fook-fook*." Jack immediately wondered why he had replied in Sunny's broken English.

"Ah," considered Werner.

"I'll leave you in Werner's capable hands, Beatrice," informed Jack. "On my first morning here I always wander down to the fishing boats. Werner here serves an excellent bacon and egg roll and a reasonably good coffee." With that he rose, handed the breakfast money to Bussy, shook Werner's hand and, putting the paper under his left arm, walked into the street and the bright morning light.

Werner stood at the edge of the table, becoming his father's waiter once more. He reached for a menu and smiled broadly at Beatrice, revealing his perfectly white teeth. "*Sprechen-Sie Deutsch?*"

*

The two English women sat across the desk from Captain Choniburshakanari. The captain wasn't tall, noted Amelia, though behind his desk he sat higher than Olivia and herself. *Must have a raised chair or a cushion,* she thought. *Position of power or mere vanity?*

The police captain held up his hand to his translator, indicating that he was not yet ready to begin. He adjusted his name plate on his desk for the two women to see clearly. He nodded to the translator seated off to the side. The meeting began.

"Captain Choniburshakanari thanks you for introducing yourselves and reminds you, you have no authority in the Kingdom of Thailand."

The women nodded. Amelia explained they were unofficially looking for an expat Englishman. The translator said to Amelia, "What is the man's name?"

"Harold Keith Brown."

Amelia and Olivia studied the captain's reaction. He simply shook his head.

"No, the captain does not know this name."

The captain spoke in Thai to his translator.

"Our captain knows all the expats here in *Sumbeach*. He makes it his business to know. He runs a very law abiding town. Part of the reason so many tourists return here year after year. They feel safe. Also many expats live here, run a business, employ our locals, marry our beautiful girls, settle down and invest in our future."

Captain Choniburshakanari again spoke in Thai.

"The captain asks: *Do you have picture?*"

"Yes." Amelia handed over the photograph of ACC McPherson. The captain studied it, his eyes narrowing as he tried to place the face. He shook his head.

"The captain says he never see man."

Captain Choniburshakanari passed the picture to his off-sider.

The translator studied it. "No. I no see him also."

Amelia and Olivia sat back waiting to be dismissed. They had done, officially, all they intended to do.

The captain raised his hand towards the translator, in the 'stop' position. He then lifted the receiver of the telephone on his desk and spoke briskly.

Amelia looked to the translator, curiously. He whispered, "Private. The captain's wife not well."

Captain Choniburshakanari hung up and asked for the photograph once more. He held it in his hand, his gaze firmly fixed on it, as he spoke to the translator.

"The captain wonders if he may now have a beard?"

"A beard? Yes, that's a possibility," admitted Amelia.

The captain held up the photo for the women to see and placed his fingers around Davey's chin, creating a 'beard'. Not happy with this image, he grunted, quickly put the photo on his desk and grabbing a lead pencil violently shaded in the face disfiguring the photograph. He held it up, proudly displaying his 'artwork'.

"The captain says to look for *this* man." The captain laughed. "The captain says you may call him Captain Choni. Everyone does."

The captain spoke quickly in Thai.

"The captain says 'you may go now'. He thanks you for coming and hopes in future he can be of assistance to the British police force."

The two women left with their destroyed photograph. Passing the front desk, Amelia noticed the pencil-thin moustachioed officer was no longer there. Outside she held back commenting until they were well away from the police station.

Finally Amelia spat, "Captain Choni! What a horrible man."

"I couldn't agree more."

"He'll be no help, not that we want it. Give me that photograph, please, Olivia." Venting her anger, Amelia took it, ripped it in two then in four and stuffed the pieces into her handbag.

They walked further away in the direction of their hotel, Amelia unable to let go of her emotions. She leant into Olivia and speaking guardedly said, "I've never been more insulted in my entire life. That was nothing more than racist and sexist belittlement."

"Yes," replied Olivia. "And you're angry, right?"

"Yes, I am. Aren't you?"

"Of course. But keep in mind racism cuts both ways."

Amelia looked at her curiously. "What do you mean?"

"Back home, we're the giver. Over here, we're the receiver."

*

The sixteen seater *All Sumbeach Golf Tours* minibus pulled up in front of the revolving doors of *L'Hotel Majestique.* Donald Randalson Jnr glanced at his wrist watch. "About god-damn time," he said to himself. The Thai driver slid down and took the American's bag of clubs, lifting them into the rear of the minibus.

From inside a Western man heaved open the van's heavy sliding door and climbed out. "Mister Randalson Junior?" he asked in his British accent.

"Sure am," the American said, extending his hand in good old southern hospitality, pleased at last to be getting his golfing holiday underway.

The Englishman took the American's hand. "Please, step in. It's air-conditioned."

The two men sat side by side in the minibus. The Thai driver manoeuvred his way past the large white and purple *Wild Orchid Vacations* tourist coach parked in the half circular driveway, bouncing across the gutter onto the narrow street.

"My name is Richard Eastman, call me 'Dickie'—everyone does."

"Richard Eastman?" questioned Donald Jnr, surprised, "Is it every day the owner of the business picks up his clients?"

"I try to the first time. I still like to meet everyone, though at the height of the season that's not always possible. And next Sunday, at the end of your golfing week, I'll try to make the farewell luncheon."

"Mighty decent of you," said Donald Jnr. "Must be all that English hospitality we hear so much about."

Dickie leant forward and said to the driver, "*Park Royal Thai Links.*" The driver nodded.

"Have you been here long?" Donald asked. "You must love golf—and the heat."

"Mister Randalson Junior, I came out here twenty or so years ago to play golf. I thought there was only the one course in the area. I was pleasantly surprised when I learnt there were three. I played them twice each and flew home a very happy man."

Donald Randalson Jnr thought that sounded rehearsed though he didn't once consider Dickie Eastman had been asked that same question countless times before.

"So, where's home?"

"Here, now. Years ago I applied for the Thai Elite Visa."

"I meant back there in England."

"In the north—Newcastle."

Donald Jnr nodded, as if he knew its geographical locale.

"I returned here the following year. My wife said 'not again!' She was no fan of the heat, nor the beach. I married the only Englishwoman who didn't wish to go to Spain annually to burn herself red-raw around a swimming pool in some resort. I tried to talk a few friends into joining me here. Sadly there were no takers, so the second year I came by myself."

"Yes siree, my wife also, God bless her, doesn't understand a thing about golf—or me."

"I returned home and that's when the big idea struck. Why didn't my friends want to come out here and play? They loved playing golf, that's how we'd all met. The reason they did not want to come?"

Donald Jnr had no idea. He couldn't comprehend anyone not liking his favourite recreation.

"Fear," said Dickie, answering his own question. "Fear of the unknown— fear of the Orient. It was then I decided to rid them of their fear. I came out here in advance, hired a van, picked them up at Bangkok Airport, and I drove them down here. I arranged their accommodation—everything. I'd costed it all for them—hotel, green-fees, money for tuk-tuks, even budgeted their potential bar bills. Sure I took a percentage, but I also took a huge gamble. They came and they loved it."

"Hell, yes. Who wouldn't?"

"And the next step was to move here and hire a couple more buses and place ads in golf magazines back in the UK. The golfers started to come—in trickles at first, mind you. I often thought in those early days, *what have I gone and done?* I'd tossed in my job, tossed in my life savings and tossed away my argumentative, unco-operative wife. Best thing I did, getting rid of her."

"Yeah, buddy. I can appreciate that."

"Now I've got a fleet of eight small coaches, with booking connections into all sorts of accommodation and I live in a condominium by the beach, which I'd never have been able to afford back home in the UK."

"Sounds like you're living the American Dream," said Donald Jnr, without the slightest touch of irony.

"Things have certainly changed around *Sumbeach*. Now there are six golf courses within an hour's drive. That's a different course to be played each day. Paradise."

"Yee-ha!" exclaimed the Texan.

*

Amelia stopped suddenly in front of the large display window of a jewellery shop. She pointed to a ring. "Ooh—I like that!" She dropped her voice. "Don't turn around. We're being followed. That police officer, the one behind the desk, *Mister Pencil-Thin Moustache* is over there, behind us, on the other side of the street. Can you see his reflection?"

Olivia moved her body slightly, as if looking at the gold ring. "You're right. He's now in civvies."

"I'll bet that was who Captain Choni phoned for his 'private' call. There is no ill wife."

Olivia laughed. "Well, let's take our tail on a bum's walking tour of *Sumbeach*."

"He had time to change, though no time to shave off his pencil-thin moustache," commented Amelia, shaking her head in disbelief. "Did he think we'd not remember that detail?"

From inside the shop an immaculately groomed woman appeared in the doorway. "Ladies, everything discounted—fifteen percent. For the right item, I could be tempted to twenty." The woman held her arm out indicating for Amelia and Olivia to step inside.

Amelia smiled at her. "Maybe later—we're just looking for now, thank you." The saleswoman smiled and shut the door to save the air-conditioning motor from over heating.

"For the sake of our tail, I think we need to appear to be only half committed to recognising our suspect," suggested Amelia. "It should look as if we've become intoxicated with Thailand—you know, play the gullible tourist."

Picking up on the suggested ruse, Olivia pointed to her left into the window and said loudly, "Ooh, I like that one. Buy it for me, mum?"

"No! Your dead father didn't leave me enough inheritance."

*

The *All Sumbeach Golf Tours* minibus headed north along the highway. The shops beneath the apartment blocks on either side of the road were beginning to open. The day's first sale was well anticipated by the many retailers because an early sale reinforced their belief in *Chokh di—good luck.*

Donald Jnr looked out his window at the people filling the footpaths in front of outlets that had no collective planning thrown over them. A tyre shop sat next to a restaurant, next to a massage parlour, next to a car repairer, next to a grocery store, next to a timber yard, next to a vacant lot with a lone tree surrounded by a previous building's rubble. He scoffed, "They're certainly in a hurry over here." He had no idea how correct he was, for he had no understanding of the effect previous economic booms and busts had had on the region and no insight into the daily struggle of most of the people's lives.

"Tips!" he commented, by way of solution. "By Jesus—some of those poor dudes could well do with a fat tip!"

Beyond the urban area, the minibus trundled forward in convoy with the fast moving motorbikes laden with pinion passengers some without safety helmets, trucks thundering around it, luxury cars of the noveau riche and open backed transit trucks all weaving in and out of the designated lanes, at times creating new ones. Dickie's minibus driver braked and accelerated often, making for a jerky trip.

Donald Jnr stared at the workers' trucks, their rear trays overflowing with men and women all dressed in the same t-shirts. Each truck had its own brightly designated colour, which made identification easy for worker and driver alike when the day's slog was over and they needed to ride the many miles back home.

"It sure as hell is not the US of A!"

Dickie Eastman smiled to himself, remembering his first experience of travelling on the roads here. What had struck him was the 'forward sight' of the drivers. Even though every vehicle possessed a rear-view mirror, no one seemed to use it. He'd been given an explanation: *Why look to what has been—we here in Asia look ahead.*

"So, Donald Jnr, you mentioned in your email, you were recommended to me by Mister Wilbur K. Jackson."

"Yes, siree," replied the American, keen that things might be, at last, moving in the direction he'd been hoping they would.

"Mister Jackson is one of my regular American customers," said Dickie. "Though I notice he's not joining me this year. Is he well?"

"I'm afraid old Stonewall's got the big C."

"Oh, that's too bad. I must send him an email wishing him well."

Donald Jnr dropped his voice. "Now old Stonewall said while I was here, I was *not* to miss out on the 'special caddy service'."

Dickie looked at him a moment. He then asked cautiously, "Would you like that today?"

"Hell, yes!" came the exuberant reply. "Let's get this golfing holiday started!"

"Right you are." Dickie lent forward and said to his driver, "Change of plans. Forget *Park Royal Thai Links*. Today we'll be golfing at *Mountain View Range*."

Three kilometres up the highway the minibus veered left towards the mountains of the Myanmar border.

Chapter 9

Jack left town and headed back to *Sumbar*. At the beach he removed his sandals. After several paces on the hot sand he began to run to the edge of the water where he slowed and strolling on, kicked water into the air as a child would. He smiled at his enjoyment of such a simple pleasure.

Off to his right, lying in the sand, tanning, he noticed the two Dutchmen from last night. He gave a wave. No wave was returned. Ahead Jack saw a man he recognised.

"Good morning. It's, ah, Michael, isn't it?" The man stopped. "We met, very briefly last night. Sunny said 'hello' down in front of *Sumbar*."

"Ah, yes. You are on holiday?" Michael asked.

"Yes. Obviously you're not." Jack indicated the covered baby in Michael's arms.

"No holiday. It was, not now. A case of entrapment, you understand. Oh, I'm not complaining—a most beautiful case of entrapment. I never thought it possible—back home, you know." Michael let that thought die as the baby began to stir. Gently bouncing the child in his arms, he said, "I must keep walking. It seems movement is the only thing that works. Mickey is teething. Good morning. Enjoy your stay."

"Thank you," said Jack. He watched the man walk off, heading in the direction of *Sumbeach*, and then gave a large boyish kick at the water in front of him. A spray shot up and out a metre and a half. A passing Thai woman in a straw hat gave him a curious look. Jack laughed at his foolishness and bid her 'good morning', cupping his hands beneath his chin and bowing his head.

Nearing *Sumbar*, Jack saw Mai bottle-feeding her baby on the front veranda, shaded by the brightly coloured awning. *No doubt Eugene's gift from last night.*

Jack waved. Mai smiled back, bowing her head, as he took a detour to wash the sand from his feet in the large concrete bowl, captivated by Mai calmly singing to Tookie. Upstairs in his room he changed to swim, picked up his electronic tablet and headed for the pool out the back.

After twenty minutes in the pool's clear blue water he moved an outdoor lounge to the corner under the ugly half plant / half tree. Some of its leaves provided reasonable shade. Opening his tablet he called up the first book he planned to read in nearly two years. Once he started nursing Jenny, the little free time available had disappeared. Today it was time to catch up on the latest fictional spy shenanigans or gripping murder cases.

He lifted his eyes from the tablet when Eugene walked into the pool area. Eugene didn't see him and Jack didn't wave or call out because he wanted to get past page one.

Eugene removed his faded blue polo shirt, baring his grey haired white chest. In long grey and black board shorts he stood on the top step of three, the water to his ankles. He walked down the steps carefully and then walked back up. Jack was no longer reading. Eugene repeated the exercise. On the third entry he quickly and surreptitiously blessed himself as he bent his knees. He walked forward in the pool holding onto its side. Bending down he immersed himself up to his neck. He stayed there—chin, mouth, nose, dark glasses and straw hat above the waterline—like a crocodile awaiting passing prey. Two minutes later he got out, dried himself, dressed and started to leave. On the way out he saw Jack.

"Oh!" he emitted, startled.

"Jack."

"Yes, sorry, Jack. I'm not terribly good around water, but it's so hot here. I was never taught—you know, back in England as a child, to swim."

"That's okay. I'll keep an eye out for you."

"Oh, no need for that. That's all I do—squat for a few minutes—my morning constitution—'to wash off the sins', as I'm sure John the Baptist would have said. I never go in that salty stuff down by the sand."

Eugene left. Jack returned to page two.

*

The large white tourist coach was the only vehicle parked in the circular driveway of *L'Hotel Majestique*. Once the *All Sumbeach Golf Tours* minibus had driven off, the driver had repositioned his large coach, taking possession of the area thereby making it difficult for any other vehicle to enter and making it easier for his tourists to access. Porters carried bags to the coach from the hotel's foyer, the driver and guide taking over from them, tossing the bags into the coach's storage area underneath. Tourists began climbing on board in dribs and drabs

Amelia stopped by the side of the coach and read its purple and pink: *Wild Orchid Vacations*. "Olivia, give me a moment."

She walked towards the two men lifting luggage. The guide stood up. "Please—on bus. We go soon."

"No, I'm not one of yours," explained Amelia. "Tell me please, where are you going?"

"Bangkok Airport," he stated, as if it were obvious. "People go home."

"And you do this every morning?"

"No—only, when we have tour."

"Yes, of course. I mean—always about the same time?"

"Yes. Same time in morning," he explained. "Otherwise, people miss flights."

"Thank you, sir."

"You're welcome, Madame."

Amelia returned to Olivia. "If the English aunt saw Harold Keith Brown from a tourist coach, it could well be this tourist coach. So we need to be around the hotel at this time each morning and maybe he will walk by with his baby like he did before."

"Maybe," said Olivia, thinking the chance of that happening was remote.

Sensing her indifference, Amelia explained, "Well, at least it gives us a start to each day. I just feel we need to structure this search, give it a framework. Chances of seeing him, I know, are remote, but us being higgledy-piggledy won't help."

Olivia touched Amelia by the wrist. "Our police tail is behind us again."

The two women moved off.

"He really needs to shave off that moustache," said Olivia, "if he's going to make undercover work his career of choice."

"Captain Choni is a very inquisitive policeman."

"And you're not?" asked Olivia. "Would you have had us followed?" Amelia didn't answer though she knew she would have.

They stopped a little way down the narrow street, where Amelia lifted from her handbag a small tourist map of the town she'd found in the hotel's lobby. The two women waited on the footpath, 'reading' the map and observing the tourists and passers-by for fifteen minutes, until the coach bumped its way over the footpath towards Bangkok. No Englishman carrying a baby walked by.

*

Donald Ranaldson Jnr stood in front of the clubhouse at *Mountain View Range* and admired the lush green course in front of him, dwarfed by the steep wooded mountain range.

I could not be further from Texas, he thought.

Dickie Eastman emerged from the clubhouse with a twentyish Thai woman dressed in a tight red polo shirt and figure hugging cream shorts. Donald Jnr couldn't say if she wore sandals or not, his eyes didn't venture any further south. *Oh my Lord—I thank thee, I thank thee.*

"This is Suzy-Q," introduced Dickie. "She will caddy for you. You will tee off in an hour."

"One hour?" Donald Jnr looked to the first tee. There were no golfers there. "What's the delay, buddy? I'm not used to being kept waiting."

"Today there will be a thunderstorm at 2.30. At that time you need to be putting on the fifteenth green or teeing off on the sixteenth. There is a small lean-to nearby. You and Suzy-Q will take shelter there."

*

Beatrice found Jack by *Sumbar's* pool. "That German kid hit on me!" she half-shouted at him. Jack closed his tablet at page ten. "I don't know whether to be complemented or offended! I'm old enough to be his—well, elder sister!" She laughed, delighted with what Werner had attempted.

"He propositioned you?"

"Yes, between serving the orange juice and the bacon and egg roll."

"He didn't waste any time."

"Guess what he said? *Life is short, baby!* Baby? I said to him *what movie did you hear that in?*" She ripped off her towel. "I need a swim." She dived in.

Jack thought, *that's a nine. No splash at all.*

The contrast between her and Eugene could not have been greater. Beatrice free-styled in four strokes, the length of the pool. He now wondered why he'd been so concerned with her swimming in the sea last night. "She'd be capable of hauling me out!" he said to himself.

After several laps, bookended with some stylish tumble turns, Beatrice stopped swimming and slid to the pool's edge below Jack. She asked, "What do you think I should do?"

"Avoid fishing nets. You swim like a dolphin."

"About what I said."

Jack considered his advice. They were after all strangers and a misunderstood comment could bring offence. He guardedly offered, "Well, if you're still thinking about it, then you haven't dismissed the idea completely."

She looked at him. "You're not a psychiatrist, are you?"

Jack shook his head. "No, certainly not anything like that."

Beatrice pushed back from the pool's wall and swam a few strokes on her back, before turning over and completing another half dozen laps. She stopped at the pool's edge below Jack again, wanting to ask a question. She decided against it and dived under, back to the centre of the pool.

Jack placed his tablet in the shade of the ugly tree and picking up his paper, searched for his favourite column of small world news items. On the times he'd been here, he'd often find a gem—genuinely reported or created by a sub-editor with a sense of humour.

After a minute he laughed out loud.

"What is it?" asked Beatrice, swimming to the pool's edge.

Jack read to her. "*Brazil. Huge power outage spreads to neighbouring countries. A local mayor, Senor Rodriguez, told reporters: 'We're completely in the dark as to why'.*"

Chapter 10

After midday, despite the heat, Jack headed out of *Sumbar*. The two Dutchmen were nursing drinks on the front veranda, disinterested in the three young women who were laughing while they unfurled their towels on the sand below. Jack skirted around them and headed along the beach to town. A little early for lunch after his large breakfast, he headed left at the hand-painted arrow up into the village for a further half hour stroll.

"I've never seen that before, have I?" he asked himself, trying to recall. "Have I even been up this street?"

Jack stood outside a wire fence, behind which some young teenagers tossed a basketball onto a back board and hoop. Five of the six shots went through the basket.

They're not bad, he thought.

A red haired priest in a white shirt, black shorts and sandals approached the boy with the basketball. As he did so, he removed his hat exposing his bald top and wiped his forehead with a handkerchief. The boy stopped mid-shot and stood erect, almost to attention, concentrating on what the priest had to say.

Off to the side a religious sister, a Westerner, dressed in cool white clothing, supervised.

"Good morning, Sister," said Jack.

"Good morning, sir," she replied in a New Zealand accent. "It is again a very warm day."

"Yes indeed, Sister. Is this a school?"

"Yes, attached to the orphanage behind."

"I've never seen it before, although I haven't been here for over five years."

"Yes. It's recent, though this building has been here for a while. It used to be an old administrative centre. The orphanage was set up by the church with donations from all around the world. Staffed mainly by volunteers, we come for three month stints."

"That's admirable of you, Sister."

"Oh, please don't single me out, sir. I am not important. We all must try to demonstrate compassion and understanding, to try to relieve some of the heartache in this world, shouldn't we?"

"Yes, we should, Sister. I won't keep you out here in the heat."

"Oh, I don't mind. I love watching children play. Innocence, sir, it is so quickly lost."

"Yes, it is. Have a nice day, Sister," Jack offered, turning to go.

"You too, sir."

*

On the intersection of the two main tourist streets, Jack found the well-established burger/pizza cafe where he and Jenny would often lunch, sharing a burger and chips washed down with a cold beer. They'd sit here for an hour or two and watch the endless array of motorbikes, mini buses, tourists and locals on foot swirl by. Once a day, around this time, the large tourist coach would appear to attempt the corner in one motion; however, the driver, having learnt from experience, would stop halfway and back up, squaring the huge vehicle and straightening it before crawling down the cross street to *L'Hotel Majestique*.

Sitting at the bench by the large open shuttered window Jack looked over to the tuk-tuks and taxi-trucks parked on the diagonally opposite corner. Placed about them were an array of photographs covered in a sheet of plastic on a large ply board, showing the tourist locations within the area. Prices were displayed prominently in baht. *That display is new*, Jack thought.

The drivers half slept behind their steering wheels, or chatted amongst themselves, or tossed dice on a small table, the heat determining their measured pace.

A strikingly dressed, middle-aged European couple stood there, considering the plethora of tourist locations listed on the board. The fit blonde woman was about ten or fifteen years younger than the tall greying gentleman. What struck Jack as being special were the clothes the man was wearing—a bright yellow polo shirt on top of a pair of bright green Bermuda shorts. Jarringly unique. *Perhaps,* Jack mused, *she's colour blind and he has no taste.* He thought a moment. *Or vice-versa.*

The couple approached the nearest driver who pointed to the sky. Puzzled, they looked up. Overhead, thick dark clouds were rolling in over the mountain range from Myanmar. The man nodded, and they walked off, indicating they'd return.

Twenty minutes later, the heavens opened and the rain bucketed down. People on the street ran for cover as the gutters filled and water rushed down the streets headlong into the four-way intersection. Daring motorcyclists getting their fix of careless pleasure, sprayed water as they charged through the intersection. The gutters began to back up and the intersection turned into a shallow pond. The rain moved on after forty minutes although the ground water kept on filling the intersection. Adults came out to observe; kids came out to splash around the edges; two young boys fell onto their bellies and flayed about laughing.

Jack spied the blonde woman he'd seen earlier in the day while standing outside *Brauhaus Helmut*. She was wading through the 'lake', her shorts rolled up high, her sandals carried in her outstretched hand.

My God, she's beautiful. I've never seen anyone so beautiful, he thought, then laughed at his foolish honesty.

Her brunette friend was laughing, enjoying their predicament. The blonde reached into the water and flicked half a handful at her companion, who turned and wagged her finger. They both laughed and moved on through the 'lake'.

Jack would have loved to have rushed out and offered her a hand, guided her out of the water, dried her legs on his t-shirt; however, he sat there, his remaining fries getting colder, as he watched the vision walk up the street and out of sight.

"Hi there, Squire, we meet again." It was the Englishman from last night at *Sumbar*.

"G'day."

"Feel like a beer?" Without waiting for a reply, he shouted to the waitress, "Two beers, *pord*!" He sat opposite Jack, before Jack could refuse or make an excuse. "How wet was that downpour? I'm used to them, but that was one of the biggest I've seen!"

Jack looked past him to the doorway. "You're alone?"

"Boonsri is working. I'm Billy, Billy Mackie."

"Jack. Jack Featherstone." They shook hands across the table. For the first time Jack looked at the man in detail. Billy had cropped dark hair, receding a little on top. He was unshaven with a face of aged lines buried in a tanned leathery skin.

"First time in Thailand?" Billy asked.

"No, I used to come here with my wife a few times."

"Used to? Divorced huh, looking for some tail." He winked.

"No, she passed away," Jack said, quietly.

"Oh, sorry about that."

"And I'm not interested in tail."

"You haven't become a shirt lifter, have you?"

"No." Jack's reply was drowned out by Billy's coarse laugh.

"That's a good looking woman you picked up on the plane."

"What are you talking about?"

Billy ignored the question. He leant across the table to Jack. "Good looking women come to Thailand for one thing."

"A sun tan?" asked Jack, knowing where this conversation was heading.

"No—a good shagging—which they can't get back home. Pleased to see you know that, and made your move. I'd have done the same!"

The waitress brought the beers. Billy spent a long time looking her over and watching her disappear back around the counter. Looking into Billy's eyes, Jack concluded this beer was not Billy's first drink of the day.

"Cold beer for a hot climate." Billy drank. "Ah, better than that flat warm piss back home." He looked squarely into Jack's eyes and confessed, "I love it here. Thailand. Never thought the women here could be so—inventive. They are nothing like the frozen tarts in the north of England. Must be the difference in temperature—loosens them up out here." He smirked and snorted. "See, I confess—Jesus, must be weeks since I've had a decent conversation—I've fallen in love. Boonsri—that means 'beautiful'—the woman I was with last night? Wow! She's got my heart around her little finger and my old fellow locked away in you-know-where. Can't understand a word she says, but boy oh boy, she sure understands me!"

He laughed and gulped his beer, snorting some back out through his nose. "Sorry." He reached for a serviette and dried his face. "Whew! Just like me when I'm in bed with her—all over the place!" He laughed again.

"Boonsri," said Jack. "Nice name, not too long, easy to remember or pronounce."

"That's exactly what I thought—easy to remember. The second time, I asked for her by name, not by number." He laughed with pleasure at the memory. "That impressed the other girls around that red snooker table, I tell you."

Jack sipped his beer, letting the statement sink in. "You met her here in Sumbeach?"

"No, further south. I brought her up here."

"You brought her here? Not against her will, I hope."

"Hell no, she wanted to come. Those bastards down there owed her money and refused to pay, so she was glad to get out of there. It just needed a man like me to take action on her behalf. Bad luck for them—she dragged her hand through the cash register just before we jumped on the train."

"Billy, hang on a minute. You've brought her here—what about her 'employers'? Don't you think they might be missing her? And the money she stole? And just maybe they might be looking for the Western guy who took her with him?"

Billy leant into Jack, dropping his voice. "They're not the only ones who'd be looking for me. I fell so hard for her I've overstayed my visa."

"What?"

"Yeah, I can't go home, can't leave her. I'm caught here. She's beautiful by name and beautiful by nature."

Jack pictured the woman from last night. She wasn't beautiful. She may have been, once; however, now she was middle-aged and hard-faced, as if she had a line for every man she'd ever satisfied.

Billy went on. "You ever have that? A woman who does anything and everything for you? Not me, I haven't, up until now. Those tarts back home!" He put on a forced female voice. "Pull down the nightie when you're finished, luv!" He laughed. "Hell, I ran out of real money six weeks ago. She lets me live off her. What woman in England would allow that?"

"You're living off ...?"

"It's okay. I know what she is. I'm not a total freeloader. I stand by her in case of trouble. I do my public service. Every two, three days I take this baby for a walk—child of one of the working girls—gets it out of her mother's hair for an hour or two. I get rewarded—a couple hundred baht tossed my way—enough for a couple of beers."

"Immigration will eventually get you, Billy," Jack warned. "One day you'll want to leave—Cambodia, Malaysia, over the mountains to Myanmar, they all have patrolled border crossings. Once deported, you'll never be allowed back."

"Yeah. What the fuck. I'm never going back to the UK. I'm enjoying life too much out here." He took a final swig of the beer. "Cold beers and hot women. What a country!" He stretched back. "How good is this?"

"Why didn't you just take the train down into Malaysia, stay a week and come back legally?"

"I tried that—got as far as the train station. But I couldn't. I couldn't leave her. What if she'd disappeared, run off with some other punter by the time I got back?"

Billy eased further back in his chair, putting both hands behind his head. "James Dean—livin' life on the edge—that's me." The bravado in his voice transformed into a satisfied smile.

"I'll get you another beer, Billy. With southern Thai thugs and the Immigration Police looking for you, it might be the last one you have for a while."

"No *problemo*," Billy said in a poor Spanish accent. "Billy Mackie knows how to cover his tracks."

Chapter 11

Amelia and Olivia walked the main tourist street away from the beach, up to the highway, glancing in all the bars and shopfronts as they went. The policeman tailing them had either lost them, returned to the station drenched, or simply given up, bored.

"Oh, my sandals are still soggy!" complained Olivia.

"Yes, I can hear you squelching as you walk." Amelia laughed. "Squelch! Squelch! Squelch! It'll be no good sneaking up on David Keith Brown from behind. He'll hear us coming!"

They side-stepped the puddles, though Olivia's face expressed the desire to be eight years old again and have a big stamp in one of them, squelchy sandals or not.

"Don't even think about it!" warned Amelia.

At the intersection with the highway, above their head was a spaghetti mess of power cables, telephone wires and thick black cables, most active, though a few long dead.

Amelia looked to her right. "Come on, we'll walk down here, the long way around, back to the hotel, and then we swim. How hot and humid is it after that rain?"

"Have you ever seen rain fall like that?" asked Olivia. "There's no wind so it fell vertically. It was so heavy raindrops were hitting other raindrops on the way down!"

They passed a muddy lane with a strip of concrete down the centre.

"Let's walk down here," said Olivia. "It feels like a short cut."

Some metal poles were stacked against one of the side walls. Two men were dragging canvas tarpaulins out of the back of a small truck, revealing open boxes of clothing, stacked tightly against the rear of the cargo bed.

"I think this lane might be a night market come dark," observed Amelia.

"A couple of bars down there," said Olivia, indicating another lane off at a right angle to the one they were walking down.

"Thank goodness, the sun's up," commented Amelia, wary of the image of two women leaning against a pool table on the veranda of the nearest bar.

Olivia smiled at her. "Well, *I've* got something to do this evening."

"Playing pool with them?" Amelia asked, askance.

"No! Shopping!"

Amelia grabbed Olivia's wrist. "Up ahead!"

Olivia looked up in time to see a Western male figure, carrying a baby, disappear across the lane's entrance with the cross street. Amelia, all concern gone, started walking quickly, Olivia a pace behind.

At the top of the lane they stopped before a large muddy hole at the edge of the tarred narrow street and looked to their left. The man was only ten metres away, talking with the owner of a bar, who was leaning on a broom. The two women stepped carefully around the mud-hole.

Amelia, taking the map from the back pocket of her rolled shorts, unfurled it, and asked in a raised voice, "Excuse me!" The two men turned. "Do you speak English?" She held up the map.

"Yes," the man with the broom said. "How may I help?"

"We're lost," explained Amelia.

"How do we get back to *L'Hotel Majestique*?" asked Olivia.

The bar owner gave verbal directions then clarified by pointing ahead and then left-right-right.

"Oh, what a cute baby!" gushed Olivia.

"Yes," the father replied, "though he loves to cry at night!"

The two women thanked them for the directions and walked off.

"Not him," muttered Olivia, disappointed.

*

The swimming pool at *L'Hotel Majestique* was on ground level in the gardens, behind the hotel's perimeter wall, by the edge of the sandy beach. From inside the pool one could see out onto the Gulf of Thailand. The afternoon shadow, cast by the high rise half-covered the area, eased the sting of the afternoon sun. Sun lounges circled the large kidney-shaped design. Most guests lay in the sun, getting red, before heading back in a week's time to their wintery homes.

"I remember seeing that swimsuit—Queen Victoria used to wear it!" exclaimed a delighted Olivia.

"Don't be rude!" Amelia exclaimed with mock offence. "It's the only one I own."

"Tonight at that market, I'm buying you a new one."

"What's wrong with it?" asked Amelia, looking downwards.

"Let me just say—no wonder men aren't knocking on your door—you dress to scare them away."

"Olivia—you're playing the obnoxious stepdaughter far too well."

Olivia laughed. "An umbrella drink?" she asked eagerly, her attention taken by a young man at the pool bar. "Hey—check out 'Super Hunk' hanging at the bar over there." Amelia looked over her shoulder. "Claim these two lounge chairs," said Olivia, "Two umbrella drinks coming up."

She removed her dress, tossed it onto a lounge chair and adjusted the bra of her bikini as she crossed to the pool bar.

"Well, hi there," the 'Super Hunk' said as Olivia slid onto a stool.

"Oh, so you *are* American. Thanks so much. I just won a hundred baht from my evil stepmum."

The young American looked past her. "She doesn't look evil."

"Don't be taken in by appearances. Her smile is lovely but her tongue is a killer."

The young man offered his hand. "I'm Donald Randalson III."

"Really? I've never met a 'three'. I've read about them in books. Now I know they're real." Olivia vigorously shook his hand.

"Friends back in the States call me 'Donny-Three'."

The barman approached. "*Sawadee.* Yes, Miss? A drink for you?"

"Two umbrella drinks, please," Olivia requested, flippantly.

"Umbrella drinks?" The barman seemed puzzled.

"I think the young lady means two Mai-Tais," explained Donny-Three.

"Yes, sir." The barman moved off.

Donny-Three said louder, after him, "Oh and put them on *my* room account."

"Yes, sir."

"That's extremely generous of you, Donny-Three."

"Yeah, it sure is."

Donny-Three eased his sunglasses down his nose and peered over the top. In close-up he liked what he saw. "So you know my name, but I don't know yours." He tilted his head slightly from side to side.

"Olivia."

"No family name?" he asked, believing he'd cast his line and was gradually reeling in his catch.

"For the moment, just Olivia. Where in the States are you from?"

"Galveston, Texas." Then turning his 'reel' he added, "My father owns a ranch."

"Wow! I've never met a rancher before."

"Technically it's his ranch, but one day …"

"You live with him?"

"Not so much with *him*, but rather with my *mum*. I *help* her. I only *work* for him. I know everything about him—financially. I'm fundamental to the smooth operation of his business."

"That must be a very responsible position."

"Hell, no. The money comes in—the money goes out. Thankfully a lot less goes out than what comes in. I just enter it into a computer. It's not very difficult."

"Oh, I think it's much harder than that," smiled Olivia, pretending to appreciate his 'talent'. "So Donny-Three are you here on business? Investing in Thailand?"

"No. My father's here playing golf. I'm here drinking in the sun and maybe meeting a few beautiful women." He winked at her.

Olivia smiled coquettishly. The barman placed her two 'umbrellas' on the counter in front of her. She lifted them, "Thank you, Donny-Three."

"So, Olivia, what are you doing tonight? You want to eat someplace by the beach and maybe fool around a bit in the moonlight? I'm in the process of tracking down some pretty high grade dope. I meet my man in an hour or two. Hopefully it could be between our lips tonight."

"Gee Donny-Three, I'm afraid tonight I have to apply the last stage of the ointment," said Olivia, with obvious disappointment.

"Ointment?"

"Yes. My stepmother brought me to Thailand for the heat. You see the dampness in England won't let me get better, won't allow my body to dry. Just quietly," and leaning in she whispered, "I had a very serious bout of the pox and it just won't go away. However, the heat here is working. So tonight, no," and with an appalling American accent she added, "but I should be raring to go by Sat'dy night. Yee-ha!"

Chapter 12

Lilly, Maggie and Connie lay on their brightly coloured, oversized towels in the sand several metres in front of the veranda outside *Sumbar*. The three English tourists, in their early twenties, had been away from home for a week and had little over two weeks remaining. They'd found a room to share in a cheap Thai guesthouse in town. Tanned and fit, being members of the same gym back home in Manchester, their bikinied bodies caught the eyes of every man who walked by, hopefully prompting them to open their wallets in *Sumbar*. That was the arrangement the three young women had made with Garry.

Garry first saw them last week when he was sculpting three bags of concrete into the large bowl for customers to wash their feet in. He'd grown tired of sweeping sand out of his bar and the old large plastic bucket had finally perished from sitting in the sun all day.

The three had placed their towels on the sand and ran, as if they were in some corny video, into the sea, laughing and splashing each other. Garry didn't fall for it, so later when he was behind the bar and they sauntered in and asked if he was the manager, he was cautious. He'd glanced to see if the cash register was closed.

"Afternoon, beautiful spot you have here. I'm Lily."

"Hi Lily," said Garry, employing his one-size-fits-all bonhomie. "What can I get you girls?"

"Well," Lily said looking around the bar, "there's not many people in here."

"Never is this time of day," conceded Garry, wondering where this was leading.

"What if we could bring some in?" she asked, smiling, flirting. Her two friends tilted their heads in a questioning come-on.

Garry took his time, not committing to anything just yet. He studied the three women. They were certainly very attractive, and not prudish about the assets they possessed. *Might be a cheaper way of attracting customers than erecting a neon sign,* he thought.

"Well?" Lily asked.

Garry leant back against the fridge behind the counter. "Go for it, Lily, hit me with your spiel."

"Every day for two or three hours, we sit in the sand out there, toss a beach ball, swim in the sea and entice men to come on up in here to drink, have lunch. The men sit on your veranda to get a closer look at us—and spend their money."

"And that will cost me—how much?" asked Garry, knowing no offer like this ever came free.

"A Mai-Tai and a Thai salad each day—for each of us."

Garry studied the girls, considering the proposal. The girls studied Garry, considering he may not be going for it.

"If the guys buy us a drink then there's no need for the free one," added Lily, attempting to make the offer more appealing.

"Only Thai salad? You don't want fries with that?" Garry asked sarcastically.

"We're looking after our figures," replied Connie, no humour intended.

Garry pursed his lips, weighing up their proposal for the final time. *If I was walking past this bar would these three girls on the sand tempt me to stop and buy a drink?* He asked, "Who provides the beach ball?"

*

"Hi, Mister. You should try the food inside, it's really good," said Connie, removing her sunglasses like she'd seen some famous actress do in a movie. "Thai beef salad is to die for."

"Cold beer—best in *Sumbeach*," added Maggie, sitting up.

"Yes, I know. I'm staying here."

Jack walked by the three girls splayed alluringly on their towels and after briskly washing his feet, climbed up the steps into *Sumbar*. "Good looking sand flies you got out there lying on the beach, Garry."

"Sand flies?"

"Yes, they put the bite on me. Tried to get me to buy them a drink."

Garry smiled. "It wasn't my idea—the girls propositioned *me*." Indicating the customers still drinking in the bar after the storm had passed, he added, "It appears to be working. Before you go, Jack, let me ask you something."

"Sure thing," replied Jack, propping against the counter.

"Mai wants a bit of a party here Saturday night. It's my birthday. I'm thinking house guests and some expats I know around town. You know, golfing connections. Don't want it to be too big and for her sake, I don't want it to be a let-down. She'll cook—you know Asian hospitality—we'll be over flowing with food."

"How old will you be, Garry?"

"Forty—the big one. That's another reason Mai wants the party. Me? I couldn't care less, but I don't want to disappoint her."

"I understand."

"Would you be interested in coming? Do you think the others would be?"

"Invite those three sand flies and it'll be a hit. Yes, sounds great, Garry. Count me in."

"Thanks. Invite a 'date' if you want and any interesting expats you bump into."

*

Donny-Three would have liked to have stopped by the three girls lying on their towels in the sand; however, he had business on his mind. *Afterwards, I'll drop by,* he decided, climbing the steps and standing on *Sumbar's* veranda, peering in.

"Hi!" he called out. Garry looked up from placing coasters on the inside tables. "Have I got the right bar? I wanna connect with Sunny? Is he here?"

"He's out the back stacking empty crates. There's a delivery truck due. What's it about?"

"Ah … nothing. Old friend of the family, Stonewall, said I should drop by, see Sunny. Have a beer; say hello; ask him about the best clubs in town," lied Donny-Three.

"Sunny's not much of a dancer," commented Garry, though he had no idea what Sunny got up to at night after *Sumbar* closed.

Donny-Three ignored Garry, looking back to the sand. "Hot babes you have hanging around here."

As Donny-Three took a few steps towards him, Garry asked, "Can you wash your feet out there before coming in?"

"Sure thing, man. I'll have a beer and a shot of vodka." Donny-Three washed his feet. He climbed back up the steps onto the veranda and looked over the sand flies below. Connie gave him a cute little wave. *I'll definitely be stopping by,* Donny-Three thought as he sat on the railing.

"Careful, that's not too secure," cautioned Garry, putting the beer and shot glass on the table.

"I'll be right, man, I know what I'm doing," Donny-Three said dismissively. He knocked back the vodka and downed half the beer. Garry walked away, hoping the carpentry would fail.

Donny-Three stayed leaning on the railing, waiting, sipping his beer, focused on the temptation below him.

"You want me?"

Donny-Three turned. "You Sunny?"

"Yes. But why? I know clubs, but I no dance."

"Can we talk somewhere—quiet?"

Sunny looked about. Garry was now in the kitchen with Mai. "Near water," Sunny said quietly. He stepped off the veranda, Donny-Three swallowed the remainder of the beer bottle, and followed. On the way down, as he passed the girls, he clicked his tongue at them.

Sunny and Donny-Three stood on the edge of the sea, water lapping their toes, their caps pulled low over their eyes. As he nudged his sunglasses up the bridge of his nose, Donny-Three asked, "You remember an old American—last year, year before—called 'Stonewall'?"

Sunny thought. "Yes, Mister Stonewall. Good tips."

"That'd be him. Well, he said to me, if I wanted some good smoking shit to look you up."

"Mister Stonewall said? He old man, how you know?"

"He's a friend of my father. Stonewall smokes to ease his pain—medicinal purposes. It's the only thing that gives him relief. Think! You remember now?"

"I remember. But—I careful." Sunny looked at Donny-Three, very closely, wary of the stranger. "What your name—what I call you?"

"Donny-Three."

Sunny studied him. "So Donny-Three, you ache? You pain?"

"Only for the good shit, man."

"Here in Thailand things change. You can grow your own."

"How can I grow my own? I'm only here the week."

"You can buy in special cafe."

"I'm here with my father. I don't wish to be seen."

Sunny considered this. "You, understand, I no sell. I help friend—he sell. I meet you and him. Three thousand baht."

"Three thousand … ah, yeah, what's that in real money?"

"It real money—it Thai baht."

"American dollars?"

Sunny did a quick calculation in his head, adding a bit of a positive transaction fee.

"Holy shit!" Donny-Three exclaimed, when Sunny whispered the amount in American dollars. "That's good, man. I'm in."

"You come here—after dark—nine o'clock. I here on front step—I stop working in bar—have cigarette. If not here, you wait in dark by beach. When I come, walk here, but go in trees—next to *Sumbar*."

Sunny left and went back to the bar. Donny-Three approached the three girls. They repositioned themselves as he neared, forming their alluringly rehearsed position.

"Hi! I've just done a survey and you girls are the sexiest girls on the beach! I'm Donny-Three."

"We've just done a survey and we're the thirstiest girls on the beach. I'm Maggie."

"Take your shirt off Donny-Three and join us," said Lily, rolling onto her back.

Connie added, "We're drinking Mai-Tais."

Lily called out. "Sunny! Three Mai-Tais, and whatever Donny-Three's drinking."

*

"Come on. It's cooled a little, time to go searching," Amelia said, running the towel over her back.

"Let me see that map, again," asked Olivia. "Perhaps we need to widen our search."

"Perhaps. Then again, perhaps not."

"What do you mean?"

"Well, out there," said Amelia, drawing an imaginary circle on the map around *Sumbeach*, "there just seems to be houses and apartment blocks. The shops are all clustered around where we are. If he's been seen in town and lives out there, I think he walks in for a change of scenery. Wouldn't you want to walk to where the 'action' is?"

"Ladies," said Donald Randalson Jnr, touching the rim of his Stetson, in a chivalrous manner. He had returned from his round of golf, happily sated. "I hope you're not leaving because I arrived?"

"No, sir, a prior engagement," Olivia lied.

"Then go with God in your hearts," blessed Donald.

Olivia glanced at Amelia, who subtly raised an eyebrow.

Donald tossed his towel on a sunbed and crossed to the bar. "Double bourbon, lots of ice." While the barman was pouring his drink he added, "Great golf courses you have around here, Buddy."

The barman agreed, though he'd never been to one. For him, playing golf was out of the question. Everything he earned went on survival.

*

On the street, Olivia pointed right and Amelia nodded. They walked in the small shadows of the buildings opposite.

"Our tail has disappeared," noted Amelia. "I guess we're no longer of interest to Captain Choni."

"I hope you're right. Back home do you think we have that intimidating look?"

"Me? Intimidating?"

"Beneath that blonde hair and sweet smile, you do have a threatening eye."

"Well, over the years you develop whatever works for you."

"Perhaps I need more braid on my uniform."

"Also, we could carry a semi-automatic weapon," joked Amelia.

"Seriously, Amelia, that Captain Choni is a piece of work. I know it was racist and belittling, but at the end of the day, we're all cops doing our job. He could've been more co-operative. Or pretended to be."

"He was proving that he was in charge and that our search is immaterial to him."

"So why have us followed?"

"Mmm. That I don't know."

At the end of the street, the strong sunlight hit them once more and on cue the Indian tailors called out from their shopfronts, "Ladies! Inside the finest

Chinese silks—feel them, feel them—you will like! Also we have Thai silks. Yes, ladies, a little heavier, but priceless."

Outside another tailor's shop, an Indian man tried a different tactic. He said quietly, "You buy my dresses, my business suits—when you go home, all the men—yes, ladies, I guarantee—all the men will whistle."

Amelia whispered to Olivia, as they walked on, "If that's what I really need in my life, right now—whistling men!"

Another Indian spruiker called, "Ah ladies, when you walk by—you break my heart!"

Olivia called back, "In time you'll get over it!"

They turned the half corner they always had when walking in this direction. Olivia stopped. "We haven't walked down there," she said, indicating a small lane off to their right. "Come on."

"There's nothing down here, just a few shops and a dead end," observed Amelia, hesitating.

"Look! Off the side of the building at the end—there are steps leading down."

Olivia descended the dozen concrete steps onto muddy sand, the tide being out. "Phew!" she exclaimed, putting her hand over her nose. She called back up to Amelia, "Stormwater drain—runs into the sea—probably a dead dog up stream—or worse. Walk the beach? Or back up to the road?"

"Is he going to be walking a baby down here?" questioned Amelia.

"You're right."

Olivia climbed back up the steps. "How many dead ends have you ever walked down, Amelia? Metaphorically speaking."

"Too many, far too many."

Amelia's eye was taken by a bright white and blue shopfront. "There's an optometrist over there." She crossed and Olivia followed. In front of the window Amelia read the price list. "Good value. I need new reading glasses."

"Then why are you hesitating?"

"They're probably a waste of money. Lose focus after a week or two. I don't really need them."

"Go on, lash out."

"Are you sure?"

"Go on, I'll be out here—window shopping."

Amelia pushed inside the optometrist's and was hit by the chill of the air-conditioning. She shivered. *I should be getting used to this by now.*

Three steps inside, she was greeted by an immaculately dressed young woman with two others standing behind, smiling and bowing a welcome. They were all dressed in their sales uniform—white shorts with a bright purple polo shirt.

"How may I help you, Madame?"

"I'd like to get tested for a pair of reading glasses, please."

"Yes, Madame." The assistant walked to the room behind the counter past several glass cabinets displaying frames. She spoke in the doorway with someone in there and returned to her position at the front of the shop.

An older Thai woman emerged from the office off to the side of the display room. "Yes, may I help you?" asked the optometrist in an educated Australian accent.

After Amelia had her eyes tested, she selected a pair of frames which she felt were rather 'swish'. She left a deposit and upon leaving the shop was hit once again with the heat. She instinctively moved her head back from its curtain.

Amelia found Olivia three shops down. Olivia commented, "That optometrist went to university in Sydney."

"How do you know that? From outside, how'd you hear her Australian accent?"

"I didn't," said Olivia coyly.

"Then how do you possibly know?"

"Her name's in the window with her qualifications. Are you really a policewoman, Amelia?"

Chapter 13

Terence McFarlane, 'Terry' to all his fellow expats, had been in *Sumbeach* much longer than the others. They referred to him as a 'pioneer', claiming he'd blazed the trail for the other Brits that followed and unlike those early ones he'd not got home sick. Terry had stayed.

When asked why, he'd always say that years ago he'd sold his house in Birmingham because his wife had died. He'd nursed her to the end, holding her in his arms as she took her last heaving breath. In the ensuing silence, lying precariously on the side of their bed, he'd decided he no longer wished to live in their house.

Immediately following the funeral he'd say he'd phoned the first estate agent in the telephone book—'Aaronsen and Abbott, realtors of choice'. He'd always touch the hearts of those listening when he confessed that he'd put down the phone and cried for days.

After a few drinks, he'd admit that he and Wanda never had children. They hadn't chosen to find out why for neither wanted the guilt of infertility to eat at their marriage of simple devotion.

Terry had claimed he'd spent his life as an accountant, rarely admitting he'd only been a bookkeeper for a local legal firm. He'd even done some 'pencilling' at weekends for an on-course bookmaker which paid very well. His party-trick was mentally dividing any two integers to the nearest three decimal places.

When asked why he'd settled in Thailand he'd say he and Wanda had never left Britain, not even for a holiday and that soon after Wanda's death he realised he wanted a complete break from the past.

One Friday evening while having a pint in his local pub a rowdy group of men in the far corner were being dominated by a man extolling the beaches, the bargains and the women of Thailand. "Cheap! For the price of this pint I stayed over there for the entire week!" the man exaggerated.

Terry had wanted a place to live, a place he could afford away from the damp and dank of Britain. Thailand sounded ideal.

Terry's was the name of the bar he'd established. It was now accessed up a small flight of concrete steps—the rickety wooden ones having been replaced years ago—jammed between the backdoor of an Indian tailor and the front door of a massage parlour which specialised in dunking customer's feet into a tank of nibbling fish.

After years of gradual development, the bar, which was once in the forefront of the narrow street, was now out of the way as the laneway had been gobbled up by buildings on either side. His bar was frequented by tourists who stumbled upon it and enjoyed Terry's 'reminder of home', the satellite television showing Premier League games and its hidden-away nature where they could drink far from the gaze of their shopping wives. Those tourists always dropped in when returning to *Sumbeach* and it became the home of the Expats Golf Society, *The Sumbeach Buccaneers.*

Dickie Eastman had been thinking of setting up the society when over a few beers one night Terry did his long-divisional trick. Dickie, then and there, asked him to be Treasurer. An informal code of passwords grew over time—Dickie was known among the golfing expats as 'Drake' and Terry as 'Dampier'. Every second Friday evening, the ever increasing membership met at *Terry's* for a drink, a laugh, a look at the upcoming fortnight's golfing draw and the handicap rankings before heading off with their wives, girlfriends or working girls to dinner and home to bed by nine. In *Sumbeach* after dark, there was always more action behind the curtains than in front.

That morning Nerida Johns slept in. She woke with a realisation, "Oh hell! I'll be late!" She showered, dressed and found her golf clubs where she'd left them the day before. She grabbed an apple from the refrigerator.

"I'll be off, Terry," called Nerida from the bottom of the stairs, lifting her golf clubs onto her shoulder.

"Let me," said Terry coming around from behind the bar.

"It's only down the lane. Dickie is sending a driver this morning."

"Lucky you. I wonder what Dickie wants?"

"Never fear, Terry, you're my one and only." Nerida laughed and placed a kiss on his cheek.

Nerida Johns lived to play golf and like the other expats had fallen in love with the courses around *Sumbeach* the first time she visited. She had taken her annual holiday, three weeks, in *Sumbeach,* hitting long drives and sinking putts which left a lot of the men gasping. She hit off a handicap of two.

At first she'd stayed at *L 'Hotel Majestique* then five years ago she got talking to Terry one night, as she'd often done, and sometime late in the night, after a few drinks, one of them propositioned the other.

Her body was welcoming and Terry initially couldn't adjust to the different motions he'd been used to with Wanda. She excited him and he her.

After three nights Terry had warned her, "I can't go back to England. I could never live there again."

"I'm not asking you to. Everything stays as it is. I'll continue coming out here each year. Are you planning on getting a live-in girlfriend?"

"Lord, no."

She laughed. "Good. Then I'll stay with you when I return next year. Okay?"

"Okay!"

"Just one thing—I'd like to replace that tatty old orange curtain."

"Terry?" asked the young woman working Terry's bar.

"Yes, Dimi?"

"Tomorrow, husband work morning. I bring in baby Sami? Like last time?"

"Yes, Dimi. I'll walk him again. I've nothing on."

Nerida smiled at him. "You're a good man, Terry McFarlane, you know that?"

Before Terry could comment, she exclaimed, "Oh! Here's Dickie's van!"

Chapter 14

Olivia emerged into the sunlight from the hotel's rotating front door, followed by a carefully stepping Amelia. They'd changed into fresh clothing for the early evening stroll. Outside they avoided the puddles not yet evaporated from the afternoon's deluge.

"It hasn't cooled much," noted Olivia. "I'm not complaining, mind you."

"Thinking back, how did you manage to get that young American to buy us drinks and not want to come over and chat you up?" asked Amelia, quite impressed.

"He took pity on me when I told him you'd brought me to Thailand for the heat—to clear up my bout of syphilis."

Amelia burst out laughing. She took Olivia's arm and they walked on. "If we don't find our man, Olivia, at least you are making this trip entertaining."

The two women stopped by a bar/restaurant to consult their town map. The outside tables and chairs sat beneath an awning, three steps up, to protect the bar from being inundated by the regular afternoon flood. While Olivia 'studied' the mounted plastic covered menu of photographed plates of food, Amelia peered inside. No one matched their suspect's description.

A young woman sat to their left, on the edge by the railing. Amelia glanced at her and took a tissue from her handbag. She smiled and quietly said, "Here."

The young woman was taken aback. "Oh, thanks. Is it that obvious?"

"That's okay," consoled Amelia.

The young woman dried her eyes as Amelia and Olivia started to move off.

"Why are all men bastards?" she called after them. Amelia and Olivia stopped.

"If you answer that," whispered Olivia, "remember, we're only here for a week."

"He brings me out here," the young woman continued, "I didn't want to come. I could have gone to Bournemouth. And then he leaves me while I go shopping. I come back laden with bags and I walk into our hotel room and there he is with this naked Thai—*whore*—riding him. He looks at me and says to her, 'Keep going! Don't stop!' And we've got to sit side by side for twelve hours on the flight home!"

Olivia tried to ease her pain. "Go on-line and change your seat."

"I have tried, the flight's full. There's a seat or two in Business Class, but who can afford to fly Business Class?"

The young woman suddenly slapped the table in front of her. "Thank you! Thank you! Whenever he goes out, he always leaves his cards behind. He's paranoid about being mugged. I know his PIN!" She stood. "Forget Business—I'm going home First Class!"

She placed five hundred baht under the glass ashtray for the waitress and hurried off thanking them once more.

*

"What a storm. I got stranded on the seventh," exclaimed Nerida. "I stood under a tree and told myself it would be over in ten minutes. But today it decided to rain on me for thirty! Mind you, I was dry by the time I completed the back nine."

Terry advised, "Have a warm shower anyway, wash it off—don't sit around in your damp clothes."

"While I was stranded there, it reminded me—I've never told you this—it's funny what comes into your mind. A long time ago—well before I started coming here, I was involved—the only time—with a married man. *I* believed he'd leave his wife, but *he* didn't believe that. So all I got from the affair was a wet, windy, dirty weekend in Brighton, stuck in a hotel room looking out at the gloom. I looked at him fast asleep at three in the afternoon, splayed on the bed, snoring, and realised that it was over. And still the rain hit the window. I didn't want to stay and I couldn't leave. That's how I felt today under the tree."

Terry nodded sagely.

"That's what I love about you, Terrence—your insightful advice." Nerida dragged her clubs up the wooden stair case to the flat above. She stopped halfway. "I don't know where that confession came from."

"Perhaps you're clearing your books," Terry offered, ever the 'accountant'.

"I don't follow."

"Clearing up things in your head before moving on—getting things out of the way."

She thought about that, then stepped up. Terry watched her climb, her tanned legs beneath her short golfing outfit, and knew this year he'd miss her more than ever when she flew home.

*

"Right, confession time," announced Olivia. "That woman back there has got me thinking about things." Amelia stopped, waiting for Olivia to continue. "You ever come across a duty solicitor called Bartholomew Davidson?"

"No," answered Amelia, after pausing for thought. "Before you tell me, let's stand in the shade over there."

Amelia took a step towards it as Olivia suddenly grabbed her arm. A tuk-tuk screamed by and a motor bike roared past in the opposite direction.

"Stepmother, you're not on a pedestrian crossing in the High Street now!"

Amelia touched her heart and laughed with relief. "I should be thankful that at least they drive on our side of the road."

"Only when they decide to." Olivia walked Amelia to the shade.

"You buy shoes?" asked a woman nearby. "Best shoes in *Sumbeach*. Come in. Come try on."

"Maybe later—after dark," Olivia said, smiling and then turning back to Amelia, "There's an expat coming towards us with a Thai woman—no baby. It's not him. How many expats are there in this place?"

"A warm climate, a beach and an affordable cost of living," explained Amelia. "How long is a piece of string?"

"We're not going to find him, you know," said Olivia.

"The chances have always been slim."

"I just feel we're resigned to following every foreigner in *Sumbeach* to no avail." Olivia lowered her voice. "Why did they send you? Why did ACC David McPherson choose you, out of all the officers in the Met? I mean any detective could have come here to look around."

Amelia waited, holding back her reply.

"Sorry for asking," apologised Olivia, "I've overstepped the mark."

"No. No, I don't mind telling you." Amelia gathered her thoughts. "He chose me, I believe, because he wanted me to get away from England. He wanted me to have a holiday, because it's the anniversary of my husband's death—the twentieth—a death that ACC McPherson had been involved in. He and Mark were the best of pals and they were shoulder to shoulder when Mark was shot."

Tears came to Amelia's eyes. Olivia put an arm around her shoulder in comfort.

"This solicitor—Davidson?" asked Amelia, riding over her emotion, returning to Olivia's previous conversation.

Olivia didn't hesitate: "Your usual solicitor marches in, arrogantly stating that his 'client', whom he's never met, is totally innocent. Then he slaps a copy of the charge sheet, which he hasn't read yet, on the table and asks to be left alone with his client, etcetera, etcetera, et-bloody-cetera."

"We've all been there."

"However, Barty knocks before entering, excuses himself and apologies for interrupting. So I hang by the front entrance and watch him sign out. As he reaches for the door handle, I say: *Thank you for coming.* He stops and says: *I don't hear sarcasm or irony in your voice at all.* I tell him: *No, I genuinely mean it, as most solicitors are real arseholes.* He laughs. Oh, Amelia, what a laugh! So I say: *Any chance of hitting on you?* He looks and says: *How do you know I'm not married with three kids under the age of seven?* I say: *Because when you said to me 'I wish to be alone with my client', I went and looked you up on a search engine.* Actually I looked him up on the criminal data base first."

"And? Don't stop there."

"We see each other from time to time." Olivia changed tack. "That young woman back there has made a stronger impact than I thought. You know what—when I get home, I'm going to suggest we come out here for our next holiday. Two weeks—I'm going to put him to the 'Thai-whore-test' and if he passes, I'll take him back home, hold my taser gun to his head and ask him to marry me."

*

Nerida turned as Captain Choniburshakanari walked into *Terry's.* The police captain held up his hand. Staying seated, she glanced at Terry, concerned, as the uniformed man crossed to the fortnightly golf draw displayed prominently beside the bar. Captain Choni studied the names listed there. Dimi held back. Captain Choni did not find what he was looking for, and came and sat next to Nerida, opposite Terry.

"Madame, good day to you. Are you well?" he asked, charmingly.

"Yes, fine—thank you," replied Nerida, uncomfortably.

"A pleasure to hear it." He smiled and bowed his head.

It was so matter of fact it reminded Nerida of Uncle Charlie dropping into her parent's home for a Sunday evening visit when she was a child. In that official uniform, she knew he wasn't Uncle Charlie.

"Terry," the captain went on, "you're also looking well."

"Captain," replied Terry, nodding. "Whenever you drop by I feel my health improve immeasurably."

Captain Choni laughed. "Such compliments! Terry you have learnt so much from our Thai ways."

"Yes, Captain, I have."

"Terry, I wish to ask one question," Choni stated simply, the pleasantness disappearing from his voice. "Do you know a 'Harold Keith Brown'?"

There was silence as Terry thought. Nerida studied both men, Captain Choni eager for an answer, Terry considering the question.

Terry shook his head, slowly. "No, never heard of him."

"The name may come from before I was posted here, from the time you were one of the first expat bar owners in our then sleepy little fishing village."

"No," reiterated Terry. "I can't recall anyone with that name."

"If you hear it mentioned, please let me know."

"Of course. Anything to reduce my rent," joked Terry.

Captain Choniburshakanari smiled and turned to Nerida. "Madame, to be honest with you, I have a few tenants and Terry here is the best payer of them all. He never fails and is always on time. It must be the English accountant in him." He turned his attention back to Terry. "Sadly this month I cannot see my way clear to offer a discount. Thank you, Terry."

He stood to go; however, he stopped and turned back. "Madame, I believe I have the pleasure to meet one of the best golfers ever to regularly play our courses here in *Sumbeach*. Your reputation is legendary in town. Over the years of your visits have *you* ever come across the name of Harold Keith Brown? On the golf course, perhaps?"

"Ah—no," replied Nerida, surprised that anyone she'd possibly have met could be part of an investigation by the Thai police.

Captain Choniburshakanari smiled at her and took his leave. Turning back to the bar he asked in Thai, "Dimi, how is your father?"

"He is well, thank you, Captain Choni," the young woman replied, unhappy with being the focus of attention.

"And your baby?"

"Well also."

"That is good. Please pass on my best wishes to your father and kiss your baby for me."

"Thank you, I will."

Choni left.

Nerida reached across the table and took Terry's hand. "He knew who I was."

"There's not much he doesn't know. No need to worry. He's okay."

She continued to look at him, concerned, rubbing the top of his hand.

"Choni has nothing over me," reassured Terry. Nerida looked back at him as if he did. "Okay, I will explain." He looked at the clock above the bar. Dimi noticed and began to pour him a beer and a glass of Italian wine for Nerida.

"Soon after I arrived in Thailand I was wandering aimlessly south along the beach, the epitome of the old clichéd Brit on holiday—long trousers, cuffs rolled up, sandals in hand, and a battered old hat pulled down protecting my eyes from the glaring sunlight. I was a sight to behold. I came upon this small fishing village of *Sumbeckarnawan*. I left the beach and slowly walked through the narrow streets, past the wooden houses on stilts, down to the rickety piers jutting out into the gulf, and stood looking over the sea."

Dimi crossed from the bar and carefully placed the drinks on the table.

"Locals passed, eyeing me curiously. Compared to them I was odd—a very pale man. I could have flown in from Mars. I remember one woman with a long straw broom sweeping a porch giving me a long stare. A boy on a bicycle waved and I waved back. With that the locals seemed to relax. I couldn't have been further from Birmingham.

"There was this sign, handwritten in Thai, nailed to a wooden building up a laneway.

"I asked a man, propped against his rusty push-bike, *English?*" He moved the fingers as if they were speaking and shook his head. He called out inside. Another man appeared.

"I asked, 'English—speak?' *Yes* he replied. 'What does sign read?' *For rent.* 'Who is owner?' *Me*."

"I wished to see inside the building. The man smiled graciously, as they all do out here, and beckoned me forward. Inside was a single large space with a crude sink and unfinished plumbing. Imagine where you are now sitting without any of the trappings.

"I pointed to the exposed pipes against the wall over there. *Water come from dam*, he said, *but shitter goes to drain.*

"Sometimes, Nerida, things seem to click into place. I asked him the rental price. He told me in *baht*, and I immediately calculated out loud in *pounds,* nodding that the price seemed to be *okay.* He was impressed with my mental calculation. I explained I was an accountant. He took me upstairs.

"I pulled open that old favourite orange curtain of yours and the Gulf of Thailand flooded in. I'd found what I'd been looking for.

"His name was Duke. He offered me a proposition. If I took the lease, he'd reduce the rent if I'd look after his books for him. He owned property about the town and felt he was losing money someway, but he didn't know how.

"I didn't take long for me to find the man who was doing the short-changing. As a thank-you, Duke refused to sign a lease with me, saying, *my word—your word—our bond. You save me, I trust you.*"

"How does this relate to Captain Choni?" asked Nerida.

"Seven years ago Duke asked me to visit him. He said, *I die soon. Now sign lease. I sell, but I want you to stay. Sign lease for—protection. I don't want you lose bar. Man I sell to may not have kind heart like me.*"

"Two days after my new landlord appeared. I showed him the lease. He studied it, saying, *I have heard about the 'first limey' in Sumbeach.* The lease I had was for twenty-five years. The new owner shrugged with acceptance and climbed onto his motorbike."

"And the new landlord was Captain Choni?"

"Yes. The newly arrived police captain rode off, accepting the fact that he'd only be getting rent from the establishment. I'd made a very early decision—there'd be no graft, as my bar was simply that—a bar. There would be no prostitution, no gambling on cockfights, no drug dealing on the premises—and everyone in town knows it."

There was a fall of footsteps at the bar's entrance.

"Dampier, what's the good police captain doing here?" asked Dickie Eastman, removing his self branded golf cap.

"His usual friendly chat," said Terry, looking up at his friend.

"Not after his bribe money?"

"Drake, you know there's nothing worthy of blackmail in my bar."

97

"Yes. Hello, Nerida. I saw your name on my office list for the week. Welcome back." He kissed her. "You're as beautiful as ever."

"Dickie, you're blind, but I'll still take it as a compliment."

Dickie badly acted 'feeling for a chair'. He sat.

Dimi was at his side. "Beer, Mister Golf?"

"Yes, please."

Dimi returned behind the counter.

"Terry, I didn't come to talk to you, so don't be too disappointed." Dickie turned to Nerida. "So, Nerida—this week I have a few struggling golfers in, and I thought that on Sunday morning, I'd like to offer something a little different— a master class—or a *mistress* class." He laughed at his joke. "I was wondering if you'd like to look at their swings and offer some tips. I'll pay you, of course."

"Take it," said Terry. "It's the first time I've ever heard him offer anyone 'money'."

Dickie offered her his hand, asking, "Interested? A deal?"

Nerida, after a brief pause, took it. "A deal," she said.

"Hey! What a great hidey-hole!" Billy Mackie, alone and on the prowl, had stumbled upon *Terry's*.

Chapter 15

Jack spent the remainder of the afternoon finding the places he used to visit and being genuinely surprised at the changes that had taken place. Thais, with money to invest, had realised that there were increasing profits to be made from the growing number of expats and Western tourists now frequenting *Sumbeach*.

Old shopfronts had been replaced with glass windows, tiled floors, securely locked glass doors and bright lighting. There were several gold stores, optometrists and dentists, all strategically placed in the tourist part of town.

He stopped outside a brightly painted supermarket, with an immaculately uniformed staff of young Thai women in deep blue branded polo shirts and tan coloured shorts. It had a section towards the front doorway of English, German and Italian books, and prominently displayed travel guides to Thailand. From inside the compact supermarket, one of the girls gestured as to open the door for him. He smiled and shook his head, waving as he turned away.

The ubiquitous Indian tailor called out to him, "Sir! Monsieur! Signor!", hoping not only to grab his attention but to ascertain his nationality. Jack merely waved and kept walking so the tailor spoke in the default language of international trade and commerce. "Three piece suit *and* two shirts for the price of one! Very good! Very good price!"

On the beach there were many empty sun beds, only the last of the days' tourists tanning themselves in the dying rays. The owner was beginning to stack them up under his make-shift tent, where he'd sleep the night after cooking his meal on a self constructed gas cook top. His three mangy dogs had already dug their beds in the sand and waited for their owner's uneaten fish and rice to be tossed their way.

The sun had set over the mountain as Jack washed his feet in the bowl outside *Sumbar*. The two Dutchmen came down the steps past him and headed towards town. Jack turned suddenly, taken by surprise as a teenage boy appeared from the bushes as if Jack's presence had startled him. His eyes were wide and enquiring.

"Can I help you?" asked Jack. The boy stared back. "What do you want?"

An elder boy followed out from the bushes. He took one look at Jack, grabbed his pal and dragged him away up the side path towards the back lot.

Inside Beatrice sat with Eugene at a table. She called to him. "Jack! Come join us for an early dinner. We're just about to order."

Jack got the impression that Eugene wasn't too impressed with the invitation; however, not particularly caring how Eugene felt, he sat with them anyway. Eugene nursed a clear combination of vodka and lemonade sans fruit peel, while Beatrice was finishing her Mai-Tai. Jack indicated to Sunny for a cold beer.

"Have you been shopping, Beatrice?" Jack asked.

"Yes! How did you know?"

"The sarong you're wearing is very bright and very new."

"I also bought Eugene's shirt. I insisted he wear it tonight."

Eugene's shirt was red with three black lines swirling their way across his chest.

Rather than offering a printed menu, Garry announced, "Tonight Mai is cooking Chicken Satay entree followed by either Massaman Beef Curry or Chicken Curry, both served with a choice of fried or steamed rice."

"That all sounds 'yum'!" said a delighted Beatrice. Garry went off to the kitchen. "Well, I've had a most interesting day," she declared.

"Any further news of the German gentleman?" asked Jack.

"Oh no, no, no!"

"German gentleman?" enquired Eugene. "I know nothing of this, Beatrice."

Beatrice sat back and simply stated, "There's nothing to know. End of discussion. So, what have you been doing today, Jack?"

"I've caught up on memories."

"And are they all still there?" she asked, wishing for him to go on.

"Some. The changes in town are staggering. The whole town I remember is basically still there, though the feeling I have of it belongs to another time. You must also feel that, Eugene?"

"Oh—yes," replied Eugene, caught drifting in and out of his own thoughts, "unrecognisable."

*

100

Amelia and Olivia sat in the foyer immediately off the downstairs bar of *L'Hotel Majestique,* people watching, listening to the Filipino trio. The last dregs of fruit peel slumped forlornly in their glasses, below the umbrellas.

The spinning door was working overtime with hotel guests coming and going. Locals, immaculately attired in colourful outfits, met with friends and after warm greetings moved to the restaurants scattered throughout the hotel. Others gathered in the foyer waiting for friends to appear from the rooms above, before continuing outside. A tourist guide, attached to the large red coach parked in the curved drive, assembled the last of his group and then walked the thirty chattering people out, down the street, saying, "I cannot guarantee it, but there might be an elephant down at the night market!"

"Those musicians are very good," commented Olivia, tapping her foot.

An overly American-accented singer joined the trio with a version of 'I'd Like to Teach the World to Sing'.

"I wish the world would teach her," commented Amelia, suppressing a giggle.

"Come on," decided Olivia, "time to wander through that night market. Come on, Amelia, don't be so hesitant. It'll be crowded out there, yes, but it'll be well lit."

"You're right. Let's go. Keep your eyes peeled."

Olivia added, "For bargains!"

*

Mai's curry was delicious, the perfect balance between flavour and heat. Eugene drained his second vodka, its effect loosening his tongue.

"When I first came over here *Sumbar* didn't exist. I don't even remember a building on this site, possibly because I only occasionally walked down this end of the beach. Back then I stayed up there in town opposite the large hotel."

"Do you recall what the hotel was called?" asked Jack. "I've been trying to think of its name all day."

"Oh—something like—Princess ... Eastern?"

"Oriental Princess!" blurted out Jack as its name suddenly came to him.

"Yes!" acknowledged Eugene. "It had a quiet little back bar away from the hotel in the gardens. I think that's where their gym is now. A select group of us used to meet there. Good conversation, good cocktails, an international flavour—

you know, a place to converse and put the craziness of the world into perspective. It was always wonderful to catch up with others—like oneself—ah, interested in global events." He paused and gathered himself. "I have an appointment. Please excuse me." He whispered, "Beatrice, I'll be back after breakfast."

Eugene pushed back his chair and walked out the back door. Jack excusing himself followed a moment later as far as the bar's toilet. He heard a car pull up onto the vacant lot behind, the car door slam shut and the car drive away.

After flushing the toilet, he washed his hands and ran water over his warm face. *I've picked up a bit of sun today,* he realised, staring at his reddening face in close-up in the mirror. He returned to Beatrice. "Is everything okay with Eugene?"

"Oh yes. He's quite a shy man. He has a friend with a house up there—somewhere." She indicated vaguely towards the mountains behind the bar. "I told him no one cares any more whether he's gay or not."

"Perhaps he feels in Thailand they still do."

"He's very private. I got a huge surprise when he asked me if I was interested in accompanying him to Thailand." She laughed. "Apparently, according to my friend at work, I'm his fag-hag!"

Garry approached and asked if they wanted another drink. Beatrice answered, "Sure!" and before Jack could say anything, she added: "I'll pay."

For a long time they sat there together. Jack learnt all about the State Library of Western Australia, Beatrice's time in the classroom and she learnt nothing about architecture or timber.

"You're a very good listener, Jack," she finally commented.

"And you're a very good talker, Beatrice."

Beatrice laughed. "I'm not usually. It must be Thailand. Back home I hardly say a word. I work in a library after all! Yes, that must be why. Back home it's all bottled up inside and over here it's simply spewing forth."

Jack finished his beer and she leant in. "Do you think you could accompany me up the beach—it's very dark out there."

"Okay," said Jack, "Where to?"

She became coy. "Maybe we could stop at a certain German Brauhaus."

Jack smiled, "So a decision has been made! Let's go."

Outside, on the sand, in the dark, they passed a determined young American heading for *Sumbar.*

*

Captain Choniburshakanari, in his neatly pressed uniform, stood in the entrance of *Brauhaus Helmut*, presenting a formidable presence. Inside diners noticed him. Locals and regulars to *Sumbeach* stiffened in their seats.

Helmut caught his eye and nodded his head. Captain Choni followed him past the bar to the storeroom out back. Werner watched them go. He held his two little sisters by their hands and in German said, "Come on, time for bed."

Safely out of ear-shot Helmut turned. "Captain?" They stood by the empty beer crates. "How may I help you?"

Captain Choni spoke in simple English as he only had a smattering of German. "Helmut—you know man—Harold Keith Brown?"

Helmut thought for a moment. "American? English?"

"English."

He thought further. "No."

"Maybe here—long time—perhaps before I come."

The two men stood in silence, the captain's eyes on him. Helmut finally said, "No. This name I've never heard." Captain Choni, seeing no movement in Helmut's pupils, believed him. Helmut added, "I know most English expats."

"So do I," said Choni, as he started to go.

"Like beer? No charge."

"Thank you, no—another time, Helmut. Let me know if you ever hear this name. Okay?"

"Okay, Captain Choni."

Captain Choniburshakanari left down the back alley, which he seemed to know only too well.

*

"Can I get a little serious?" asked Nerida.

Terry wondered, *Serious about what?* "Mmm—maybe," he offered cautiously.

"If Sunday is successful, do you think Dickie could make it a regular job?"

"You're only here for another three weeks," rationalised Terry.

"Well, I've been thinking. Work back home is getting tedious and the new manager is at times unreasonable. I have money stashed away. I could quit in six months and live here with the aid of a semi-regular 'golf-pro' job."

Terry continued to look at her, "So you *are* clearing the books."

"Maybe." She'd planted the seed and knew it needed time to grow.

"I'll consider it, Nerida. Though—expats can't work in Thailand."

"Oh, I hadn't thought of that."

"Maybe Dickie could deposit money into your UK bank account if you invoiced him rather than he employ you."

Nerida smiled, "You *are* an accountant."

"Don't take my word for it. Check on-line. I'm not an immigration lawyer."

"Can I show you something? You see if I did come for a longer stay we'd soon get in each other's way upstairs. It's too small. However, there is a new development up towards the *Park Royal Thai Links*. Separate houses built around a communal swimming pool."

Terry looked at her. "I'll consider it."

"Look," she said, placing a coloured brochure on the table between them. "Consider seriously."

*

"Those jeans are tight and very low waisted," observed Amelia. "They certainly leave nothing to the imagination."

Olivia had emerged from the canvas curtained make-shift change booth. "Might just be what I need to arouse Barty and get him to commit," she said in a loud pronounced voice, trying to be heard above the crowd's hub-bub and the pumping sounds of Asian pop music. She nodded to the lady that she'd buy them and went back inside to change out of them.

Amelia studied the faces in the crowd slowly streaming by. *Most of these men would be far happier back in the bar of their hotel, rather than fighting their way through this packed alley at their wives' insistence.*

Opening the canvas curtain, Olivia handed the jeans to a teenage girl, who slid them into a pull-string bag. She then handed baht to the lady in charge of the stall.

Amelia reminded herself again that they were trying to balance shopping with searching for their suspect, though tonight Olivia had tilted the balance in favour of the former. *She is certainly making use of the excellent exchange rate.*

They jostled their way through the throng crammed into the unrecognisable alley they'd walked down that afternoon. The brightness of the exposed light bulbs strung above the hastily erected stalls made every face, passing through their halos, clearly visible. Snatches of German, Italian, Japanese, Chinese and English were caught, as one slipstream passed by the other.

"Oh mum, look, over there!" Olivia pointed to a row of brightly coloured swimsuits.

"No! They'll expose bits of me, even I haven't seen for twenty years."

Olivia stopped moving. Amelia bumped into her.

"Off here is that laneway with the bars down the end," said Olivia. "He might be down there."

Before Amelia could say a word, Olivia headed off. She followed quickly, trying to catch up. A large man cut across her path, bringing Amelia up short. By the time she'd side-stepped him, Olivia was quite a way in front.

"Olivia!" Amelia yelled. "Olivia!"

Within ten metres the bright lights and the noise of the shoppers had disappeared behind her. Ahead was the silhouette of Olivia, caught in the red and amber light coming from the bars further down the laneway. On the veranda of the first bar, over the pool table they'd seen that afternoon, two Western men were now holding cues, drinking and laughing. Three local girls in tight slit leather skirts were hanging about pretending to be interested in the game's outcome. Another girl massaged a man's foot as he sprawled back on a sun lounge, a large bottle of beer in his hand, a wide smile across his face.

The bar girls sensed Olivia's approach and turned expectantly. She stopped as they did so, Amelia catching her up. Disappointed at seeing two women, the Thai bar girls returned to the game at the pool table and the sprawled man's inner-sole.

A Thai man saw Olivia approach and he stood—in front of her. Across the alley from them another Thai man stepped forward from the dark into the amber pool of light behind Amelia. The two Thai men spoke rapidly to each other and laughed pointedly.

"Come on, Olivia," hissed Amelia. "Let's get out of here."

"Hello, Olivia!" said an American-accented Oriental voice, coming from behind Amelia. The two women turned. This third man was silhouetted by the bright lights of the market behind him.

I must have walked right by him, thought Amelia, feeling her body tense, hoping to protect herself from whatever was coming her way.

The three Asian men stepped in. Amelia reached for her badge. Her badge was back in England.

Memorise their faces, she advised herself and silently cursed her blonde hair.

"Olivia, do you and your friend like satay?" asked the first Thai man. "Inside, we have the best satay in *Sumbeach*—cheap, but good." He reached inside his trousers pocket.

Oh hell, thought Amelia, *a gun.*

A knife, thought Olivia.

The man took out a business card and offered it. "Olivia—it true—very good satay in here."

Olivia took the card. It read: *Sami's Bar.* She breathed easier.

The two Westerners playing pool stopped their game and turned. "Hey blondie," said the taller, in a broad Australian accent, "Wanna shoot some pool with us?"

"No thanks," Amelia said, stepping to take Olivia by the arm.

"I'll buy you that satay, afterwards."

"We're looking for our husbands," explained Olivia. "They're six foot, body builder types. Haven't seen them pass down here, have you?"

"Nuh! Don't wish to either," laughed the Australian's fat mate.

Amelia and Olivia waved and slowly walked back. The men behind laughed. One of the Australians let fire with a piercingly loud wolf-whistle.

"Australian men," said Amelia, as they were once again lit by the market's overhead globes. "How could a woman ever fall for one of those?"

Chapter 16

Donny-Three stood in the dark, off to the side of the light from *Sumbar* spilling onto the sand. It was nine o'clock and Sunny was not standing on the front veranda, as promised, smoking his cigarette. Donny-three kicked his left foot, impatiently.

A thirtyish Thai man walked out of the darkness, through the edge of the shaft of light and into the darkness on the other side. Donny-Three watched him go, the man speaking a brief message into his mobile phone.

Donny-Three turned to the sea behind him and the green-lit boats far out on the water. He counted fifteen, gave up and turned back. Sunny was now on the veranda, lighting a cigarette as arranged. Donny-Three did not move immediately. He hesitated, allowing Sunny to emit several puffs of smoke. He glanced about into the darkness. The passing Thai man had disappeared.

Sunny watched Donny-Three, approaching, silhouetted against the moonlit ocean. He tossed the cigarette into the smoker's box at the edge of the veranda and met him below *Sumbar's* steps.

Once together, Sunny turned so he could keep an eye on *Sumbar*. "All good—follow me," he said, moving off.

"Wait! In there?" Donny-Three realised that Sunny was leading him past the outdoor shower, into the bushes and trees next to the bar. "I don't know," the young American said, warily.

"You must—trust. I cannot be seen. Garry would tell my sister and she would beat me."

"Your sister?"

"She raise me—like mother. I must not do wrong that she see."

Donny-Three thought about it and in a split second decided he'd trust Sunny. The two young men walked into the trees. Sunny said something in Thai and from the darkness came a reply.

Around a sloping tree was a very small clearing, the sandy vegetation underfoot trampled. The man who'd passed Donny-Three on the beach, stood upright, one extended arm resting against the sharply angled tree. He took out of his pocket a plastic, zippered packet and opened it for the young American to see and smell. He held out his hand for the cash. With his right hand Donny-Three placed money into the hand of the Thai man who simultaneously placed the dope into Donny-Three's left. The man checked the money and patted Sunny on the shoulder, giving him a five hundred baht note before heading off, picking his way carefully through the undergrowth and bushes.

"Wait. We no move," said Sunny. The two stood. In the quietness surrounding them, muffled noises could be heard coming through the side wall of *Sumbar.* "Okay," said Sunny at last, "you go."

Donny-Three was hesitant. "No Sunny. You go that way. I'm going the back way." And Donny-Three stumbled through the bushes, some cutting his legs, as he found the side concrete path up beyond the swimming pool. He gathered himself and crossed the vacant lot, avoiding the mongrel dogs, taking the road back to *Sumbeach.*

*

Twenty metres from *Brauhaus Helmut*, Beatrice turned to Jack and tentatively asked, "Am I making a mistake?"

"Beatrice, who am I to know—and who am I to judge? If worse comes to worse, put it down to 'one of life's lessons'."

"You *are* a psychiatrist!" She looked at the sign above *Brauhaus Helmet's* open entrance. "Don't tell anyone back in Perth!"

"Who do I know to tell?"

Beatrice moved a step and stopped. She turned back to Jack. "I'm actually nervous. But I think this sure beats hanging out for a divorced man with three kids and a mortgage in South Fremantle."

"Beatrice, go!"

She took a step and turned back again. "My heart's pounding! Okay. I'll be okay from here. Thanks for the escort." She kissed his cheek. "Wish me luck." She hesitated, "Ah, the folly of the unattached woman."

"I'll wait over there by the police station for fifteen minutes. If it doesn't work out, I'll walk you home."

"You're a really nice guy, you know that. Just like my father."

Jack crossed the street. Beatrice took a couple of steps into the restaurant's light and stopped at the first table.

Helmut approached. "Madame? I help you? It is too late for dinner. Kitchen closed."

From further in the restaurant Werner turned and smiling broadly said, "It's okay, Papa. She is here to see me."

*

After the promised fifteen minutes, and with no re-emergence of Beatrice, Jack decided to walk home via the streets, rather than retrace his steps along the beach. He dipped his head underneath the low hanging spaghetti of power cables and crossed the intersection, dodging the stream of motor bikes, before stepping up onto the uneven footpath.

In the darkness Donny-Three swerved suddenly, avoiding a collision with Jack. *Clearly that young man's mind is on other things.*

A kilometre down, he was walking on gravel, a section of the path in the process of being concreted. Several steps on he realised he had a stone in his sandal. He suffered it as he neared where he had to turn left down the laneway through the vacant lot behind *Sumbar*. Finally having had enough of the annoying pain, he leant against a shop's wall and attempted to flick the stone out.

A dark coloured sedan pulled up a little in front of him. A teenage boy emerged from the back seat and quickly pulling a singlet over his head to cover his thin torso, he started running towards Jack. He soon slowed to a brisk walk. Jack had thought him to be about fifteen; however, as he neared, Jack believed the boy to be closer to twelve and then he recognised him. It was the younger boy Jack had seen earlier out the front of *Sumbar*. Another boy opened the car's front passenger door and alighted. The rear window was rolled down and he stuck in his hand. He walked confidently away towards Jack and past him.

That's the basketball boy from the orphanage!

Jack sat on the pavement, removing his sandal, ridding the stone and rubbing his foot. The car didn't move.

A bald headed man climbed out of the front seat and as he stepped away, the rear side window was lowered. Someone from inside called him back. Words were exchanged. The bald headed man then walked in the direction of Jack.

That's the priest from the orphanage!

The priest stopped next to Jack. "Disgusting! Drunk and in the gutter! You insult this fine country and these fine people."

Jack, biting his tongue, glanced up. The moonlight caught the silver crucifixes on both collars of the priest's white shirt. For that moment Jack was back in school being castigated and ridiculed by the brother who'd taught him mathematics, brandishing a heavy wooden ruler!

"You should be ashamed of yourself," the priest continued. "From your eyes I see it's not liquor it's … As I have said from the pulpit, legalising marijuana will bring to this beautiful country all the world's riff-raff and turn its citizens into a nation of drug dealers. Cleanse yourself my son, before it's too late."

The priest walked on.

"Stupid idiot," Jack muttered after him.

He watched the priest stride away then looked back to the dark car. Eugene appeared from the back seat and hurried into the vacant lot behind *Sumbar.*

A large man struggled out of the back seat and stood by the vehicle. He lit a cigar, spat once and puffed violently. To Jack the man seemed vaguely familiar.

Watching the cigar smoke being shot into the night sky above the man's head Jack wondered, *What are you guys up to?*

Eugene returned, wearing a fresh shirt. He'd changed out of the red and black one Beatrice had bought him.

Jack studied his sandal and his foot, pretending to pick out another stone, in case the cover of darkness failed him. When he raised his head, the two men were once more in the back seat of the car. The rear door slammed. The car slowly drove off.

The cigar was still smouldering on the ground where it had been tossed. Jack stood on it, contemptuously, extinguishing it. The identity of the large man played on his mind as he crossed the empty lot, under the single light and past the swimming pool. It was, as always, a warm night so he decided he'd change and jump in.

In the pool Jack stopped mid-stroke. *An Australian politician!* He couldn't recall the name, though he'd worked out the face.

*

110

After Werner had finished his shift in the restaurant, Beatrice walked with him hand in hand down the beach. They crossed the shaft of light from *Sumbar* then walked in the darkness on the other side to the large bowl where they washed their feet. Up the side path, she led him in through the back entrance and up the stairs, thankful she didn't bump into anyone.

In the room she said a little nervously, "It's so hot. I'm going to need a shower."

Turning, she noticed Eugene's red and black shirt, tossed onto his side of the bed. She picked it up and went to hang it in the wardrobe. *Oh, Eugene's spilt something on this!* She took the shirt into the bathroom and rinsed it in the sink, explaining to Werner who Eugene was. She then carried the shirt and hung it to dry overnight on the chair on the balcony. She returned inside. "My god! You don't waste your time."

Werner was standing naked leaning against a chair. He approached her, easing down her shorts.

Beatrice uttered, "Easy, easy," more to herself than to him, all thoughts of South Fremantle well behind her.

*

"I have to admit, I was very concerned back there," said Amelia opening their room door.

"No need," replied Olivia. "His satay was probably okay."

"That's not what I meant!" Amelia tossed her small market bag onto the bed "A couple of steps off the well lit path—we could have been in big trouble. We let basic safety awareness fly right out the window—just because we're too caught up in 'being on holiday'!"

"Yes," agreed Olivia, knowing the 'we' Amelia referred to was her. "Yes, I threw caution to the wind. Sorry." She began searching through her many purchases. "I never thought surveillance could be such fun," she laughed, trying to ease Amelia's concern, before collapsing into the arm chair.

Amelia looked at her, surrounded by her shopping.

"I'm the Queen of the Night Market!" exclaimed Olivia.

"I should never have let you talk me into buying that swimsuit. Red and black is far too gaudy for me! Where will I ever wear it?"

"In your deepest fantasy," said Olivia, in a spooky voice. "As pool playing Australians cart you off into their den of iniquity. Doo-doo-doo-doo!"

*

Jack sat alone on *Sumbar's* front veranda, looking into the black nothingness of the gulf, his hair drying in the night air. From inside Sunny sang an unrecognisable pop tune while hand washing dirty glasses. The sound of Tookie's crying grew nearer. From behind, Garry joined Jack on the veranda quietening her, gently rocking the baby back to sleep.

"It's a wonderful spot you have here, Garry."

Garry nodded, maintaining the gentle rocking of his arms.

"You must have pinched yourself when you found it."

"Yes."

Jack heard the weariness in Garry's voice and realised he'd probably heard that comment a million times.

"And Mai and the baby," Jack went on regardless, trying to kick start a conversation. "You are one happy man."

"Oh, yes."

Out of the darkness, Michael appeared carrying his baby. "Evening Garry, how's tricks?" he asked. He nodded his head to Jack, this time recognising him.

Garry replied, "The same as last night and the night before."

"Yes, my sentiments exactly," said Michael. "I hear it's raining back home with an expected blizzard at the weekend." He turned to go.

"Michael," said Garry, "Saturday night. I'm turning forty. Mai's idea. Come along, bring Vanh."

"I'll see what I can do. Good evening." Michael disappeared back into the beach's darkness as silently as he'd entered it.

The quiet of the evening returned, the only sound the background noise of the gentle sea.

"Garry, that land there," said Jack, pointing beyond the outdoor shower, "no one's ever tried to develop it?"

"I'm told it is land owned by the military."

"If they ever put in a base there it could kill the peacefulness of *Sumbar*."

"Thankfully, they have no plans."

"And the land on the other side?"

"It's owned by a Thai dynasty and has been caught up in a legal fight between family members for the past ten years or more."

"So things can stay as they are for quite a while yet."

"Happily, yes."

Jack stretched back. He lifted his feet onto the railing. "What price paradise, eh?"

The question remained unanswered. Garry and Tookie had returned inside.

*

Donny-Three finished rolling the third joint, hoping the girls would keep their promise, when there was a knock on his hotel door. He scooped back the bed cover, put the joints and plastic dope bag under the sheet, covered it quickly and moved to the door. He removed the door chain and turned its handle. "Hey, you came."

The girls didn't move. Lily said, "You get the stuff?"

"Sure," he whispered.

The three girls entered. They looked about the room, impressed.

"You wanna have a smoke in the spa bath?" Donny-Three asked.

"You got a spa bath? Cool!" said Connie.

Lily opened the bathroom door. "How hot do we like it?" she asked, turning on the taps.

Donny-Three pulled back the sheet covers and put a joint in his mouth. Before he could light it Maggie suddenly removed it. "Look! You've got a smoke alarm."

"Ah, shit!"

"Does the balcony door open?" Maggie asked.

"Yeah."

"Outside then. Turn off the spa, Lily!" called out Maggie.

The four sat on the balcony, Lily and Connie on a chair each, Maggie and Donny-Three cross-legged at their feet.

Donny-Three lit the joint and inhaled deeply. "As promised—quality stuff."

Maggie extended her hand and taking the joint, inhaled. She coughed slightly. "Yeah."

When the four had smoked that joint, Donny-Three went inside and returned with the other two. An hour later the four were happily conversing nonsense, overlooking the dark Gulf of Thailand.

Lily whipped off her top and said, "Let's hit the spa!"

The other three followed and they sat there ruminating in the hot tub. Donny-Three couldn't wait to get back to the States to tell his friends.

When the girls were drying themselves, Donny-Three asked, "One of you like to spend the night here?"

The three exchanged looks.

"Drop that towel. Let's get a close-up of what you're offering," said Maggie. Donny-Three did. "Okay," she said.

The other two whooped and Connie reminded her, "Don't forget we have to be at *Sumbar* around noon!"

*

Morning.

In front of *Sumbar*, Jack watched the sun rise from the sea.

To the north, on a fishing pier, Amelia did the same.

Jack stood in the water, moving his toes up and down, enjoying the simple pleasure. "Jen, it's still as beautiful as it always was."

Amelia was on the old wooden slats, letting the light and cool morning air take her over. "Yes, Mark, we should have holidayed here. I'm starting to feel my fear was unfounded."

Jack and Amelia let the quiet of the day's awakening creep over them—a pleasure one could have when far from home, not pressured by the timetable of the day's appointments.

Amelia shattered her own calm. *I have to pick up those reading glasses today!*

*

As bright daylight was trying to make its way around the drawn curtain, there was a knock at the door. Donny-Three, half asleep, called out, "Yeah?"

"I'm heading off to golf! Breakfast is over in an hour. Move your fucking ass! Stop wasting your life."

"Whatever," Donny-Three answered quietly.

After a while, Maggie whispered, "Who was that?"

"My fucking asshole father."

"Why do you hate your father so much?"

Donny-Three considered whether to tell her or not.

"My father is the same," admitted Maggie. "Gets drunk, screams at me, hits mum. I left the minute I found a job."

"Only *screams* at you?"

Maggie waited for Donny-Three to continue.

"When I was seven I caught him beating up on my mother. I stepped between them. He undid his belt and whipped me and moved to hit her again, but his slacks fell down his fat belly and he tripped forward hitting his head on the bed. Ma took me downstairs and into the car to her sister's. He came crawling, 'Come back, come back! I let the devil in! Forgive me. The Lord forgives all sinners and there is no greater sinner than me!' We went back. He never touched me after I'd turned fifteen because by then I was strong and I could fight. I don't know what happened to my mother after I was sent away to junior high. All I know—she was never the same again. She's still alive, but different to what I remember—a shell of the woman she could have been."

"Why did he bring you to Thailand?" asked Maggie, genuinely curious.

"To ease his conscience? To convince himself he's a good father? Who knows. I guess he thinks we'll do some father-son bonding over here. But that's not going to happen."

"Why come with him? Why stay with him at home?"

"He's very, very rich and one day it will be mine. So I pretend and wait."

"Might be a long time before he dies."

"He doesn't have to die for it to become all mine. You want a gold necklace?"

"A what?"

"Our family company pays my American Express card. Tax minimisation. Come on, get dressed. We'll have breakfast downstairs and go to the gold shop. It won't open until after ten."

As she pulled last night's top over her head, she asked, "Where in the States are you from?"

"Galveston, Texas."

"Galveston? It really exists? I thought it was an old song!"

Chapter 17

"Have you planned anything today?" Beatrice asked Jack over a cup of coffee on the front veranda of *Sumbar*.

"Not really—that's the beauty of *Sumbeach*. Take each day as it comes."

"Well, I've been seeing that red light blinking at night from way up there on the mountain top. Want to share a tuk-tuk to the top to have a look?"

"Sounds good."

Their attention was taken by the sound of suitcases being dropped on the floor behind them. The two Dutchmen were checking out. Garry moved from behind them to the bar where he presented them with their account. The taller of the two paid by credit card. The other handed Garry a wad of baht without commenting.

Bloody big tip, thought Jack.

The two picked up their suitcases and headed out to the back lot to wait for their Bangkok transfer.

"Two very unfriendly men," commented Jack quietly to Beatrice.

"I wouldn't say that. They knew Eugene from last time they were here. They said a few words to him the other evening before you joined us for dinner."

"Maybe I'm not their type," joked Jack.

*

Jack and Beatrice walked the beach, turning at the arrowed sign and then into the centre of the village to the intersection where all the tuk-tuks waited patiently.

Beatrice pointed to the communications tower and jumped in the back of a very keen driver's vehicle. Before setting off Jack pointed to the top of the mountain. He held up his hand, indicating that the driver should wait once they were up there and then pointed back down to the town. The driver nodded he understood and they agreed on a return price.

The tuk-tuk jerked as it took off, Beatrice squealing with delight as the stream of blue smoke spewed out behind them. On the highway they idled at a set of traffic lights next to the wheels of a large truck, Beatrice's face inches from the rear wheel. She tried to look up to the top of the truck, around the canvas canopy of the tuk-tuk.

"Watch yourself," Jack warned. "Don't put any body part out of the tuk-tuk."

She soon understood why. The tuk-tuk roared off zig-zagging in front of the truck and behind a motor bike with a pillion passenger who was carrying one long piece of timber under his arm. The tuk-tuk braked suddenly, the plank almost smacking into its windshield.

Three hundred metres down the highway, the tuk-tuk driver braked hard, tossing Beatrice forward.

"Hang on!" yelled Jack as Beatrice grabbed onto one of the thin metal struts holding up the canopy. After several huge trucks lumbered towards them, there was a momentary break in the traffic. The driver jerked on the accelerator and the little engine roared a high pitch expulsion as the tyres squealed, successfully turning off towards the mountain. The road narrowed and steepened; the tuk-tuk coughed and spluttered.

Beatrice sang a child's song, "I think I can, I know I can."

Jack appreciated the change in her. Her first night's apprehension, following Eugene across that deserted lot had now well and truly disappeared, and had been replaced by a sense of fun. *Familiarity of locale and Werner are better than any prescribed tonic*, he thought.

At the summit, there was a parking area and over from it an old concrete block and timbered cafe. The driver bumped the tuk-tuk over the rough terrain to a spot of shade. The two climbed out and Jack bought a single bottle of fizzy orange.

"Where's mine?" asked Beatrice.

"Later." Jack walked past her and handed the drink to their driver. He pointed at his watch and made a circle, indicating time. The driver nodded.

Jack returned to Beatrice, "Come on, an hour should be long enough." They set off to explore the clearly marked paths and lookout areas.

Off to the side of the path, below a sign which read: *Khao Hin Lek Fai*, three dogs lay sleeping in the shade of a tree.

"Huh," commented Jack. "That yellow dog looks remarkably like a dingo."

"Oh, look over there. Monkeys!"

117

"Don't go near them," warned Jack.

"No, I won't."

They walked a wide arc around them.

"That was really kind of you to do that back there—buying our driver a cool drink."

Jack tilted his head, shrugging, "It was nothing."

"If I could put you and Werner together I'd have the perfect man."

"There's no such creature, Beatrice. Keep walking, and don't trip over the edge. It's a long way down and this perfect man may not catch you in time." Beatrice laughed.

They stood looking south over *Sumbeach*, the golden Buddha at the end of the long bay and into the haze that seemed to gradually engulf the remainder of Thailand. As they moved away Beatrice exclaimed, "Wait on! I want a photo!" She took out her phone and took several rapid shots.

To the west, the mountains forming the border region with Myanmar towered ruggedly in front of them. Jack pointed down below. An immaculately manicured golf course wove its way beneath them. Tiny figures swung their clubs and climbed in and out of little white carts. He started to move off.

"Wait on!" exclaimed Beatrice. "I want another photo!"

Facing north, Jack said, "I can see Bangkok and there's my favourite Thai restaurant on the Chao Praya River."

"Where?" Beatrice asked, eager to see. Jack didn't answer. "Oh, very funny," she said. "One day I'm going to stop being so gullible."

She held the phone in her outstretched arm. "Come on—a selfie!" she demanded. "You hold it—your arm's longer!" Jack bent his knees so their heads were together in the frame, and he tapped her phone several times.

Back at the car park, Jack bought three more drinks, and after they stood in the shade of a tree drinking them, he collected the empties and dropped them into a trash can. The tuk-tuk driver took off happily. Beatrice held on for dear life as the vehicle gathered momentum and hurtled down the winding road.

"He took that corner on three wheels!" she shouted.

"It only *has* three wheels!" shouted back Jack.

"Dear god—he took it on *two*! Wheee!"

*

118

"Which one do you like?"

Maggie held Donny-Three by the arm as she stared unbelievingly at the array of gold earrings and chains in the glass cabinets before her, the length of her body woven into his side. "I can't make up my mind," she admitted, having never been in a situation like this before.

"Then I'll buy the most expensive." Donny-Three scanned the price tags, pointed to one, and handed his American Express card to the sales lady.

"Won't your father have a fit when he reads his credit card statement?"

"He's never interested in checking the small details."

Small? thought Maggie, not believing what was happening. In her world no one had that amount of money in the bank, or under their bed—let alone that amount which could be thrown away on a gold necklace after a one-night stand. *Maybe,* she thought, *I should stay with him a little longer than planned.*

*

Beatrice climbed out of her side of the tuk-tuk and felt like kissing the ground beneath her feet. "Wow!" was all she could utter. Jack smiled, "A bit scary on the way down?"

She nodded. Her eye was taken by a photo on the large plastic covered board. She moved towards it to get a closer look.

The brightly dressed European couple Jack had noticed the day before, stood studying the board of photographs. He'd left the bright green shorts behind in his hotel room and was wearing a conservative silver polo shirt with bright fire-truck red shorts. She, by contrast, wore a simple white summer dress, sans bra—her hair tied up loosely under a straw hat.

The woman and Beatrice pointed to a photograph simultaneously. The supervisor of the 'depot' looked at it, trying to bring to mind its location. He called out to another driver. That driver studied it as well. Then another came to look. A fourth driver exclaimed that he knew where it was.

The supervisor, after consultation with him, said to the two women, "No today." He pointed at the European woman's watch. "Much time, much time." Then he pointed into the distance. "Very far. Very far!"

"How much—tuk-tuk?" asked the European woman in accented English.

"No tuk—tuk," the supervisor explained. "Taxi-truck—very far—only taxi-truck go there."

While the women bartered, Jack greeted the brightly attired gentleman. "Hello!"

"*Gutten tag!*" the man replied. "Is hot, yah?"

"Yes, very hot."

Walking away, Beatrice informed Jack, "We're going tomorrow, leaving here at 10am. I think the four of us are sharing the benches on the back of that blue taxi-truck."

"They're all blue," joked Jack.

"Pedant," said Beatrice. "That okay by you?"

"Sure. Where are we going?"

"North, beyond Cha … something."

"Cha-am. And what are we going to see?"

"Monsters in the sea!" explained Beatrice, gleefully.

"I hope the German gent doesn't scare off the monsters with his Bermuda shorts!"

They walked on, laughing.

"Weren't they bright!" commented Beatrice.

"I'd even say they were 'lairy'."

"Lairy? That's an old fashioned kind of word."

"I'm an old fashioned kinda guy," said Jack, flippantly.

They were now on the sand heading back to *Sumbar*.

"Jack, apparently we need all day to get there and back. I hope he's not late."

"Who? Herr Lairy-Shorts?"

*

Amelia and Olivia sat in the foyer's coffee shop looking out at all those who walked by the large tourist coach in the driveway of *L'Hotel Majestique*. No male expat with or without a baby interested them.

"Needle in a haystack, is correct. Oh, come on mum, let's go shopping!"

"Wait—after the coach pulls out. You're as impatient as your dead father!"

They sat back in their chairs. Olivia laughed a little.

"What is it?" asked Amelia.

"Across the street, over there, to the right of the coach—there's our moustachioed friend from the police station."

"I'd forgotten about him," admitted Amelia. "Captain Choni hasn't given up after all."

Olivia leant in and added, "Let's take him on a wild goose chase in this heat."

"He's Thai—we're English," explained Amelia. "Which one of us do you think, in this heat, is going to tire first?"

*

"Eugene's asleep in the room. I had to change very quietly," said Beatrice as she walked into the pool area, placing her towel on the sun lounge by Jack. He returned to reading the *Bangkok Daily*, shaded by the ugly tree.

She pulled over her head the simple dress she was wearing, revealing a black and yellow bikini which she'd purchased up town yesterday. She wiggled her barely covered bottom and cheekily asked, using a dreadful American accent, "Is my *ass* big in this?"

Without taking his eyes from the newspaper Jack said, "Yes!"

"No, it isn't!"

Jack put down the paper. "If you already know the answer, why ask the..."

However, Beatrice had dived in. Jack watched her swim the first lap and again envied her skill as she executed a tumble turn.

Beatrice stopped beneath Jack's lounge and held herself against the pool's edge. He lifted his dark glasses, saying, "I'm not going to finish my paper, am I."

"Jack—Werner is ..."

"It's okay Beatrice. Enjoy your holiday."

"No, nothing like that. I intend to enjoy it! I was just going to say: Werner is so honest!"

"All men are honest, Beatrice."

She laughed out loud. Jack folded his paper and dropped it onto the tiles.

"I was concerned—you know, about me being a bit older. So he tells me a story, hoping to put my concern to rest."

Jack now knew he wasn't getting to his newspaper for a while. "So, what's the story?"

"Werner came here via India. He loved it. He could have stayed there forever because India is loose and easy going while Germany is rigid and uptight."

"It is a well worn cliché, Beatrice, about travel and the width of one's mind."

"He'd found a beach to stay at and each morning he would wave to the large Shiva on the hill spending the day swimming and basking in the sun."

"Sounds ideal—not unlike here."

"He'd budgeted carefully…"

"No German is ever going to give up a lifetime's habit."

"Are you going to continually interrupt?"

"Sorry, continue."

"I shall!" Beatrice poked out her tongue and dived under the water. When she emerged she asked cheekily, "Is the suspense killing you?"

"No."

She smiled, "Got you hooked, have I?"

"Beatrice! The bloody story!"

"Okay, okay! Werner would eat a cheap curry for lunch then have another swim, before spending the late afternoon back at his hotel reading in a comfortable hammock, one of his prescribed texts for next year's final semester. That is, until he met Mrs Kingston from Nebraska—then his afternoons were spent in her bed."

"And that's what he wanted to tell you?"

"Yes, that he is not fazed by being with an older woman."

"And that makes you uncertain about exactly what?"

"How easily could he be drawn to *another* older woman?"

"Beatrice, what are you considering?"

She didn't answer. She swam away, feeling she'd said too much. Eventually she returned after three tumble turns, and as Jack was reaching for his paper she stopped and said, "The only thing not keeping him in India was that Mrs Kingston had to return home to Nebraska to teach third grade."

Chapter 18

Amelia pushed open the optometrist's front door and braced herself. She closed the door and shivered as she adjusted to the hit of air-conditioning. Through the glass door she waved 'bye' to Olivia, who headed down the street to one of the stalls where she hoped to find bright sarongs.

The three assistants inside bowed and together said, "*Sawadee*, Madame."

The optometrist emerged from her office and smiled broadly. Amelia greeted her and then by way of chit chat said, "Excuse me for asking—I see you trained at Sydney University."

"Yes, Madame. The most enjoyable four years of my life."

"In Australia? How could you cope with those men?"

The Thai doctor smiled and confided, "I fell pregnant to one."

"Oh, dear," consoled Amelia.

"Yes, Madame, after we married and we'd both graduated. Later, I fell pregnant to him a further two times. He teaches at the Institute for Foreign Languages, two hours up the highway on the outskirts of Bangkok. We are very happy together."

"Oh, Madame, I'm sorry. I didn't mean to cause offence."

"No offence, Madame. Prejudice is universal," she said, smiling sweetly, "not solely reserved for us Asians."

"Ahh—I think I'd better pay you for my glasses," said Amelia, embarrassed.

"Yes, Madame, of course."

On the way to find Olivia, Amelia stopped outside the open annexe of a restaurant. An older teenage girl and her younger brother, in immaculately attired school uniform, sat at the nearest table to the footpath unconcerned by her presence, doing their school homework. She noted their concentration and remembered sitting around the small kitchen table still dressed in her school uniform trying to absorb the mathematics lesson of that day.

The children's father placed before each of them a tall iced lemon flavoured water. Amelia couldn't remember her father ever doing that. She smiled at the man and walked on.

*

Amelia stopped outside a wire fence behind which boys played basketball. She realised she had stopped near a nun, watching them play. "Hello Sister. It's a very warm day."

"Yes it is. Then again it usually is here."

"You should be inside out of the sun."

"Oh no, I'm supervising. Then again I do love the difference in weather from back home."

"And where would that be?"

"Christchurch, New Zealand. And you?"

"Bath, England."

"Oh such a beautiful town."

"You've been, Sister?"

"No. I have seen many pictures of it though."

"So, Sister, what brings you to Thailand?"

"Oh, I've been volunteering for many, many years. I always take my vacation to aid some church charity. I have no family back home to visit, you see. This is my first time in Thailand and I'm not affected by the heat as much as I thought I would be. Here the heat is humid. I have been to Africa and the dry heat there is accompanied by dust."

"Sister Sheelagh!"

Amelia turned to see a red headed priest wiping his bald top with a handkerchief, walking towards them.

"Father Aloysius, you should stay indoors," suggested Sister Sheelagh, concerned. "Your skin is not suitable for this sunlight."

"I'll be fine, Sister. I wish to give you a gentle reminder that you promised to sing your solo at Evensong tonight. All the children are looking forward to it."

"Oh, Father, I assure you I haven't forgotten. I'm starting to get a few butterflies about it."

"I'm sure you'll be wonderful, Sister." Father Aloysius turned to Amelia. "You're more than welcome to join us, miss."

"Thank you, Father. And thank you for referring to me as 'miss'. It's been a long time."

The priest smiled and moved away, standing by the boys playing basketball.

"Father Aloysius is a very good man. He also devotes his vacation to charity work, though unlike me he comes here regularly, whenever he's free. I think he's from your way."

"Bath?"

"No, I meant he's English. Canterbury I believe. I remember when he first told me I recognised the name. You know Chaucer's tales."

"So this is a school?" Amelia asked.

"Yes. It is attached to the orphanage behind. I do a bit of music teaching and a lot of trying to teach them to sing. I'd love to be here long enough to put together a small choir."

*

That evening, after he'd walked Beatrice along the sand to *Brauhaus Helmut*, Jack ate some satay sticks in a Thai restaurant which, sometime in the past five years, had moved from a side-street corner to a better location in the tourist part of town. On a whim he stopped outside *L'Hotel Majestique* and realising that he'd never been inside, decided to wander in for a beer or two before heading down the beach to home.

He waited for the European couple circling the revolving door. The woman exited; however, the man upon seeing Jack, grinned devilishly and went around a second time, dancing comically inside and finally emerging with an extended hand and a glorious laugh. The two men shook hands like long lost brothers. The woman, now dressed in a long tight fitting multi coloured sarong with her long hair cascading over her shoulders, looked as if she'd emerged from a South Sea Island dream. She said something in German. The man jokingly cowered and obediently shuddered.

"Until tomorrow," the German gentleman said, and waved to Jack as he took off after his wife, his bright pink Bermuda shorts disappearing into the evening's throng.

Jack uttered quietly, "*Auf Wiedersehen, Herr Lairy-Shorts.*"

Inside the revolving door, the foyer opened before him. To one side was the reception desk, and opposite, on a raised section of the foyer was the bar area where a band was playing. From inside one could look out onto the street; however, the windows outside were tinted a dark grey, offering the patrons privacy from prying eyes. Jack took a stool at the dimly lit bar.

From down the other end came a loud, "How'd ya be, fella?"

Knowing they were the only two in the bar, Jack looked about and pointed to his chest. "Me?"

"Yeah, Buddy—you!"

"Well, I'm a hundred percent—if you discount the rheumatic fever, the wonky left knee and the in-grown toe nails," Jack offered by way of friendly entree into the conversation.

Completely missing the humour, the American said, "Take up golf—cures everything. You'd never know I was sixty-five, would you?"

"No, you wouldn't."

"Say, you South African, aren't you?"

"No, Australian."

"A kangaroo!" The American waved to the barman. "What you drinking, Buddy?"

"Beer."

"A Bud for my buddy, Buddy!" the American said loudly to the barman, before laughing loudly at his joke.

The barman looked at Jack. "A Singha, please," Jack qualified.

The American picked up his double bourbon with ice and slightly stumbled to Jack. "I'm Donald Randalson Jnr—from Galveston, Texas."

Shaking his hand, Jack said. "I'm Jack Featherstone—from Lake Cathie, Port Macquarie."

"Say Bud—there's a thing I'd love to ask you. You really an Aussie, right?"

"Right."

The barman placed a tall frosted glass of cold beer onto a coaster in front of Jack.

"This here thing's been bugging me for years. When we have summer, you have winter. Is that correct?"

"Yes."

"Why do you guys do that?"

Jack, unable to answer for fear of laughing, merely uttered, "Mmm," and buried his smile behind his glass.

"Exactly, it's a real brain-fucker, ain't it!" Donald Jnr raised his glass. "As the Ruskies say: *prosit!*" Jack clinked the Texan's glass.

Donald Jnr didn't take long before he ordered another for himself and Jack. Jack told the barman that he'd pay; however, Donald Jnr insisted that it all go onto his tab. Indicating two lounge chairs over by the window, the American said, "Join me over there. Those seats are more comfortable on my old ass! I'd love to tell you about my week so far."

Once in the chairs, and after the barman had delivered the drinks, Donald Jnr said, "Those musicians seem to be good, though I'm not a fan of their music. Why don't those Asians play good old Country and Western?"

"Too difficult to master?" Jack asked cheekily, adding seriously, "They're Filipino. They're the musicians of Asia."

"Un-huh." Then without drawing breath Donald Jnr ploughed on. "I love golf. I came here to play golf every god-damn day. This local limey guy's company picks me up at the airport and drives me here, picks me up from this here hotel and takes me, every day, to *The Mountain View Golf Course.* I pay him of course. He thinks he's charging me a fortune, but in US dollars, it's like ordering a banquet at McDonalds!" He paused. "Though it's sure a lot tastier here in Thailand." He leant in, nursing his drink, the ice melting from the heat generated by his sweating palm.

"So, back home I've an old, long time buddy, old 'Stonewall'. He's been here many times. Me? I've always had to work so this week's my first time. He says to try the 'special caddy service'—ask the golf tour owner. So on my first day we're out there putting on the fifteenth green when right on cue this huge storm tumbles all this rain over us. Did you get that rain here in town?"

Jack nodded, "Yes, water rushing everywhere. It's a regular occurrence."

"This caddy—did I say she was a woman? No? Well, she's not just a woman—she's one of those beautiful Thai women—not much in the way of tits, but man, what an ass! An ass to die for! So she drags me over under this tin roofed thing. She says: 'Give thousand baht.' I start to say 'a thousand?' but I stop because I'd forgot—over here their money's like cheap as Jack Shit. So I dig out this coloured note—why the hell can't they have greenbacks like you and me, eh? She puts the note into her pocket then she goes down on me. Man, right then and there. Hell, no one can see because it sure as hell is a-raining hard. I looked to the heavens and I called out: *Praise Be To Ye O Lord! You sent to earth your only son and now you send this here angel.* No lie, by the church I finance back home, all that is not a word of a lie."

Jack nodded slowly, sipping his beer, looking at Donald Jnr.

"And Buddy, let me tell you, the next day I played the same golf course and she caddied and right on cue the rain came a-fallin' and I gave her a thousand and she reacquainted me with the heavenly delights created by my Lord."

He drained his glass.

"So today I asked her: *How much for ficky-fick?* And she says: *No. I no do ficky-fick—I good girl!* Well, I just laughed and laughed and laughed. Another round, barkeep!"

*

Amelia noticed every Western male's face as they brushed by her. Men who walked with Thai women, she particularly studied. Some carried babies, or holding the hands of youngsters, while the women bought fresh food from the produce end of the laneway. The children had in common a delightful mix of East-West smiles and a bubbling Thai happiness. The more Amelia looked into the eyes of the expat fathers, the more she noted the number who wore vacant looks, a seeming lack of connection with the immediate world around them, a distant yearning. Some came alive when they chanced upon a fellow expat. She overheard snatches of conversations and promises to catch up in the near future; however, to do what, no one really seemed to say.

The night crowd began to thin. Amelia had walked up and down the alley past the same stalls several times. She took Olivia by the arm. "That's enough. Leave some clothes for the other tourists to buy."

"Mum!"

"Olivia!" The cry came from off to the side. It was the English speaking Thai man from the laneway. "Was the satay this afternoon good or was it good?" he asked, laughing.

"Yes!" Olivia shouted back. "You were right. The best I've ever tasted!"

"And the cold beer?" he asked.

Olivia mindful of Amelia's presence, merely bowed in his direction and waved, 'goodbye'.

"When did you have satay?" asked Amelia. "While I was getting my glasses? No wonder I couldn't find you at that sarong stall!"

Olivia laughed. Amelia walked her out of the tightly packed laneway and back towards their hotel, continuing to keep her eye on every Western male she passed. They both suppressed a gulp of laughter as they passed a silver haired gentleman wearing bright pink Bermuda shorts.

*

"And another thing, we have Christmas on December twenty-five. When do you Aussies have it?" Donald Ranaldson Jnr was now on the downhill side of sobriety.

Jack saw her—the blonde woman from the flooded intersection—walk across the hotel's foyer—heading to the elevators—she and her friend laden with shopping bags.

"Yeah, they've got great asses too," commented Donald Jnr, "though I think my Thai caddy's ass is better."

The Filipino trio began to play the introduction to another number and Jack hoped the blonde woman might return after dumping the shopping. "You feel like another?" he asked the American.

"Yeah, sure thing, Bud. But be *my* guest. Just quietly, my company is paying for this—not me." He laughed as he waved to the barman then confided to Jack, "I gotta spend the profits somehow. You can't take them with you. A piece of advice, Bud, raise beef and sell it at a high price."

*

Beatrice was helping Werner wash up dishes in the restaurant's sink. Helmut hovered, studying her thoughtfully. She sensed his presence. "It's okay," Beatrice explained. "I'm happy to help out."

"Werner, there's a customer out front," Helmut said. "I know him. He will have a vodka chaser and a black beer. Sit with him. Talk German to him. He is Canadian but likes to practise."

"Okay, Papa." Werner dried his hands and left. Helmut looked at Beatrice. She stopped washing up and dried her hands also.

"You wish to tell me to stop seeing your son?" she asked, putting down the hand towel. "Or not to get too carried away with a holiday romance?"

"*Nein*. He is old enough to do what he wants. Who am I to tell him of the choices he should make in life?" Helmut took Beatrice's eye. "All I hope for is you do not mean too much to him, that when you go home he does not have a broken heart."

"More like, I'll be the one with the broken heart," admitted Beatrice. "Your son, Helmut, is very intelligent, very well read, a very sensitive young man. When he's back home he'll find a pretty girl. I'm under no illusions."

Helmut pulled out two stools and from the fridge two bottles of German beer. He offered Beatrice one. She nodded and they sat.

"I was worried when I hear Werner wants to come here, to meet me after all those years. I was never a father to him. I ran away. It's no excuse, but his mother and I, we argue, argue, argue. It was better I leave. If I stay, who knows—maybe I hurt her."

Beatrice said nothing as Helmut momentarily relived snatches of the arguments.

"Yah, it was better to run. Now my feet are settled in *Sumbeach*." He tapped his chest, "But in here, part of me always run, never settle."

He took a mouthful of beer.

"I left Deutschland. I travelled—aimlessly drifting. I thought I'd go to your country—Australia. I have a cousin in city called Newcastle. His parents emigrated there. They worked in the steel works and bought a house on the lake and lived a good, safe life. I never got that far. Here I meet a Thai lady—before Achara—beautiful like her—like all these Thai ladies—and I let my Willy Brandt do the talking and—well, I stay because the weather is much better than Germany and the beach is right there and the women … well, you know." He took a long drink.

"I take train to Malaysia to renew visa. I look around down there but I decide to come back. This woman is now in someone else's bed. For long time here I stay with no woman. I go regularly to Malaysia and come back with new visa. Then I apply and get residency because my wife back in Germany meet a man, she want divorce, so she finally send me my German money and I set up a bar down the wrong end of *Sumbeach*. I meet Achara—her mother has a house and I move my bar into their front car port and put tables and chairs in their garden. Now I am in a better area of *Sumbeach*. Achara cooks, I teach her German flavours, I find German beer in Bangkok and have it delivered here, first on train and later by truck. *Brauhaus Helmut* is born." He waved his outstretched arm slowly around, taking it all in.

"Now my Willy Brandt do more talking and babies are made. Too much talking—I make twins! I move restaurant to here. I do the right thing—I marry Achara—legally—my friends here say I'm a fool. 'Pay her bills, yes, but only sleep with her! No marry her!' But I want to make good, after first marriage was bad. I live upstairs with Achara and her mother and her sister and our two babies. Her mother was old, and I pay for hospital. Sadly, she die three years ago. She was a decent woman, a kind soul. I am thankful her daughter takes after her. Sister Bussy needs new clothes, I pay. If you talk with Willy Brandt—there is always price to pay. Do not misunderstand, I love baby Gretel and baby Hannah, but I will never be wealthy—too many people live off me."

He opened the fridge door. "Not for me, thank you," said Beatrice. Helmut took another.

"I drink too much. At times I am my best customer, though I don't always put the money into the till, which makes me my worst customer. I'm important here—a big man in this small corner of Germany. They come to eat and drink here often, some every year to play golf and to carouse over my famous Bratwurst Platter and Lowenstein beer. But I can never forget Munchen. I want to stand below the Rathaus-Glockenspiel and watch those figures dance and carry on one more time. I want to sit in the Augustiner Kellar with my old school friends—those who haven't died yet—and listen to the Oom Pah Pah band and sing along with their songs, and ogle the beer hall maids in their frilly blouses and flouncy dresses."

He paused, lost momentarily in a time that was perhaps never real.

"I often think of just going back. But back home I'd be a no body. Here, at least, I am somebody. I have a bar, a restaurant—a beer house!"

Helmut pointed at a framed photo of a snow scene on the wall. "I think I should throw that away—it never helps when I look at it."

He focused back on Beatrice. "So, Werner come here and I see him with you. I know he is my son—I recognise me in him—because now *his* Willy Brandt do the talking."

Without blushing Beatrice said, "He's a very good conversationalist." She leant in to Helmut and put her hand on his shoulder. "But the difference between you and him is me. I'm not going to trap him into a pregnancy neither of us want."

"Missus—I want him to *not* be me. I want him to go back to Germany and go to university and finish the course. Get the letters behind his name. Then—I don't care! I just don't want him to waste his life like me!"

Outside, Werner pressed against the wall, backed away, quietly returning to the restaurant.

Chapter 19

Amelia and Olivia stepped from the elevator, across the hotel's foyer to the bar.

Donald Jnr leant into Jack and whispered, "Hey Bud, they're back."

The American wasn't telling Jack anything he didn't know. He'd seen them. As she crossed the foyer, Jack kept saying to himself, *Don't go outside, don't go outside, stay in here, sit in the bar.*

The Filipino trio began their next set. It was as if their music was a call for the two women to walk in and sit at a table. The waitress came over and took their order.

Jack thought, *Now all I need is to get up enough courage to go over there and ask her to dance.*

Olivia leant into Amelia and said, "Don't look now. There's a man over there unable to keep his eyes off you."

"Stop it!" chided Amelia. "There is not."

"True. Just tilt your head a little to the right. That's it, not too much."

Amelia's glance landed on Donald Jnr. She turned back to Olivia. "Err," she whispered.

"Don't like him?"

"Not much."

"Looks okay to me. Oh, he's coming this way."

"Excuse me, would you care to dance?"

Amelia glanced up, slightly flinching at the unexpected Australian accent. The man asking the question wasn't the man she'd seen. This one looked quite presentable.

"Ah. No. Sorry." Amelia glanced towards the band. "There's no one dancing."

"We could be the first—start a trend."

"No." Amelia smiled. "Sorry."

Jack deflated, turned to go.

"I'll dance with you," Olivia said.

Jack turned back. "Great!"

He held out his arm, old fashioned style. She took it. They walked to a small square of parquet flooring in front of the band and started to move in time to the music. When the number ended they applauded gently. The band began a slow number and Jack offered to take her in his arms.

"I'm not very good with organised steps," Olivia said placing her left arm gently on his shoulder and taking his outstretched left hand.

"That's okay. I'll lead, you follow."

They danced arm in arm, and on every turn Jack had great difficulty not focusing on her blonde companion. Mid-song Olivia stopped. "That's enough for me, I'm all at sea. Come and dance with Amelia. She's older—she'll know the correct steps." She dragged him over. "Amelia, your turn. This is?"

"Jack."

"Jack knows all the steps, all you have to do is follow. No excuses."

She reached forward, dragged Amelia to her feet and moved her into Jack's arms. On the dance floor he picked up with Amelia where he'd left off with Olivia. When Amelia was looking her way, Olivia gave her a cheeky little wave and smile. On the next turn she pursed her lips and on the third turn shook her hand, mouthing: *Hot, baby, hot!*

An excited shout came from outside the bar. Herr Lairy-Shorts had spotted Jack. He raced in, waited for his wife sedately following behind, then eagerly joined Jack and Amelia on the dance floor.

The Filipino band, pleased at last to have enthusiastic guests enjoying their music, picked up the tempo. The two couples jived a little, and then Olivia joined in with Donald Jnr as her partner, deliberately bumping into Amelia and laughing.

Twenty-five frantic minutes later the set ended and the six slumped around the same table, swapping stories about the last time they danced like that! How much younger they'd been! What a lot of good old fashioned fun it was!

Jack passed on Garry's invitation for Saturday evening's birthday party at *Sumbar*. The European couple promised they'd be there, as did Donald Jnr. However Amelia wouldn't commit and Olivia whispered to Jack, "I'll talk mum into it."

"I'm sorry, I don't feel well," said Amelia, standing and heading for the elevators. Olivia concerned, excused herself and followed.

Not a word passed between them in the elevator. Once inside their room, Olivia leant on the back of the closed door and stared at Amelia, waiting for an explanation.

"I got frightened. Okay?" Then much softer and to herself she repeated, "I got frightened."

"Frightened?" asked Olivia.

"Yes, good old fashioned frightened!" admitted Amelia. "He scares me."

"Scares you? I can sense insincerity, sniff out falseness and too readily acknowledge the two-bit conman; however, Jack is one of the nicest men I've ever met."

"Yes, I agree—and that's why I was frightened. It was like I was seventeen again." She sat in the armchair.

Olivia studied her. "And that's how old you were when you first met Mark, right?"

Tears welled in Amelia's eyes. "Yes."

*

Beatrice lay in Werner's arms back in her room above *Sumbar*. The sliding door was open onto the small balcony. A gentle breeze slowly moved the curtain.

"Werner, are you awake?" she asked, knowing he was.

"Mmm—yah."

"Werner, I can't have you follow me back to Australia." She turned from him.

Werner lay there thinking, *Has this come from the conversation with Papa?* He lifted himself onto his elbow to get a better look at her. "So honesty, please," he said. "No lies." Werner wiped Beatrice's cheek with his index finger. "Why you cry? Don't I make you happy?"

"Too happy," she admitted.

"Honesty—yah? I hear some things Papa say."

"Your father—he doesn't want you to waste your life—I'm older than you."

"So? Three? Five years?"

"Werner, I'm a widow!" Werner looked at her, waiting. "He was killed, tragically, in a motorbike accident."

There was silence. Outside the ocean lapped onto the shore.

"I sorry for you. Sorry for loss of husband. But I Werner. I not him."

"Yes, I know you're not and I don't want you to be him. I meant, I know what sudden loss is like. There is no time to say goodbye. So it is better for us that we grab what we have now and only now. No future. You are not to follow me back to Perth. Okay, Werner? When the time comes you must walk away from me and not look back."

That will be difficult, thought Werner.

"And I will do the same."

Werner stood and crossed to the balcony door, looking out into the blackness. He turned back. "Honesty—how old you?"

"Thirty-one."

"Honesty? You seem older. Ah, not in face—ah, not in body—ah, you know—in head! You very sensible, very grown up."

As Werner weighed up his thoughts, Beatrice crossed to him and tickled the hairs on his chest. "So are you—too grown up for your age."

"You know—you special. In bed I can just lay with you. No need to sex. You first woman I ever hold, and have no need to sex."

"I'll take that as a very strange compliment."

"I like talking to you. I like my feeling for you—is very different. I feel no need to sex you all time." He paused. "Is that love?"

"Love? Holding a woman, talking and not wanting to sex her?" laughed Beatrice. "Well, it's certainly different, special, and love is supposed to be special."

Werner lifted up Beatrice and gently lay her back down on the bed. He stood gathering thoughts. "So—I go back Germany. I go university. I study—easy—because it snows there, no beach, no need to go outside to play. I no have sex. Then I graduate and we together—in Perth, in Munchen, in wherever. We sex together for rest of our lives."

Beatrice studied him. *Is this young man for real?* She kissed him. "Okay" she whispered, though she feared it could and would never be.

After a while, when she heard his breathing settle and become regular, she slid past the curtain and stood in the darkness of her balcony. There she thought of her married life, the suddenness of love lost, the past few days with Werner and wondered whether it *really* could be.

No. Back in Perth, I'll return to my world of the silent librarian, my well-established routine. In Munich he'll bed the first leather clad Fraulein he stumbles across and after time I'll be just a notch in his gun, a distant volley fired in a foreign land.

*

Jack walked the beach back to *Sumbar*. It was the slowest trip home he'd taken in the several days he'd been here. He stopped to splash sea water onto his face. He was feeling quite hot; however, it didn't seem to cool him. Troubled, he kicked his feet in the water as he walked, with none of his previous childishness.

Maybe I should never have danced with her. Maybe she should have just stayed a vision—well, two visions actually—the vision getting out of the tuk-tuk in front of the police station and the vision of her with rolled up shorts crossing the flooded intersection. Maybe I should never have put my arms around her. Why did she feel so comfortable there?

He stopped and to relieve his concerns tried to count the green lights out at sea.

Now I have a third vision to contend with—the vision of seeing her beautiful face in close-up, dancing with her as she disturbingly looked away.

As he approached *Sumbar* he made out the silhouette of Beatrice standing on her balcony. He gave her a wave. She waved back.

That one would have been so less complicated, he thought. *Too young, though much less complicated.*

On the balcony Beatrice thought, *that one would have been far less complicated. Too old, though far less complicated.*

Chapter 20

Herr Lairy Shorts introduced himself as 'Gerhardt' and his wife as 'Angelica'.

"You don't like to dance?" he asked Beatrice who looked back uncomprehendingly.

Jack explained, "Oh, we're not together—we're just staying at the same hotel. We're sharing the expenses of the day trips."

Gerhardt nodded. "Beatrice, last night Jack danced with the most beautiful woman in the whole world!" Angelica nudged him in the ribs. "Sorry—*second* most beautiful woman." Gerhardt laughed then smiled at Beatrice, "Third."

A little after ten, the four climbed onto the benches on the tray of the taxi-truck and the driver bounced over the gutter onto the road way. He stopped at the lights on the highway intersection, the poles with the spaghetti wires overhead. Next to the footpath, a lone cable slung a lot lower to the ground than the others.

"Last night we walked. In the dark I did not see. The cable hit me—here!" Gerhardt drew his finger across his throat and poked out his tongue, emitting a strangling sound.

Angelica gently smacked his knee. "Unfortunately he did *not* strangle."

Gerhardt feigned hurt. They all laughed.

Bouncing down the highway, leaving the centre of town behind, Beatrice asked Jack, "So who was this woman?"

"A vision," Gerhardt said, "A dream!"

"Was she?" asked Beatrice, tapping Jack's knee.

Jack looked at them all. "Well, sadly she is."

"Why sadly?" asked Beatrice.

"Because there's nothing I can do about it."

The taxi-truck roared on and turned off the highway between closely built shops. The driver yelled something in broken English, which no one in the rear understood above the truck's engine. He pulled up at a plain building, in front of which stood a woman with two small children.

"My wife," the driver explained. "She speak good English. She tell today you."

The woman lifted the children onto the front bench seat next to their father and said, "Hello—good morning—we drive for an hour and half—longer if traffic busy or husband loose his way!" She climbed in. The taxi-truck did a u-turn on the spot, roared back to the highway and headed north to Cha-am, dipping under the runway of the Hua Hin airport.

*

"Mister Ranaldson Jnr, today you will play the *Park Royal Thai Links*," said Dickie Eastman, matter of factly.

"What?" Donald Jnr was taken aback. "For Pete's sake—why?"

Dickie indicated that the American should get into the van. He did so. Dickie asked his driver to get out from behind the wheel and to wait in the shade of the hotel. Dickie climbed in and settled. He whispered, "Mister Randaldson Jnr, you must not proposition Suzy-Q. She is very sensitive."

"Sensitive? You have any idea what she did to me?"

"Here in Thailand I have *every* idea and *no* idea."

"What the fu ... what is that supposed to mean?"

"Mister Ranaldson Jnr, Suzy-Q is my employee—she caddies—that is all. There are whores in every bar in town who will fuck you. If you wish that, then that is where you must go. Suzy-Q is so upset she is not at work today. That is why you're playing the *Park Royal Thai Links*."

"If this is a question of money—hell and damnation, I'll fling green backs at the bitch!"

"Mister Ranaldson Jnr…"

"Jesus H. Christ! Have you seen the ass on that girl?" He paused and looked at Dickie. "Oh, I get it—you're keepin' her for yourself. You're fuckin' jealous she might wanna fuck me!"

"Mister Ranaldson Jnr…"

"Okay Buddy—how much do *you* want for me to fuck *her*?"

Dickie looked at him with contempt and slid open the van's door. Getting out, he motioned to his driver, who climbed into the cabin and turned over the engine. Dickie did not turn and watch the van bounce over the gutter, head away towards the piers and then beyond, away from *The Mountain View Range* and towards the *Park Royal Thai Links*.

*

"Where'd you steal that?"

"Who you calling a thief, Connie?" Maggie knew the other two would be envious.

Lily grabbed Maggie by the arm. "If you didn't steal it—who gave it to you?"

Maggie shook her hand off. "Who do you think? Donny-Three!"

Connie tried to touch the necklace, commenting, "It looks real."

Maggie pulled her head away. "It *is* real, you doubting bitch! This is what gold looks like."

"Gold?" questioned Connie. "If it's gold, why are you wearing it to the beach?"

Maggie stopped. "Our hotel room's not safe. I can't leave it there, someone will steal it."

They walked past the arrowed sign onto the sand. Connie asked, "Where were you yesterday? Garry was pissed off."

Maggie confessed delightedly, "Fucking Donny-Three. How'd you think I got this necklace?"

Lily turned on her. "You're a slut!"

"Who you calling a slut, you slut?"

"You!" Lily spat at her.

"You coulda had him—only had to put up your hand like back in school. Oh yeah—just like the time you sucked off that arithmetic teacher!"

"That's a fuckin' lie!"

Connie came to Lily's defence. "She's not a slag like you!"

"Who you calling a slag, you slag?"

"You, you slut!" Connie spat back.

They walked on a way, the tension seeming to calm. Then Lily turned on Maggie. "You fuck him all day yesterday? You didn't even turn up at *Sumbar* late!"

"Donny-Three likes me."

Connie from behind Maggie asked, "Are you going to see him more?"

x

140

"Yeah—he's loaded and I know exactly what he likes."

Lily danced in front. "Yeah, yeah—a slut who knows what a guy wants—as if that's breaking news around the world!"

"You coulda had him. You both coulda stayed."

"You offering us a foursome with your boyfriend?" asked Lily.

Connie pretended to be shocked. "Ergh, that's so gross! What a slaggy slut!"

"Who you calling a slaggy slut, you slutty slag? And keep your eyes off my necklace, you thief!"

Lily in front turned back again. "Who you callin' a thief, you bitch?"

"You're jealous because Donny-Three wants me to fly to the States to meet him in—Galveston."

"Ain't that a song?" queried Connie.

"Dumb-arse! It's a town in Texas," said Maggie. "Everyone knows that."

The three walked on to lie in the sand in front of *Sumbar* and earn their free Mai-Tai and Thai beef salad for the day.

*

At *Puek Tian Beach*, several statues stood in the water.

"Those are stunning!" exclaimed Beatrice. The others agreed.

The driver's wife said, "At low tide you can walk to them."

The dominating one was a large, overweight, fearsome, black, god-like woman. She faced the shore with her right arm extended in an unwelcoming pose. The driver's wife explained, "Legend statues. Come from very long Thai poem—*Phra Aphai Mani*—Thai poet—name: *Sunthorn Phu*."

The four tourists stood beneath the open squared arch in its shade, looking to sea. Around them there were very few people, and they were local Thais whose children were playing in the sand and the water, oblivious to the legendary threat just off shore.

Gerhardt offered, "Thailand's best kept secret." He then held out his arm like the statue and monster-like stumbled towards the women, groaning with menace.

*

"Cover your tits—there's a Thai family on the beach." Garry was standing on the front veranda of *Sumbar* looking over the three girls. After they managed

141

to look less obvious and no less appealing, he added, "Tomorrow night, I'm having a birthday party. You three want a job waitressing?"

"How much?" asked Lily, adjusting her bikini top.

"Five hundred baht each."

"I do." Lily looked at the other two. They nodded. "We'll be here."

Garry came down onto the sand and handed them some baht. "Buy some bright coloured sarongs this afternoon—give the party a bit of life."

He returned to his bar after washing his feet, passing four young men drinking on the veranda. One of them said, "We'll have the same again—and whatever the girls are drinking."

Garry went behind the bar, pleased.

*

They walked *Puek Tian Beach* and had lunch in a cafe across the road, asking the driver, his wife and two children to join them, the four tourists paying. When leaving to get back in the truck, the elder of the two little girls, picked some flowers from the side of the road and gave them to Beatrice and Angelica who thanked both girls as they put the flowers in their hair.

"What side means I *am* available?" asked Angelica, looking cheekily at Gerhardt. He laughed. The women put the remaining flowers into the hair of the Thai children who beamed with delight. Their mother bowed deeply, her hands in the prayer position.

Beatrice, climbing onto the back of the taxi-truck, commented, "Such innocent pleasure," and after the truck had set off, added, "That's what I'm going to strive for, or at least reclaim."

"A most worthy pursuit," commented Gerhardt.

The taxi-truck returned home via the beach at Cha-am. Jack was surprised as they drove the esplanade by the water. The Cha-am he knew always seemed like every other Thai town—an intersection on the highway surrounded by apartments and shops. However down here, the trees by the sea made it memorable. Not a Westerner in sight, the area was heavily frequented by Thai families.

"Another hidden secret," said Gerhardt.

Back in *Sumbeach* at the tuk-tuk depot, they paid the driver and refused the change. How could they put such a small price on such a wonderfully enjoyable day? Gerhardt tapped Jack on his arm and showed him two 100 baht notes. Jack found the same and they surreptitiously gave the girls two hundred baht each. Their parents noticed, bowed and thanked them. The little girls waved happily as the taxi-truck drove off.

"I need a swim," said Jack.

"In the sea?" asked Gerhardt.

"No, the small pool at my hotel will do."

"Why don't you join us in the large pool at *L'Hotel Majestique*? Do you have your bathers with you?"

"I wore mine", said Beatrice, "I forgot to swim with the statues!"

"Come back next year," said Gerhardt. "Do it then!"

"Yes," thought Beatrice. "I just might."

Jack joked, "I must warn you, Beatrice has a new bikini and we have to be prepared for the pandemonium she will cause at the hotel pool."

"My wife has already caused three pandemoniums!" declared Gerhardt. Angelica smiled, moving her head from side to side, knowing that she probably had.

Beatrice, ever the librarian said, "I think that's three pandemon-*ia*!"

The others groaned.

"Then it is agreed," said Gerhardt. "Everyone to the pool bar! Follow me!"

They traipsed towards the revolving door. The two women entered first and came out the other side. The two men shared a segment and continued around twice, making out they were blind and could not find the exit.

After they'd finally emerged, Angelica said, "I apologise for Gerhardt. The Berliners think they have a superior sense of humour to us Viennese."

The late afternoon was spent swimming and drinking cocktails in the superior quality of *L'Hotel Majestique's* pool.

"I could get used to this," Beatrice said to Jack. "The only thing stopping me from living the life of an international jet setter is money."

"You can't have both. That and the simple pleasures you said you now craved."

"I'm very adaptable."

As Jack left with Beatrice, he reminded Gerhardt and Angelica about Garry's invitation for the following evening.

Half an hour later Amelia and Olivia walked into the pool area. Gerhardt turned to Angelica and asked quietly, "Should I tell the blonde English woman what a great guy Jack is?"

"No!" snapped Angelica. "You are not cupid!"

"But Cupid has a belly like mine."

"Not as big!"

Chapter 21

"Friday night and you're not up town?" a brightly dressed Beatrice commented as she walked from the stairs into the bar at *Sumbar.*

Jack looked up from his tablet. "No. I think I'll have a quiet one at home."

"You don't want to maybe go to that big hotel and catch up with that fabulous dancing blonde Gerhardt was talking about?"

"No—too much uncertainty there, I'm afraid. She's better left alone. I mean, I'm better she's left alone. No, that's not quite right either. Whatever, I'm playing hard to get," he joked.

"Jack, it's not *hard to get* if she doesn't even know *who you are.*"

She messed his hair, as if he were a child, and laughingly departed.

"You'll be okay out there?" he asked after her.

"I know the way!" Beatrice called confidently as she stepped down onto the sand.

Jack closed the tablet and watched her disappear into the darkness. He climbed to his room and changed into his swimming trunks and grabbed a towel. After dark, the pool was always deserted. He did some simple laps of breast stroke, not even bothering to kick his legs. *Of course, I'd be thinking of her!* He climbed out and with his towel wrapped around his waist stood in the warm night air looking over the back lot, across the dogs eating a scrap of food someone had tossed them, towards the fast moving lights of the endlessly flowing cars on the main road.

The dark car drew up at the top of the back lot. Instinctively Jack eased back from the reflected light and watched from the shadows.

Eugene got out of the car. Cigar smoke began to drift from the open door as he stood bent over it, talking and looking back inside. A Thai boy climbed out and walked away in the direction of the orphanage.

The large Australian politician climbed, with exertion, from the back seat, cigar in his mouth. He said nothing to Eugene who stood by the rear door and watched him walk across the empty lot to the rear entrance of *Sumbar*.

In the shadow, Jack studied the big man walking confidently down the path by the pool beneath him. He put on his shorts over his damp swimming trunks, pulled the t-shirt over his head and followed the politician into the bar, calling, "Garry! Did I leave my tablet in here?"

Garry, startled, turned. The large Australian paid no attention to Jack. "This bar bill will be the financial ruin of me," he laughed.

"It won't be of me," Garry managed to say, accepting the wad of cash, before turning his attention to Jack. "Ah, no, Jack, haven't seen it."

"That's not it over there, is it?" sneered the politician.

What he really means is don't interrupt while I'm speaking! Jack crossed to look on the corner table. "No. Thanks, mate. Oh, I've left it upstairs on the floor by my bed." He climbed the stairs. *A bar bill? I haven't seen him in here drinking all week!*

*

"You go, Olivia," said Amelia, stretching back on her bed. "I've searched enough for today. I'm beat. It's been a long week."

Olivia, dressed, waiting by the door looked back at Amelia lying there. "Amelia, nothing can happen if you just bump into him out there. He isn't going to attack you."

"I know that—I'd just rather not. I think I'm over Thailand. I'm virtually resigned to the fact that on Sunday we'll leave without the identification."

"That was always the most likely scenario."

"Yes, I know that. I still hate losing though. You go. I'm perfectly happy here."

"Amelia, you can't live your life running from interesting men, particularly the second man in your entire life who has actually affected you."

"Affected me? I had my guard down. And besides, who said I can't? Of course I can. It's much easier and safer this way."

"God, I wish I understood myself as well as you think you understand you."

Amelia sat up and looked at her. "Is that a complement or a criticism?"

Olivia smiled enigmatically and opened the door. "Bye!"

Outside the hotel the hot evening curtain of air hit her. Olivia stopped and took it in, now enjoying its familiarity. There was movement and colour and life on the street, just like any Friday night throughout the world. Motor bikes and tuk-tuks jostled for space and pedestrians dressed for the evening, stepped quickly up onto footpaths as they zoomed by. The restaurants she passed were full, the bars lively.

A couple argued over the price of a dress, the woman finally handing the shop assistant her credit card. When taken she turned to her husband and poked out her tongue. Tourists walked with arms around each other, though not the locals—the public display of affection not part of the culture.

Three gaudily dressed showgirls surrounded Olivia, forcing her to take a pamphlet for a show beginning in an hour's time. She took it, noticing that the back of the hand which had given it resembled more the hand of a male than a female.

A small truck took her attention as it bounced by with a noisy commentary from the speaker on its roof, its sides emblazoned with a garish advertisement for local Thai kick-boxing. *I won't be going to that!*

"Ev'ning, Gorgeous!" said the drunken Billy Mackie. "Where's your blonde girlfriend?"

Olivia walked off quickly.

The evening's movement, the couples together, the sense of enjoyment in the air, the anticipation of a special night, led to her wishing Barty was here with her. *When I get back, I need to have a serious talk with that man. It's time to lift this relationship to a more secure footing.*

*

"Friday night is golf club night," Jack remembered out loud. He changed his plans. Pulling on a clean shirt and not wishing to bump into Garry, or the large Australian in the bar, he took the back way to *Terry's*. The large Australian had left the bar. The dark car had gone. In the back lot only the two mangy dogs were moving, settling into their hole.

The nearer Jack approached the town centre, people thickened around him. He passed a bill board advertising white condominiums squared around a bright blue swimming pool. Even though he had no strong ties back home he knew he could never settle here like so many other Westerners had. He wondered exactly where he'd end up after his planned time in France.

Deliberately avoiding the street where the orphanage was, he ducked his head underneath the power cables at the main intersection, recalling Gerhardt's recent experience, and turned right, down past the police station and beyond *Brauhaus Helmut.*

*

"Yes!" Terry had made a decision.

"Yes?" asked Nerida, not quite hearing. "What are you referring to?"

"Yes!" Terry shouted again to Nerida trying to be heard above the packed hub-bub of drop-ins, regulars and the members of the *Sumbeach Buccaneers.*

He took her aside by the arm and spoke into her ear. "I'm agreeing to your moving over here permanently. Tomorrow at eleven there's an inspection of a new place up there on the other side of the highway. No communal pool though. It's got a private one!"

"Yes!" exclaimed a delighted Nerida.

"Terry?"

Terry looked up; Nerida stepped back. Terry gradually thought he remembered the face, though couldn't recall the name.

"Jack—Jack Featherstone. Australia. Last time I was here would have been six years ago."

Terry studied him. "Yes!" he clicked his fingers. "Your wife loved that crazy Australian Football game, if memory serves me correctly." He began to move his hand up and down as if conducting his thoughts. "She hated the black and white team. You both sat here and the three of us watched the grand final." He looked about. "She's not with you?"

"No, sadly, passed on."

"Ah."

Nerida broke the awkwardness. "Jack, I'm Nerida. I'm new here—after your time. For *my* crimes in England, like you early Australians, I was sent away. The judge said: *Go to the Orient, find an expat bar owner and fall in love with him.*"

*

Olivia stood on the street along from her hotel and heard from behind her raised voices discussing, in English, international cricket—specifically English/Australian cricket—*The Ashes*. She looked up a small flight of concrete steps to an innocuous sign which simply read: *Terry's*.

Harold Keith Brown may be up in there. Friday night, he's got to be somewhere.

A group of men and a Western woman stood on the edge of the small bar clearly enjoying themselves. Olivia recognised 'Dancing Jack' from the night before. She climbed the uneven concrete steps towards them.

Jack waved to her as she emerged from the shadows. "Ah", he said to the others, "let me introduce you to the best dancing partner in all of *Sumbeach*." Olivia feigned embarrassment although smiled genuinely. "Olivia, meet everyone else."

"Hello, everyone else!" said Olivia, happily.

"Hello, I'm Nerida. What would you like to drink?"

Three men in unison exclaimed, "I'll get it!"

Nerida looked at them, "Settle, boys, settle. Beer or wine?"

"Ah, it's a very warm tonight—a cold beer, please." Nerida didn't move. She simply waved to Dimi, wearing a red *Terry's* emblazoned t-shirt, behind the bar.

"Actually, I'm not the best dancer; however, Jack here is very good. He danced so well with my stepmother last night that he knocked her off her feet. She's sprawled on the bed back at the hotel unable to get up!"

"She's okay?" asked Jack, concerned.

"Sure she is. I'm only kidding." Dimi handed Olivia the beer. "Oh, thanks." She sipped from the bottle, remembering to cast her eye over every male in the room. "Lot of expats," she noted, as if for the first time.

"Fortnightly golf club social gathering," Nerida explained. "You looking for anyone in particular?"

"Only my future dream lover."

"Aren't we all," quipped Nerida, winking at Terry.

Jack wanted to ask her more about Amelia. *Not the place, not the time, not the anything*, he thought.

A tall thin white skinned man leant into Olivia. "I'm Julian. So what brings you to *Sumbeach*, Olivia?"

"Just a holiday, Julian. My stepmother read about it in a magazine."

A man pushed by the group. "Good-night. Must run. I'll see you all tomorrow night at Garry's birthday party?"

"Yes! Sure thing! I'll be there!" The responses from the group were rapid.

As the man moved off, Julian called after him, "Hey Drake! Give my love to Suzy-Q!"

Dickie Eastman waved and called back, "Will do!"

*

"Guess who I stumbled across, in an out of the way bar, tonight?" Olivia asked as she let the hotel door close behind her.

"Oh you didn't, did you?"

"I did."

"What did you say?" asked a concerned Amelia. "Tell me you didn't talk to him about *me*."

"Gee it's warm out there. I've just *got* to have a shower."

"Wait a minute," ordered Amelia; however, Olivia had disappeared into the bathroom.

Amelia rose from the bed. At the bathroom door, over the running water she asked loudly, "Was he alone? You didn't embarrass me, did you?"

"Sorry!" shouted back Olivia. "I can't hear you. I've water in my ears."

"Poke your head out! Look at me!"

"Sorry—soap in my eyes."

"Sometimes, Olivia, you're just far too childish."

"I heard that!"

Amelia returned to the bed. She lay there a moment then silently went back inside the bathroom, removing all the towels and tossing them onto Olivia's bed.

"Hey!" called out Olivia, when she'd turned off the shower. "Where are the towels?"

"What towels?"

"Oh, who's being childish, now?" Olivia started to brush the water from her body with her hands. "Okay, okay. Hand me a towel and I'll tell you everything."

With a towel wrapped around her torso, another wrapped around her hair, and drying between her toes with a third, Olivia started her tale. "Amelia, from the outset I want to say—you are mad! Australian or not—and I do not know

150

why you are hung up on them—Jack really is such a nice guy." She ceased speaking to concentrate on the little toe of her left foot.

"That's it? What kind of 'gossip gatherer' are you?"

"Business time—the bottom line is: we're going to that birthday party tomorrow night. I've got a feeling every English expat in town will be there."

"Yes, of course. I couldn't agree more."

"And while we're there, if you run into Jack because that's where he's staying, talk with him, bury this 'fear' of the 'man who's meant for me' because he's such a great guy and he's had a tragic life. A couple of years back he buried his wife and before that a still-born child. He's an architect by trade and he's recently sold his timber mill for an enormous amount of money and he's heading to Paris on Wednesday and then will drift around the world with no thought of returning to Australia."

"You learnt all that? How long did you 'bump' into him for?"

Olivia ignored the question. "So he doesn't need any childish carrying-on from you, O Evil Stepmummy. Did I say he's a really nice guy?"

"If you say that one more time I'll put you over my knee and smack your bum! Baby Olly! It's a wonder you didn't find out what room he's staying in."

Olivia thought a moment and lied, "Number seven, overlooking the ocean!"

Chapter 22

To Garry, the three sand flies had miraculously transformed. They'd spent time on their hair and make-up and their new sarongs matched his intentions perfectly. He watched them emerge from the beach's darkness into the spilling light of *Sumbar* giggling as they walked towards him, arm in arm, sandals in their hands. *They don't look too bad*, he thought, *better than their usual foul-mouthed whorey demeanour.*

He looked into the darkness beyond them to the green-lit fishing boats on the horizon and to the silhouettes of storm clouds edged by moonlight. *They will pass over*, he reasoned, supported by years of weather watching from the veranda.

How long ago has it been since leaving England? And today—another birthday. Forty-four! Who'd have believed it?

Back home Garry had only ever worked for others. Here he worked for himself, with a finger in a few pies which paid well. Back then he couldn't have dreamed he'd one day settle down in Thailand, a model citizen of the *Sumbeach* community.

Outwardly pleasant to all, he'd kept himself to himself and that's the way he liked it and more importantly, how his 'special clients' liked it. That's the reason they came back time after time—trust. They knew he'd keep his mouth shut, and they needed his blind eye when it came to matters concerning the pick-up and drop-off area in the empty back lot. It was all 'business' to Garry.

He had no intention of letting on to Mai or Sunny that there was extra money around the place; no intention of revealing his secret stash in the dirt around the large half plant / half tree by the swimming pool out the back.

It might be time to re-visit Bangkok, to place orders personally and keep Sumbar's suppliers of cheap liquor happy. That's what he told Mai, whenever the urge hit him, three, four times a year.

A large handful, from beneath the ugly plant, bought first-class whores, top grade Irish whiskey, massages with benefits and, at a particular gym in Patpong, a violent bout of Thai boxing. There he could batter a fighter into submission, smashing his head and kicking his guts in. His victim would be assessed for damages and the price, in cash, paid. You can't ever truly say goodbye to a violent youth—a grown man needed to let his hair down, release the pressure valve, after being couped up in domestic bliss for too long.

Maybe next week—yes, I'll take a train to Bangkok for two days, he decided.

The three sand flies stopped below him on the beach. "This okay, Garry?" called out Lily. They did a short modelling parade in the sand.

"Yes." he said. *Back in England,* he mused, *I'd have taken all three of you tarts to bed and given you a time you'd never forget.* They adjusted the sarongs that had been hitched up when walking down the beach in the water. *Especially that one with the gold necklace. Christ, she does something for me, even now. Yeh, I'd take you out the back to the empty lot, darling, and give you one up against that wire fence! I'd leave an impression on your back you'd never rub out. Talk about a birthday present!*

"Garry!" called out Sunny, obliterating his reverie. "Mai want you."

"Tell these tarts what to do—get serving trays for them," ordered Garry. "And don't try to fuck them behind my back!"

Garry obediently went to Mai in the kitchen.

Fook them? No way! thought Sunny. *Combined, they don't have enough money to buy me a tyre for a red motor bike!*

*

"Garry, hold Baby Tookie. She no sit still." Mai was trying to remove fish cakes from boiling oil.

"Where's the baby sitter?" Garry asked, checking his wrist watch.

"She no come. Maybe late. I must cook. Not long. I finish soon. Tookie no stay under feet. I drop food."

"Yeah, yeah, okay." He picked up his daughter in his arms and carried her outside, out the back to the deserted lot. Suddenly he turned back inside. "Lily!" he called out. "Want to make 200 baht?"

Connie called back, "Who she gotta fuck, Garry?"

"Hey! This is a family bar!"

"Sorry," said an immediately contrite Connie.

"Yeah, sure, Garry. What do you want me to do?" asked Lily.

"Take Tookie out back until the baby sitter gets here. Mai needs thirty minutes to finish cooking."

"Sure." Lily took the baby from his arms. "Hello, Tookie." She carried her outside.

"Sunny?" enquired Garry, "You explained everything to the girls?"

"Yes, Garry, all on control."

"Under," Garry corrected. Then he muttered quietly to himself, "Idiot."

*

An imposing figure walked up the steps onto *Sumbar's* front veranda. He wore pressed white slacks and a floral ironed shirt. He carried two pairs of designer sandals in his hand.

"Captain Choni!" Garry called out, "You came! Welcome! A pleasure to have you here!"

Then from behind the man a small, middle-aged, coiffured woman appeared. "Missus Choniburshakanari!" Garry went to her and bowed before her. "*Sawadee.* So pleased to see you. I am honoured by your presence."

The captain's wife smiled and returned his bow. Garry knew that was all he had to say and do. She did not speak English.

Sunny was by his side, bowing and smiling and in Thai said something along the lines of "Missus Choniburshakanari! You brighten my humble life by your appearance here tonight. All the stars in the sky are dimmed by your radiance."

The captain looked at Sunny and whispered in Thai, "Somsak, though very respectful, you are full of shit."

"Yes sir, I know," admitted Sunny, nervously. "Thank you, sir."

The captain spoke in English, "We are early because we intend to walk along the beach a little—we haven't done something like that for many, many years.

My wife thought it would be romantic. And I agreed. So, just to let you know, we'll be back and for you to reserve a table."

"Ah," Garry looked about wondering which table; however, Captain Choniburshakanari knew he wanted to sit where he could take in all of this evening's guests. It wasn't everyday he got to see them collectively and he wanted to put a face to the names he had on file and hopefully the one name he had inside his head.

"There, I think," he said, pointing. "I will sit in the corner at the bar on a stool, and my wife on a chair at the table next to me."

"Won't she feel isolated?" asked Garry, wanting to successfully accommodate both of them.

"Sorry, I no tell you. Wife's sister and brother-in-law will be attending also. Mister Garry, they thank you so much for the invitation you did not send."

Uncharacteristically Choni genuinely smiled. He gave a small wave of 'goodbye' to those around him and then stopped his exit. He approached Maggie, studying her necklace. "A beautiful necklace," he deliberately said, "for a beautiful young woman."

He studied it—perhaps lingering a little too long—trying to recall any report of theft from a gold shop in town.

Turning to everyone he said, "Where else in the world would you find such a combination? A beautiful sea, a beautiful moon and a beautiful woman." He turned to go, then back again. "Of course I meant my wife." He smiled at Maggie and left.

Sunny stood next to Garry, not moving, watching the captain leave. Connie, moved to Maggie and held her by the arm. They all stayed like that for a moment until it was broken by Billy Mackie, bounding up the steps.

"Holy Shit, who was that guy? The local mafia chief?"

*

Jack climbed out of the pool and dried himself. He'd fallen asleep in the late afternoon reading his tablet on his bed and only woken an hour ago. Now, after several laps, he felt refreshed. He stood by the fence near the single lamp post illuminating the vacant lot.

"Jack!" He turned. Beatrice was walking with Werner up the three steps to the pool "Not at the party yet?"

"I'll be there in half an hour or so."

"Do you stay—to swim?" asked Werner.

Jack looked suspiciously at them. "Why?"

"Well, Werner and I thought we might take a dip—starkers! You know, the old 'skinny dip' in the creek."

"I'll leave you to it, Beatrice."

"You can join us if you like."

Jack walked off. "Bye."

By the staircase he saw those inside talking to a well dressed, middle-aged Thai couple on the front veranda. He moved to the staircase, paused and then crept back, retracing his steps. He stopped at the wall before the pool, hearing Beatrice and Werner in the water, splashing each other and giggling like children.

What the hell! He dropped his towel, flung down his swimming trunks and ran into the area naked. Screaming, he leapt into the air, holding his knees up under his chin, as he cupped his hand around his testicles to protect them from rupturing on impact.

Beatrice and Werner screamed with delight as water convulsed from the pool onto the surrounding tiles. When Jack came up, Beatrice pushed his head back under and laughed. When he surfaced the second time one of the sand flies, nursing a baby in her arms, was looking at them from outside the fenced wall, her back to the empty lot.

"Looks like fun—pity I gotta work," said a disappointed Lily.

A young Thai girl rushed out of the darkness into the light of the single lamp post. She spoke rapidly to Lily, bowing and pointing to the baby and herself.

*

"About time! You're late!"

The young Thai girl smiled apologetically to Garry and bowed her head, walking in from out back.

"Give her the baby?" asked Lily.

"Yes, yes," said an annoyed Garry, interrupted from welcoming the first group of expats. "Then tell your friends to go get the spring rolls."

Sunny overheard and ordered the other two, "Girls—go get spring rolls!"

Garry looked at Sunny and wondered if his wife's brother was a fool, a parrot, or a 'piss-taker'. Never once had Garry considered Sunny to be clever, ignorant of the fact that Sunny was operating in two languages. Garry had never learnt more than a few words of Thai in all his time in *Sumbeach*.

Sunny returned to his preferred position on the front veranda and spoke into the darkness. "Good Evening Mister Michael. How is Little Mickey?"

The expat emerged from the sand's darkness. "Finally asleep." He carried the baby to the steps. "What's going on tonight, Sunny?"

"Birthday party—Garry."

"Oh, I forgot. Garry invited me earlier in the week. Did I just see Police Captain Choni walking the beach?"

"Yes, Mister Michael. He come to party."

"Mmm. I'll just go back home and drop off Little Mickey."

"You come back! Do not forget!"

The man turned and went. Sunny wondered why he never stopped longer than to say the usual brief greeting. Sunny didn't think he would return. *Mister Michael is sad man—never unfriendly, though not cheerful. He carries many worries in his head.*

"Gutten Tag!"

Sunny's thoughts snapped back. "Gutten Tag!"

Before him stood an older man and an elegant woman, long blonde hair falling beyond her shoulders.

"Is this birthday party? Jack invite us."

"Yes. Mister Jack. He inside—somewhere," said Sunny, wondering where he could buy a pair of bright yellow shorts like those the man wore.

Gerhardt and Angelica dunked their feet in the large concrete bowl and climbed the steps, their smiles illuminated in the bar's lighting.

As Lily passed, Gerhardt asked, "The Australians, Jack and Beatrice they are … where?"

"They're out the back in the pool!" replied Lily, pointing the way through the bar area.

"Ah, Angelica, it's a pool party." And before Lily could add, *They're starkers!* Gerhardt and Angelica had moved on, waving a greeting, "*Tag!*" to the gathering expats and Garry behind the bar.

As they walked by him, Billy Mackie raised his beer bottle in the air and offered a half-swallowed, "I won't mention the war!"

Coming into the pool area, Gerhardt called out in English, "So this is your own private party!"

"Gerhardt! Angelica! You came!" called out a delighted Beatrice.

Recognising the accent, Werner said, "*Wir wurden gerne auftauchen, aber wir sind nackt.*" ("We'd love to get out, but we're naked!")

Gerhardt laughed. Beatrice and Jack looked at each other, puzzled.

Angelica ordered, "Gerhardt, come away." However, Gerhardt laughed louder and put his hands to his eyes as if surveying the scene through binoculars. Angelica insisted, "Gerhardt!"

"I come also!" he shouted, delightedly, and started to remove his turquoise polo shirt.

"Gerhardt! Nein! Nein! Nein!"

"That'll be twenty-seven!" quipped Jack. Beatrice laughed out loud.

Angelica dragged her husband away, shirt half over his head, causing him to kick his toe on the ugly half plant / half tree. He turned, whipped off his yellow shorts and running, leapt into the pool, without protecting his testicles.

"Aaaahhhh!"

*

Jack could hear a large group of noisy guests arriving on the front steps of *Sumbar* as he stood drying himself. He passed his towel to Gerhardt who took it, thanking him.

"Will Angelica speak to you again?" asked Jack.

"Oh—yah! We marry—long time. She used to me. She always say she marry child." He laughed and passed the towel back to Jack. He gathered up his scattered clothing, hurriedly put the items on and left, calling out, "I be in bar!"

Beatrice and Werner were taking their time, wrapped in each other's towels, their bodies pressing. Jack dressed quickly and with sandals in hand, stopped by the stairs to dry his hair. Climbing up he opened the door to his room and tossed the towel into the darkness. *I'll find that after the party.* He locked the door and left, bumping into the kissing couple slowly climbing the stairs.

"The party's down here, Beatrice, not on the stairs!"

*

Terry and Nerida stood tentatively on the front steps of *Sumbar*. This evening would be the first time the two had been out together at a special event, away from *Terry's*. The apprehension they felt immediately disappeared as they were welcomed by Julian and his golfing buddies like a newly arrived bridal couple.

Billy Mackie sat excluded. It didn't bother him. He had a second cold beer in his stubby holder and drinking by himself wasn't a one-off experience. "Aussie! Aussie! Aussie!" he shouted when Jack walked in through the rear entrance to the bar.

Jack caught his eye and returned a very uninspired, "Oi! Oi! Oi!"

"So, Nerida, is it my grip or my swing?" asked Julian.

"Come to the class tomorrow and find out," teased Nerida.

"Drake's charging 500 baht!"

"I'm worth it." The circular group of expat golfers 'oohed' at the innuendo.

Terry looked at her, as the conversations continued and thought, *Yes, you are. You are totally different to Wanda, but you are most definitely worth it. How did I manage to strike gold twice in one lifetime?*

There was a grunted stumble on the steps leading onto the veranda. Julian looked up. "Hey! I played with that American chap today!" He broke from the group and crossed to the entering Donald Ranaldson Jnr. "Donald Jnr! Long time, no see."

"Long time? Didn't we meet today, Buddy?"

"Yes, you're right. My mistake. Julian—Julian Fields—remember?" He offered his hand. Donald Jnr ignored it. "There's the bar," said Julian, and with that he stepped back to his friends and summed up the man with two quietly spoken words, "Humourless prat!"

Unbeknownst to the loudly speaking expats, Captain Choniburshakanari was now seated, listening and watching intently from his selected position in the corner of the bar, his wife and his guests sitting at the table by him. Sunny had seen the return of Captain Choni's party and had whisked Mai-Tais in front of them before they had time to settle.

Gerhardt noticed Jack being accosted by a loud mouthed Englishman. He touched Angelica on the arm and went over to save him. "Ah—Jack! All dry at last. Your two friends are still cavorting with mother nature?"

"Yes, though no longer in the pool. This is—Billy, isn't it?"

"Sure am, Squire. Billy Mackie, lately of the Old Dart."

"Billy—Gerhardt and Angelica," said Jack.

"Here they are!"Gerhardt had caught sight of Beatrice and Werner entering from the stairs.

Jack remembered the first time Beatrice had entered this room—nervous, protective of her luggage, unsure. Was it only six days ago? Now she shone, her natural poise and sense of humour, which he admired, fully released. She and Angelica were very similar in the way they carried themselves. *If only Amelia were here*, he thought. *What a trio they would make. And Olivia? That would be a plethora of riches!*

"Tell me," asked Gerhardt. "I have always wanted to know this. What is 'piss taking'? I am told you Australians do that a lot. Is it a medical procedure?" Beatrice and Jack laughed loudly. "What do you Aussies always find so funny?"

"Too hard to explain," Beatrice managed to say.

"Try me. We Germans also have a wonderful sense of humour."

Jack and Beatrice looked at Gerhardt, then at each other, and burst out laughing again.

Their explosive outbursts had an immediate effect on the other guests, as conversation levels rose to compensate for the noisy joy of the rear table.

Billy Mackie uttered, "I'm outa here." He sidled off, everyone oblivious to his staggered departure.

The five settled at the table. Gerhardt insisted on buying everyone drinks and went off to organise it.

Angelica leant into Jack. "You know Gerhardt dragged me over here, because he saw that Englishman was not really your 'friend'. My husband is very understanding of human relationships—for a dentist."

*

Billy Mackie saw an empty spot at the bar next to the well dressed Thai gentleman seated on a stool in the corner. He plopped himself noisily onto the stool next to him.

"Evening Squire, I'm Billy Mackie from his Majesty's Realm." He offered his hand. The well dressed gentleman merely bowed his head. "Ah, that's right. I keep forgetting—you guys don't shake hands, do you?" Billy exaggeratedly bowed his head and cupped his hands beneath his chin.

Captain Choni smiled. "I … buy … beer you?" he faked.

"Mighty decent old son," said Billy, as a smile emerged. "Mighty decent."

"Is … yes?"

"Yes. Oh, yes. I never say 'no' to a free beer."

Captain Choniburshakanari caught Sunny's eye and indicated a beer for Billy. Sunny was onto it straight away. Connie carried a tray of spring rolls towards them. Captain Choniburshakanari indicated she should first serve the table to his side. She did so, then returned and Captain Choni took one in a small napkin, while Billy took three, tossing one immediately into his mouth.

"Shit that's hot!"

Chapter 23

Donald Jnr sat by himself in the centre of the bar, empty stools either side of him, fiddling with a coaster in the fingers of his right hand, nursing his second double bourbon with ice in his left, unconcerned by those behind him talking and laughing noisily. He'd scoffed the first bourbon, still seething over being admonished by Dickie Eastman yesterday. His eye was taken by a colourfully clothed waitress, brushing by him. "What's your name, lil' darlin'?" he asked, gruffly.

"Connie," she replied, immediately. "What's yours?"

"Donald Randalson Junior," he said, stretching up his stooping shoulders.

"Hey! I met a Donny-Three. He any relation to you?"

"My lay-about son." He knocked back the remainder of his glass.

"Lay-about? He's very active, from what I hear."

Donald Jnr was not in the mood for listening. "I'll have a third!" he called to Garry, passing over his empty glass. "My son?" he asked, realising what Connie had said. "Where'd you meet him?"

"Like a Spring Roll?" she asked, moving her tray closer to him.

"Hell no! Only the Lord knows what's inside those things! How'd you know my boy?"

"Sorry, can't chat, got to serve. I'm a working girl tonight."

"That's what I was hoping to hear. That you're a *working girl*." He gave a forced leer.

Connie teased, "What do *I* have to do to get a gold necklace?" She walked off deliberately wiggling.

Donald Jnr looked after her, giving her a lingering assessment. *Nice ass— but not as nice as Suzy-Q. Lord, why do you send me this temptation?* Garry put the third drink on the bar before him. Donald Jnr handed over 500 baht. "Keep the change, Bud!"

"Hey!" exclaimed Billy Mackie. "You must have connections around here. That beer arrived like," he attempted to click his fingers, "very fast."

Sunny had placed the beer in front of Billy and backed off. Captain Choni had taken his eye and nodded his 'thanks'.

"So, matey, you from around here?" Billy asked, after drinking heartily and plopping the bottle down on the counter top.

"Around—here?" asked the captain.

"Yeh. You—live—here?" asked Billy, emphasising each word.

"Yes—close," Captain Choni emphasised back.

"How do you local guys stand it? How do you manage to go to work with all this great looking tail on the street? I mean, every Thai woman I pass in the street is just so gorgeous!" Captain Choni looked blankly at him, pretending not to understand. "So—what's your name?"

"My name is—Choni."

"Connie?"

"No. *Cho*-ni."

"Well, *Cho*-ni, I have to tell you that I so love it here in your country. This Thailand caper is okay by me." He dropped his voice and confided, "Cold beer and hot pussy—what a combination." He touched the side of his nose knowingly and drank from his bottle. Captain Choni waited for him to go on. He knew he would and Billy Mackie didn't let him down.

"I got this woman—Thai woman—wow, she knows what I like! I don't mind she has to work for a living—you know, on her back—I'm a very liberal minded man. So we're down south—that's where I met her in his third rate, flea ridden whorehouse. I convinced her to scarper with me, see? Easy to do, because she's in love with me and I confess, I'm in love with her. I cannot leave her behind—anywhere I go—I want her with me. Those dumb arses down there weren't paying her properly. So as we're heading to the train station late at night, early in the morning, who can tell, eh?—it's all dark outside—she runs her fingers through the cash register and lo and behold all this money just sticks there. We get off the train up at Hua Hin and settle in here. Those thick heads have no idea where we got to."

Choni, pretending he was thinking about this, innocently asked, "Men—danger—no?"

"Nah," dismissed Billy, taking a swig from his beer bottle. "No problemo!"

"They look—you?"

"Hell, they're the least of my worries. I've already overstayed my visa by two months." Billy laughed. "Any chance of another beer, Mister *Cho*-ni?"

*

Sunny was heading into the kitchen when he caught sight of Donny-Three hiding in the back corridor, fidgeting, looking out into the darkness. Upon turning, Donny-Three raised his fingers to his lips and beckoned Sunny over.

Sunny whispered, "You okay?"

"Yeah, yeah. Call your pal. I want some more of that good shit."

"What? You smoke already?"

"Not all," he admitted. "I want to take some back to the States. It's seriously good shit."

"What?" whispered Sunny, alarmed. "You crazy man! This is Thailand. You get caught airport with drugs …"

"Come on, man, it's only dope." Donny-Three looked furtively down the corridor towards the noisy bar. "You said its legal."

"Here in Thailand!" reinforced Sunny. "Not to take out! Don't you read papers?"

"Sunny, I pay double price. Call your friend. Get him here."

"Why so fast?"

"My asshole father has cut my holiday short, just when I was getting some serious good fucking happening. I don't know why. There's no golf tour transfer next week, we got to take a car transfer tomorrow. That's why it has to be tonight. Enough questions—phone your friend. I'll be waiting out there by the pool. Come tell me. I need it, so, double price, okay?"

Sunny walked to the back lot taking out his mobile, and no longer caring why Donny-Three was so desperate. *Double price* was all he heard.

*

Captain Choni turned to the open doorway as Amelia and Olivia stepped from the darkness and stopped at the top of the step, looking inside. He nodded surreptitiously as Amelia caught his eye. She returned his enigmatic glance.

"I've seen these two women all week," Billy said to Captain Choni. "Everywhere I go, they're there. Anyone would think they're searching for me." Billy leant in. "Bloody hot though, aren't they?"

Beatrice seated at the back of the bar, tapped Jack with her foot. "Is that your dancing blonde?" Jack turned around. He didn't know if his heart leapt or sank.

"Now I understand," said Beatrice. "Women like her should be arrested and locked away. They don't give the rest of us a chance."

Chapter 24

"You ladies looking for me?"

Olivia recognised Billy Mackie. "No, sorry, we've saved enough lost souls this week." Seeing Jack down the back of the room, she took Amelia by the arm before she could object, leading her in past the clusters of party-goers and their animated conversations.

Billy watched the two women pass by him. "To hell with it!" he spat. Ignoring Captain Choni, he knocked back the remainder of his beer and stumbled outside to fall asleep on the sand.

Jack stood as they neared, Amelia's eyes finally resting on his, after hurriedly surveying the male faces in the room. Without thinking, she genuinely smiled at Jack. The others at the table made space for the two women to join them, Gerhardt lifting two unused chairs from another table.

"What would you ladies like to drink?" asked Gerhardt.

"No," Jack said, "I'll get them, Herr Lair—Gerhardt!"

"No. I have money!" Gerhardt insisted.

"So do I."

"Yes—but Euro much stronger than Aussie Dollar!" He dug Jack in the ribs.

Olivia said, "We'll have two umbrellas please!"

"Umbrellas?" asked Gerhardt.

"Mai-tais. Olivia's not very funny joke," explained Amelia. Gerhardt headed to the bar while all the necessary introductions were made.

*

Out the back near the single lamp post Donny-Three waited, peering into the gloom beyond the pool of light. A mangy dog stood, stretched, shook himself, and fell back into his hole with a grunt. Donny-Three turned suddenly.

"Well?"

"Soon—he come," whispered Sunny. "Same place. You go there—now."

"Now?"

"He no wish you see where he come or where he go."

"Okay, I understand," nodded Donny-Three.

*

When Gerhardt returned, followed by Maggie with the drinks on a tray, he announced, "A toast to good times."

Captain Choni, with his perfect sight line, watched them stand and clink glasses.

*

Sunny turned back towards *Sumbar*. Garry stood in his path.

"Who's that guy?"

"Friend," replied Sunny.

"He's a tourist. Since when …"

"I meet him on beach—he good customer—he know sand flies—buy them drinks."

"Yes," nodded Garry, recalling. "A smart-mouthed American. Maybe he buys them drinks in the day, but what's he want at night?"

"Maybe he want sand fly at night also. He ask what time party finish."

"If you're selling drugs behind my back I'll beat the shit out of you. You know I get my cut."

"Yeah, Garry, I know."

Sunny pushed by and went into the bar. *Giving you a share will not help me buy a motorbike.*

As the young American disappeared up the laneway, Garry looked about and sensing nothing of concern, followed Sunny.

*

Jack's table clinked glasses, took a sip of their drinks and sat. Amelia and Olivia didn't. Their eyes widened as Garry walked by them.

Captain Choni noticed the ladies' bodies stiffen ever so slightly. He looked over at Garry, looked back at them and knew they'd stumbled upon Harold Keith Brown.

"Don't stand on ceremony," Jack said to Amelia and Olivia.

Beatrice added, "You're allowed to sit. We won't bite."

Captain Choni watched the two English policewomen sit and settle back into their chairs.

Under the table, Olivia lightly gripped Amelia's knee. Amelia's hand tapped twice on top of Olivia's and she withdrew it.

Captain Choni settled back, leaning on the wall behind him, fixing a prolonged stare on Garry.

Amelia and Olivia sipped their drinks and listened distractedly to Gerhardt's story. At its conclusion they laughed with the others on cue, though they had no idea what they were laughing at. All they knew was their holiday was over— mission accomplished.

*

Julian saw him arrive first. "Drake! *Entrez, mon ami!*"

Captain Choni turned his attention to the veranda.

Dickie Eastman stood on the front steps. He waved to Julian and waited there. From the darkness around the foot wash, Suzy-Q walked up to join him.

Donald Jnr saw her appear from the darkness. She was as she looked that first time—her cream shorts and tight pink t-shirt advertising Dickie's Golf Tours—her dark skin, soft and smooth and highly desirable. He drained his fourth double bourbon and asked the passing Lily for a re-fill.

Dickie, placing his hand on Suzie's back, gently easing her forward, said with surprise, "Dampier, what are you doing here? This is a once in a century event!"

"Nerida and I are, at long last, hitting the town together."

Dickie turned to Nerida and kissed her on the cheek. "Are you still okay for tomorrow morning?" he asked.

"Of course," she smiled back.

"Drake, if these lessons are successful," Terry said, "we should talk about making them a permanent fixture."

"How so?" asked Dickie, cocking his head, curiously.

Nerida looked Dickie squarely in the eye. "In six months I'd like to settle here and I'm going to need some source of income."

"Of course, that's wonderful!" Dickie winked his 'congratulations' at Terry. "Everyone—I'd like you to meet Suzanna."

Donald Jnr watched on bitterly as Lily placed his double bourbon with ice on the bar in front of him. He knocked back half of it in one gulp, the tapping fingers of his left hand working overtime.

*

The nondescript dark sedan drove carefully down the laneway and stopped on the empty back lot. In the rear seat the Australian ex-senator removed the cigar from his lips and savagely exhaled a cloud of smoke. "What the fuck's going on in here tonight?"

Eugene thought for a moment. "Oh—I'd forgotten—Garry's birthday."

The Thai boy seated between them, not understanding English, followed their conversation like a spectator at a tennis match.

"Eugene, get inside and get your wallet," said the larger man. "Pay the kid." Eugene climbed out.

"You!" the ex-senator spat contemptuously, "Out as well." He pushed the boy forcefully behind Eugene. "Get your money," he shouted at Eugene. "You shouldn't have left your wallet back there in the first place. I'm off. If you desperately need your turn with him, then fuck him in those bushes over there— perfect cover with a noisy party going on."

Eugene shut the car door as gently as he could, trying not to bring attention to it. He watched the sedan drive off then pointed to the far wire fence where the darkest shadows were, indicating the boy should go over there and wait.

"I get baht. Wait! I go upstairs." He pointed. "In my room—baht—for you. Wait! Wait!" Eugene walked towards the single lamp post. He gathered his public face.

The two mangy dogs watched the boy cross to the darkest corner of their domain and stand there, looking about, his head half bowed onto his chest.

*

169

Amelia leant into Beatrice. "That man who just walked by, do you know him?"

"Oh, yes. He owns the bar. That's whose birthday party this is."

"Of course. Has he owned it for long?"

"Jack?" Beatrice asked. "How long's Garry owned *Sumbar*?"

"Ten years, maybe. Maybe more. Why?"

"Just curious," said Amelia, not wishing to appear too inquisitive. "Wondering what brings these Englishmen out here to settle."

"Many reasons," added Gerhardt. "Many reasons and all to do with biology!" he laughed.

Under his outburst Olivia leant into Beatrice and asked quietly, "Has Garry got a last name?"

"Sutherland," replied Beatrice, reflexively.

Amelia stood, cutting across the conversational flow. "I'm sorry, I must go."

Olivia, in sync, stood also. "Yes, we've a big day tomorrow."

They started to thank everyone.

Jack couldn't believe how quickly it seemed to be over. He saw his chance disappearing out of *Sumbar* and never returning. He'd been very happy, very content sitting there in Amelia's company. He couldn't let her just walk away.

Jack stood and followed, watched by a concerned Beatrice. On the steps outside he called out, "Amelia!" She didn't turn; Olivia did. He went down onto the sand. "Ah—could I buy you both dinner tomorrow night?" he asked, making it up as he went along.

Without turning around, Amelia said, "No! We can't."

Olivia took charge. "What she means is—we're leaving tomorrow night— flight to Heathrow—4 pm transfer from our hotel."

"Oh," said Jack, his expectation flattened. "I'm sorry, I didn't know." He stood there watching Amelia walk off and out of his life, wanting to shout after her, again, though what could he say in three seconds that didn't ring of desperation? There was no way he could ever tell her not to go, to turn around, to stay.

Olivia turned back to him. "Invite us to lunch?" she asked loudly, so Amelia could hear. "Why yes, of course we'd love to accept. Though *I* have a previous engagement, Amelia would love to be there. Top floor of our hotel—that's *L'Hotel Majestique*—there's a highly rated Thai restaurant up the top. Sensational views. Twelve noon, you say? I'll make sure she's there."

Then she walked to Jack and kissed him, whispering, "That's from Amelia."

Olivia ran back to Amelia and they walked off into the enveloping darkness. "Did I do good, evil Stepmummy?"

Amelia couldn't speak. She had tears in her eyes. Halfway down the beach, she confided in Olivia, "I *hate* you so much, you know that?"

"And what do you really think of Jack?"

"I *detest* him!"

Chapter 25

Captain Choni had watched the two policewomen leave *Sumbar*, impressed with the control he'd witnessed. They hadn't caught his eye as they passed him. They hadn't glanced at Garry after their initial identification. They hadn't looked back from the steps of the veranda for a last minute memory of the scene.

What are they now intending to do? He asked himself, concerned, mulling over their identification of Harold Keith Brown and how he'd address this revelation. *On Monday morning will the two policewomen be in my office bright and early demanding I act? If so, demanding of me to act how?* Choni knew Garry had not committed a crime in *Sumbeach*. *I have no reason to arrest him. I will wait for my superiors in Bangkok to tell me what to do legally about Harold Keith Brown, if and when those two from Scotland Yard inform me they've found their suspect.*

Choni watched the Western male who'd followed the two women return, noting he was now happier than when he left.

Garry was still behind the bar. *He's not going anywhere*, reasoned Choni. He studied Sunny working diligently, between the bar and the kitchen, organising the three Western waitresses with their trays and serving drinks. *I've never taken much notice of Sunny before. He'd always seemed to be an immature young man doing what he'd always been told to do by Garry. Sunny is more than capable.* The police captain thought long and hard, as he formulated his approach to Garry.

Sunny answered his mobile and left the bar.

*

"Hey! Where you?" Sunny called in a loud whisper.

"Here."

Sunny found Donny-Three in the small clearing by the leaning tree.

"Okay, he come," said Sunny. "Wait here."

Sunny returned inside. Donny-Three felt exposed in the moonlight. He left the clearing for the bushes, crouching and waiting.

*

Donald Ranaldson Jnr couldn't contain himself any longer. Temptation would not be denied. He stood drunkenly, knocking over his stool, staggering to Dickie and taking Suzy-Q by the arm. He spun her to him.

"Just like I thought!" He exclaimed, dramatically. "You won't fuck me because you're fuckin' the boss. The same the world over—fuckin' the boss! Fuckin' the boss!"

Julian moved in, grabbing Donald Jnr's arm and tossing it forcefully off Suzy-Q. He snapped at the drunken American, "How dare you!"

Dickie took a gentle hold of Suzy-Q. "Thanks, Julian." He walked her onto the veranda, away from the embarrassing incident, calling as he went, "Sorry lads! Must away. See you all in the morning for Nerida's master class!"

Donald Jnr shouted, "No, you don't! This ain't over!" He followed them out. Standing on the top step of the veranda he shouted after them as they walked into the darkness, "I'm Donald Randalson Jnr!" He followed them down onto the sand.

Choni watched it all. He reassured his wife and guests, "Expats— Imperialism—all solve problems with confrontation. Let Westerners fight it out amongst themselves."

The expats gathered on the veranda, eagerly watching. Julian started to move down; however, Terry took him by the arm. "No lad, let things work themselves out."

Blinded by anger, Donald Jnr ploughed on. He didn't see the sleeping Billy in the sand and fell face first over him. The expats on the veranda cheered like schoolboys. Billy stirred enough to mumble, "Mine's a cold one, thanks!"

The American picked himself up and drunkenly screamed, "Thieving bastard! Bring her back—what are you worried about?" He stumbled after them. "She's just a common old garden-variety whore!"

Dickie stopped. Suzy held his arm. "No. No, Dickie."

Dickie Eastman walked back to Donald Jnr and calmly said, "You belittle yourself when you say those things." He turned to go.

173

Donald Jnr exploded, threw his right fist forward and smacked Dickie on the back of the head. The blow knocked Dickie to his knees.

"Get up you mother fucker!" Donald Jnr quickly unthreaded his belt and whipped Dickie on his shoulders! "You don't deserve to be a son of mine!" he flogged the Englishman a second time. Dickie cried out, the savage sharp whip cutting through him. The American raised his belt again. "I said get the fuck up, Donny-Three!"

Suzy stepped quickly through the sand and let fly with a perfectly timed kick to Donald Jnr's groin. Howling and clutching his testicles, he screamed in rage, "Bitch!" He fell to his knees, dropping his belt on the sand. Suzy clipped him with an exquisitely delivered karate chop to the base of his neck. Donald Jnr screamed and fell face down.

The expats on the veranda cheered and applauded.

Suzy helped Dickie stagger to his feet. "Okay? You okay?"

"Yes, Suzanna. I'm okay."

Donald Jnr raised his head. "Fuckin' bitch-whore!"

Suzy let go of Dickie. She bent, picked up a handful of sand and as the American opened his mouth to scream another invective, threw it in his face, yelling, "Shut mouth, Mister!"

The expats whooped with glee; Donald Jnr coughed and spat. Those on the veranda applauded as if one of their pals had hit a boundary on the village green.

"Happy now?" asked Terry of Julian.

"Very. You old chaps are certainly wise."

Nerida laughed at Julian's humour.

A figure quickly walked past the sand-spitting American, making an arc towards the sea to avoid being caught up in the altercation. Once around, he continued towards the bushes beside *Sumbar* and the small clearing within.

Suzy held Dickie as they moved away down the beach. She'd never held him before, had never been this close to her boss.

Dickie ached from the blow, his shoulders stinging from the whipping, his bones throbbing from the fall. Stopping to rub the back of his head, he groaned, "I'm so sorry you had to experience that tonight."

"It okay. It okay. I know they think me whore. But I tell you—I never *ficky-fick* anyone. I wait for man I love. Man I want to give me babies. Other stuff—it job—money paid, job given. No man ever *ficky-fick* me."

174

"That's okay, Suzanna," Dickie managed to say, breathing deeply. "You don't have to justify yourself to me."

They turned from the beach towards town. "You the one I love. You the one I want to make my babies."

*

"Here. I'm here." Donny-Three stepped from the bushes. "Same quality as before?"

The dealer opened the plastic bag and Donny-Three sniffed. "Here." Donny-Three handed him a wad of notes. As the man counted it, he heard something behind him and turned abruptly. It was Sunny.

"Double pay?" Sunny asked the dealer. "You get double pay?"

The man nodded, handing Sunny twice his usual commission. "Double pay. I like double pay," said Sunny, holding up the thousand baht before stuffing it into his pocket. The dealer skulked off into the shadows.

"You wanna try it?" asked Donny-Three.

Sunny looked back at the party and then at the young American. "Yeah, sure."

Donny-Three began to roll a joint. "Over here, in the bushes. There's too much moonlight around this tree."

*

The expats returned inside *Sumbar*, pleased with the outcome. Ordering a round of drinks, Julian commented cheekily, "Best birthday party I've ever been to. When's Garry cutting the cake?"

It was time. Easing himself down from the stool, Capt Choni brushed imaginary sand from himself, then straightened his shirt by flexing his shoulders and lifting the back of his collar. Simply prepared, he smiled at his wife and indicated to the group that he had to go through the restaurant and outside.

Lily asked, "Another drink, sir?"

Choni shook his head, again looked at his wife's table and indicated to Lily that she should replenish their glasses. Choni sat again while Lily delivered the order to Garry and waited for Garry to fill it. Once Lily returned with their drinks Choni moved to Garry. They locked eyes and with a very small head movement

Choni indicated that Garry should meet him outside. Before leaving the bar, Garry bent and took a thick envelope from behind a box of coasters under the counter.

Garry led the way. Passing the bottom of the staircase, he looked up as Eugene stepped onto the top step. Garry quickly shook his head at him and Eugene stopped moving. He waited there and eased back.

Following Garry, Captain Choni passed across Eugene's line of vision. Remembering the boy outside, Eugene exhaled, "Shit."

The two men stopped by the deserted pool. Choni felt the area was too well lit and so indicated they should continue several metres into the back lot. The boy in the far corner saw them and slunk back into the darkness.

Away from the single lamp post Choni stopped and turned.

"Can't you make your usual time tomorrow?" Garry asked, handing him the envelope.

Choni felt its thickness and put it into the left side pocket of his white slacks. "A good week," he commented to himself, not knowing the impact the three sand flies had had on the bar's takings. The bulge in his pocket was pronounced. He took it out again, split it in half and returned the money to both side pockets. He patted them simultaneously. "Better," he said.

Lifting his head, he stood staring at Garry.

"What's your concern?" asked Garry. "You want me to buy out your share in *Sumbar*?"

Choni shook his head. "No. You—sixty-five; me thirty-five—is very good. It will stay that way."

"What then?"

Choni simply said, "Harold Keith Brown."

It was as if Garry had been simultaneously smacked in the face and kicked in the guts.

Choni dropped his voice. "I will help you. You have been very good for me. I'm not throwing away you and my investment." Garry took a backward step. "No," continued Choni. "Stand still and listen." Garry began clutching for air. Choni took hold of him. "Did you see those two English women who came to your party tonight?"

"No," Garry managed to utter.

"Well, they saw you. They are from Scotland Yard."

"Shit!"

"They have no power of arrest. They will merely report back to their bosses or come to me. I believe the former is what they will do. By the time their people talk to our people you will be well and truly gone. Remember—I do not let down those who have been good for me."

Garry agitated, nodded that he understood, beginning to doubt whether he could really trust him.

"Tonight you must go. I do not want them seeing you again around *Sumbar*. When they are on the plane back to England, we will meet again and we will think this through—calmly and logically." Garry nodded again, holding back the rising emotion. "Now go pack a bag."

Garry hissed, "What about Mai? The baby?"

"No worry. I tell them you called away. They will understand. You are not the first expat to suddenly leave his common-law Thai wife. You will be back here in a week or two, once the British policewomen realise you've gone. A month at most."

Garry knew he wouldn't be back, not in a week, not in a month. What had Mister Fingle said? *Once you disappear, son, you have to stay that way.* "What about *Sumbar*?" Garry asked.

"Money for Mai will always be here. I will see to that. *Sumbar* will keep operating."

"Operating? How?"

"Sunny."

"Sunny? He's a fucking loser. No, not Sunny. He now gets what he's been dreaming of. All those years—watching me behind my back, taking note of details, chatting to the delivery men, waiting for his moment and now we hand it to him—on a plate!"

Choni held Garry tighter by the arm. "Listen to me. It is only for a week, a month, until you return. I watch Sunny tonight. He knows what to do. I will keep an eye on him and on *our* investment."

Garry's lips tightened. He looked flustered as his eyes took in all he was about to lose—his beloved *Sumbar*.

Choni reiterated. "Pack a bag—you'll be gone for a week, a month, no more. Train north, south, it doesn't matter, just get out of *Sumbeckarnawan* tonight. It's not just you. Too many questions will be asked of me. What if those English policewomen walk into my office Monday morning with a Government official? You are too hot to stay here—for now—only for now."

Garry blurted out, "Jesus! What about the special clients?" He turned and quickly headed for the stairs.

Choni looked after him. *Special clients? What special clients?*

On the stairs Eugene was still waiting, caught between ascending or descending.

Garry startled, whispered, "Oh—Eugene, you gave me a fright." Putting on a brave face he said, "All good, carry on."

Chapter 26

On the stairs Eugene waited for the well dressed Thai gentleman to return inside. He stepped softly down hoping the stairs would not give away a tell-tale creak, and once past the swimming pool, crossed to the far corner of the empty lot. The boy was still there. Eugene took out his wad of notes and split it in half. He held up one half for the boy to see and pointed to where the sedan had been. He waited until the boy nodded, understanding. He gave the boy the money. He then held up the remaining notes and pointed to himself. He took a step back and pointed to the bushes beyond the single lamp post. Turning to the boy, he repeated the gesture. The boy nodded.

Eugene put out his hand and the boy took it. He then walked him across the empty lot, skirting the areas where light fell. It was as if Uncle Eugene was walking his nephew home from school.

*

Donny-Three and Sunny lay on their backs in the bushes looking at the stars in the night sky, listening to the boisterousness of the party inside. They didn't speak, they let the shared joint work its magic.

Sunny thought he heard something. He craned his head. Donny-Three looked curiously at him. Sunny shrugged, *nothing*. He eased back down.

He heard it again. He indicated to Donny-Three to stay where he was and not to make a sound. Sunny, very carefully, rose.

Both now heard a sharp soft whimper—a suppressed cry—followed by a slow crescendo of heavy breathing and muffled voices—one low, the other higher pitched. Sunny looked back at Donny-Three, who began to stir uneasily, recognising the combination of sounds.

Donny-Three quickly climbed to his feet unbalanced and fell forward several steps into the small clearing. In front of him a boy with pants around his ankles was being buggered by a grey haired man, his back against the leaning tree for support.

In an exploding rage Donny-Three screamed and grabbed the boy, flinging him away onto the ground. He hit the man as hard as he could in the stomach and chest—again, again and again. The tree held the man in a half upright position. Donny-Three pulled back his right fist and smashed it into the side of the man's face just below the left eye. The man toppled sideways and landed heavily onto the sandy ground.

Sunny stood, transfixed, stunned by the violent outburst.

Donny-Three knelt in front of the boy and pulled up his pants. He gently brushed tears of pain from the boy's eyes and then moved to the prone body of the man by the tree. Searching his pockets, he found the wad of notes and gave them to the boy. "Get out of here. Go!" The boy didn't move.

Sunny managed a translation. "*Winghni!*"

Gingerly the boy left the clearing.

Sunny watched the boy go, looked across at the man on the ground, studied Donny-Three standing there breathing hard, shaking. He crossed to Donny-Three and said calmly and quietly, "Go hotel. Do not come back."

The young American looked at him and then at the man on the ground. He wrung his aching fist. "Shit. Holy shit. I'm sorry Sunny—I just snapped!"

"Go! Now!" hissed Sunny. "Get away from *Sumbar!*"

Donny-Three patted his back pocket checking he hadn't lost his newly purchased stash, and like the Thai boy before him, stumbled out of the small clearing, the tingling memory of the whiplashes on his back and the weight of his father pressing him down, the pain of penetration in his arse.

Sunny watched him go. Of all the thoughts racing through his head, he settled on, *Come back later. When party over.* Then he groaned remembering Captain Choni was inside the bar. He looked about and slowly walked back to the place where they'd been smoking. It was there on the ground—the very small butt of the joint. He picked it up, carefully blew the dirty sand off it, tossed it into his mouth and swallowed.

*

"Donny-Three! Donny-Three!" Maggie was on the front steps peering into the darkness, making out the silhouette of her lover walking erratically down to the water's edge. She put the tray on the veranda's railing and leaving the noisy party guests, ran down to him. Donny-Three looked at her and smiled vacantly, not breaking stride. Maggie fell in step alongside him.

"What's the matter?" she asked, concerned. "What's wrong? What's happened?"

He couldn't tell her. He could never tell anyone. He hoped Sunny would keep his mouth shut. "Go back to the party", he managed to say.

She looked back to *Sumbar*. "No!" She took Donny-Three by the arm and helped him walk.

*

Sunny stopped by the staircase, gathering himself before entering. In the kitchen Mai was cleaning up, Tookie was being rocked to sleep in the arms of the baby sitter. Inside everything was normal, no one had heard. "Mai! Have you seen Garry?"

"No," she replied, drying her wet hands. "In the bar?"

Sunny entered the bar and looked around. "Mister Jack," he asked, disguising his concern, "have you seen Garry?"

"Last time I saw him he went out the back with that Thai gentleman up the other end of the room."

Sunny didn't like hearing that. He looked to the front of the restaurant. Garry wasn't with the police captain. "Lily, why you behind bar?" he asked.

"Getting drinks," she explained, annoyed. "Someone's got to keep the party going. Where've you been? Where's Garry?"

Sunny shrugged.

"Tend the bar, Sunny! There's only me and Connie—Maggie's pissed off somewhere!"

Sunny began serving drinks. He placed the third Mai-Tai on Connie's tray and left, going back past the kitchen. Movement at the top of the staircase caught his eye. "Garry?"

Garry ignored him. He hissed into his mobile, "Now! Hurry!" He put the mobile back in his pocket and picked up his bag.

"Garry, where you go?" Sunny asked, not comprehending the image of him holding his travelling bag on a Saturday night. And on his birthday!

Garry climbed quietly down the stairs concealing himself from Mai in the kitchen. He studied the young man. He nodded, conceding. "It's all yours. You have it at last."

"What you mean?"

"Talk to Captain Choni about the details. Look after Mai and Tookie."

Sunny watched him walk away, not believing, unable to call out, silenced by the seriousness of what he was witnessing. Garry stepped into the pool area. Sunny crept along the wall and peered around the corner.

At the back of the ugly potted tree, Garry took out a trowel. He scraped away dirt from the edge of the large ceramic pot, then dug deeper. He dropped the trowel, dug with his hands and tugged at something. Standing quickly, he opened his bag and tossed in the thick dirty plastic bag of money.

Sunny quickly stepped back down the corridor, climbed up three rungs of the staircase and waited until he heard Garry leave. Then he walked carefully back down past the pool. In the small spill of light from the single lamp post he could make out dirt by the pool's edge. He stayed in the shadows around the pool, creeping to the edge fronting the empty lot and looked out over it.

Garry stood in the centre of the vacant lot waiting, churning over thoughts. *When Choni gives me the all clear to return, will I be walking into an Interpol trap?*

Garry knew Choni would always have something over *him*. However, those others—his 'special clients'? Garry knew he'd always have something over *them*. It was better *he* determine his life—not Choni. *Not only will I insist those special clients take me to the Hua Hin station, but that they get me another identity, another protection,* Garry reasoned. *Even if I don't really need it, no matter, let them believe I do. I've been protecting them long enough, it's time they returned the favour.*

The advice that Xavier Fingle gave him had worked well. They'd been sitting in his car—Garry behind the driving wheel, Mr Fingle in the rear with another distinguished looking gentleman. Outside, the rain hit the roof so Garry was not privy to what they were saying. As the rain eased Mr Fingle handed the gentleman a packet. The other gentleman climbed out, opening his umbrella and disappeared.

"Drive on, Mr Fingle?"

"No hurry lad. Let's enjoy the sound of the rain." After a time, Mr Fingle had said, "Harry, you're a good lad—loyal—I like that." Then settling back, self satisfied, he said, "You know, if you ever want to keep something hidden—really hidden deep down—find someone in a position of influence and pay him, or her, to protect something else. Let him think the smoke screen you devise is your real concern."

And that's what Garry had done—the thirty-five percent investment in *Sumbar* for Choni, perfectly legal and honest—had been the best protection he'd ever made. He knew Choni had been blinded by their financial arrangement. Garry's special clients came and went unhindered with a safe place to stay when visiting *Sumbeach*. And the large Australian politician kept Garry sweet, bought his silence for far more than Choni ever took legally from the bar.

Mr Fingle you'd be proud of me!

Waiting in the dark, Garry knew what he now must do—bury Garry Sutherland's bonhomie and rediscover Harry Brown's cunning.

I'll take the 'pool' cash and hole up in Bangkok for twenty-four hours. There I'll go to my safety deposit box and remove the identification papers and passport, the renewed entry and exit visas for 'Mister William Norton' and head to where? Myanmar? Cambodia? Then maybe buy a bar on Lombock? No, too touristy these days. Get a bar somewhere quieter, off the beaten track—maybe that kingdom down near Malaysia—or a backwater in Vietnam—who knows?

In that desperate phone call he'd made, Mr Fingle had been very generous. "Why just one passport? To really disappear you need two—and never forget to renew both. Go back home son and quickly get rid of anything that may identify you. A family photograph album in particular. Bring the gun and get yourself down to London. I'll solve the rest. Then fuck off, forever, and live a long and prosperous life."

Whoever that gun had killed, thought Garry, *must have been important.*

The dark sedan entered the vacant lot and turned off its headlights. It bounced over the ground's unevenness, did a u-turn and stopped. Garry tossed his bag onto the front passenger seat and climbed into the back.

"Get me out of here," he said, pretending to be afraid. "I can't explain. It doesn't concern you and your pals. It only concerns me. Train station. I need to get to Cambodia," he lied. "I'm going to need a new ID."

"A what? I don't know about that."

"Senator, I've helped you all these years and now it's time for you to help me. It doesn't have to be Australian—but hey, that's not a bad idea." Garry stared at the Australian politician, his eyes full of incriminating knowledge.

"Drive on," the Australian said to his Thai brother-in-law, accepting, believing Garry.

The car drove off. At the top of the laneway the headlights were turned on. It glided up the highway, away from *Sumbeach*, away from Sunny, away from Mai and away from Baby Tookie.

The large Australian patted Garry on his knee, saying, "Maybe the passport could be a New Zealand one. We've been fucking them for years." He laughed.

"I'll be back in Bangkok in ten days. Have the passport ready. I'll contact you when I get there."

As the car drove on, Garry stared out the window at the brightly lit shops and bars flying by. For the first time he really noticed the people—the tourists walking arm in arm and laughing and heading back home in a few days time. *Home. If I only knew where that was.*

There would be no more taking Tookie for her morning walk along the beach and up into town where he'd bump into an acquaintance and pass the time, telling lies about his life back in Britain. He'd actually been happy with Mai at *Sumbar*.

"Shit!" he muttered quietly to himself, knowing he'd never see them again.

*

Sunny had watched Garry get in the car and drive off. He continued to stare into the emptiness. His conscience getting the better of him, he felt a sudden urge to go and see Aussie Gene. Walking from the pool under the lamp post, he cut into the bushes. The area around the bent tree was empty. He breathed out, relieved, *He's alive!*

Chapter 27

Eugene had stirred, aching. His ribs felt shattered, his cheek bones throbbed. Carefully touching his face, he withdrew his fingers and stared at the blood on them. *I can't stay like this*, he thought, *not here!* Lying on the sandy ground, he reached for his pants around his ankles. *Pull them up! Pull them up!*

For a man who'd always taken care of his appearance, Eugene was at a loss. He'd never been assaulted; he'd never sought out rough sex; he'd never played a contact sport; he'd never felt the repercussions of physical violence at all. *I need to clean myself up.* He struggled against the pain and his body weight, as he pulled his pants up over his lower torso. *I can't let Beatrice see me like this.*

With pants up and belt tightened, he held out an arm against the tree to help balance himself while he attempted to stand. Unable to do so, he fell back, hitting the ground hard. On his back he exhaled deeply and breathed in as quietly as possible, listening.

He heard the noise of a party somewhere, out there. Then he remembered Garry's birthday at *Sumbar*, the car dropping him and the boy off in the vacant lot, how he came to be where he was and the attack by the young stranger.

Eugene began to shiver. *Get up, come on, get up. You can't stay here.*

With one arm against the sloping tree, he tried again to stand, pushing against it, taking his weight as he rose, carefully, painfully. Disoriented, covered in blackness, he stumbled out of the bushes and down the slope of the sandy beach in the direction of the dark ocean. *The salt water will be good for the wound, won't it?* At the water's edge he stopped. *Care. Take care.*

He stepped forward and knelt in the gently lapping water. After making a slow sign of the cross, he scooped up a handful and patted his cheek. It stung. He gave a sharp intake of breath and did it again. Each time the sting was less. *Oh, that feels better!* He splashed water over the rest of his face. Looking out at the fishing boats on the horizon he'd never realised how reassuringly calm those green lights were. *Serenity, that's what I need.*

A bolt of chest pain threw him face forward. He struggled. His body weight pinned him down as the water caressed his face.

*

For Jack the party was over when Olivia had given him 'Amelia's kiss'. Back inside he sat with his friends, large portions of the conversation passing him by. A flustered Lily served behind the bar and a distracted Sunny came and went. Jack eventually excused himself.

Beatrice looked at him concerned, extending her hand towards him.

"I'll be okay, Beatrice," he reassured. "Fresh air. I'll just be outside."

Jack patted Gerhardt on the shoulder and rising, crossed the bar past the boisterous expats involved in a drinking game and by the imperious well dressed Thai gentleman. Standing on the front veranda, he peered into the blackness broken by the green lights dotted on the horizon and thought of Amelia and tomorrow's possibility.

He made out the shape of a body on the sand to his left. He studied it; it didn't move. Very slowly Jack eased himself from the veranda pole he was leaning on. The body rolled over, half stood and vomited. It was Billy Mackie.

The drunken Englishman belched loudly and wiped his mouth. He poked out his tongue. "Arrgh!" He saw Jack standing on the step. "Evening Squire, just taking a well deserved rest. Those spring rolls must have been off. Mouth tastes like ... Errgh! Gotta wash it out." Billy stumbled off towards the ocean.

Jack, concerned, followed. Billy knelt over and scooped water into his mouth. He gargled and spat it out. He did it a second time. On the third gargle he noticed a mass to his right. He stumbled to it and spat the water over Eugene.

"Holy shit! Holy shit!" he screamed. "Squire! Squire! Dead body here!"

Chapter 28

Jack stood over the body, recognising Eugene's red and black shirt from the evening they'd had dinner together at *Sumbar*. Taking a deep breath he knelt and peered closely at the side of the face, the water continuing to lap. Yes, it was Eugene.

"Who is he?" asked the dishevelled Billy. "Was he at the party?"

"Billy, go up inside and ask Garry to phone the police."

"Who's Garry?"

"The owner—the Englishman who runs the bar. If you can't see him then ask Sunny, the young Thai man who works for him. Quietly! We don't need everyone down here staring."

"Sure thing, Squire. Billy Mackie to the rescue." He stumbled off.

Jack studied Eugene's face. He had forced himself to do that when his father had died and had been pleased he'd done so, allowing himself to have that final memory. And for Eugene, whom he'd never known before a week ago, he felt he owed it to him, having died so far from home, so unexpectedly, so alone.

Jack's mind wandered. He was kissing Jenny on their wedding day, her white ensemble flowing behind her, surrounded by family and friends. *Where have all those friends disappeared to over the years?* He was holding Jenny as the doctor told them their child was still-born. *What kind of a person would our child have grown into?* He was walking down this very beach for the first time with Jenny, arm in arm, on a night similar to this.

"Eugene, Eugene, Eugene," he slowly whispered, consoling himself, as well as his fellow dead Australian. *Is all life some warped Greek tragedy? How many of us are taken from this world by what we fear and avoid the most?*

From up near *Sumbar* he heard Billy scream, "Call the police! Dead body on the beach!"

*

"I'll take over from here."

Jack turned. "Who are you?"

"Police Captain Choniburshakanari."

Jack looked at the neatly dressed, stockily built man who'd been sitting at the other end of the bar. "Do you have identification?" Jack asked.

"I don't need identification. Move away from the body."

"I'll move away when a uniformed policeman turns up."

"Move away from the body or I'll have you arrested," stressed Captain Choni.

"And charged with what?" asked Jack reasonably. "Compassion?"

The captain thought a moment and refrained from insisting once more. Jack returned his gaze to Eugene. The three stayed, as if caught in a freeze-frame— Eugene face down; Jack kneeling by his side; Captain Choni standing, overseeing the two of them.

People gathered around. Choni held out his arm keeping them back.

Rather like that 'monster in the sea' at Puek Tian Beach, observed Jack. *He is the police chief!*

Beatrice worked her way to the front. Her eyes widened, placing her hand over her mouth in disbelief. "Eugene!" she managed to utter.

Jack stood, nodded to the police captain, went to her and held her.

"My god, what happened?" she asked, unable to believe the image of Eugene lying dead at the water's edge in front of her.

"It looks as if he drowned."

"Drowned? He hated the water!"

Uniformed police and paramedics arrived. Eugene was photographed lying there and then on Choni's command rolled onto his back and rephotographed. Jack noticed the bruise on Eugene's face.

Captain Choni stepped forward, moving Jack and Beatrice further away from the body.

Eugene was lifted onto a stretcher and carried from the sand, up the side path, under the rear lamp post and into the ambulance parked on the block lot. Jack supported Beatrice as they followed behind.

"It was less than a week ago we walked this path, dragging our suitcases behind us," commented Beatrice, trying to comprehend the enormity of the situation.

The ambulance left. Choni stood with his two uniformed officers. Turning to Jack and Beatrice he asked, "Which of you knew the deceased?"

"I did," said Beatrice. "I flew here with him."

"He was your husband? Partner?"

"No—a friend, a work colleague."

"Tomorrow morning at ten, come see me at the police station." He looked pointedly at Jack. "I am the police chief—Captain Choniburshakanari." Then he asked the small group of Westerners, "Do you know where the station is?"

"Yes," said Werner, "Opposite my father's restaurant."

Choni looked at him, seriously, for the first time. "You are Helmut's son, Werner, from Munich?" he asked.

"Yah."

The captain nodded and the three policemen walked through the back lot and to their waiting car.

*

Jack and Beatrice sat on the steps of the front veranda of a near-deserted *Sumbar*, the only sound the low voices of Gerhardt, Angelica and Werner conversing in German from the back table. All the expats had drifted off, the buoyancy in the party well and truly deflated.

Sunny sat at a table wondering, *Garry gone; Aussie Gene dead. What is going on?* He glanced up to see his sister approach carrying Baby Tookie. She sat opposite him.

"Where is Garry?" Mai asked. Sunny looked at his sister and shrugged. "Where?" she asked, louder.

"He's gone. He had a bag, the bag he takes to Bangkok."

"Bangkok? He didn't tell me. Bangkok? It's his birthday party! He always tells me when he goes to Bangkok. Oh no! Another woman!"

"No. No woman," said Sunny, trying to placate her. "He'll be back. I look after you and Tookie until he is back."

Mai began to rock back and forward, trying to hold in a growing wail.

"We've finished the last of the washing up," called out Lily as she and Connie came from the kitchen. "Where's Garry? He promised to pay us."

"Follow." Sunny left Mai at the table, rocking, holding her stomach. At the cash register he asked, "How much? What did Garry say?"

"Five hundred. Each."

Sunny gave the girls their money as Mai's wail could be contained no longer.

"Thank you. We'll see you tomorrow," said Connie, giving Mai a concerned look.

Sunny returned to his sister.

Gerhardt, unsettled by what he was witnessing, tapped his wife and Werner on their arms and indicated they should leave.

"Where's that slag Maggie gone?" asked Lily as she and Connie went down the front steps, Jack and Beatrice watching them disappear into the darkness.

"I suppose—I hope—the embassy will take over. Jack, how does one fly a body back to Australia?"

"I don't know. I guess the embassy will be closed for the weekend. You could ring on Monday morning."

"Yes, I'll do that. You know, I don't even know who Eugene's next of kin is. Though he did say he had an aunt in Kalgoorlie. How could he possibly have drowned?"

"I don't know—he just did." They sat in silence, lost in their thoughts.

There were footsteps on the veranda behind them. Gerhardt, Angelica and Werner once again offered their condolences to Beatrice.

"We go now," said Gerhardt to Jack, smiling ironically. "*Sumparty* at *Sumbar* on *Sumbeach*."

Jack shook their hands and kissed Angelica. "Thank you again for the wonderful day at 'The Monsters in the Sea'."

"If you ever get to Berlin," Gerhardt said, placing a business card into Jack's hand, "You come see the best dentist in Charlottenburg."

"Will do, Gerhardt, will do."

Werner kissed Beatrice. He held her, letting her know how he felt. She watched him walk off with the other two. "I'm not going to get much sleep tonight, and for all the wrong reasons."

Sunny had managed to get Mai to her feet and taking Tookie in his arms he escorted his sister and niece to the stairs and up to their apartment above.

"I cannot believe what has happened," said Beatrice. "I don't know if I'll ever believe. Oh, of course I know it happened, but how?" She looked into Jack's eyes and asked rhetorically, "Why? Why would he go down to the sea?" They sat in silence.

"It's so unfair, Jack. He was such a decent man." Jack looked at her. She caught the doubt in his eye. "What aren't you telling me?" Jack didn't know how to begin. "Come on," Beatrice prodded. "Out with it."

Quietly he said, "There was a cut on his cheek and his face was swollen."

"Oh god. A gay bashing, do you think?"

"I don't know. Maybe it's not that simple. Let me just say this—a few nights ago I saw him get out of a car with a very young boy."

"Oh Jack—he's gay, he's not—you know."

"I think he was, Beatrice. And this may be totally innocent and totally irrelevant, but I saw a suspicious connection between the man Eugene visits and Garry."

"Garry? What, regarding children—and men?"

"Yes."

"No, Jack, no. You're right—in that there's bound to be a simple innocent explanation. But you're not right about Eugene. Where *is* Garry?" Beatrice asked, suddenly aware of the deserted bar.

"I've no idea."

"There's a drowning in front of *Sumbar* and he's not here?"

"I haven't seen him for a while."

She sat considering. "Oh, Eugene was gay—I have no problem with that, but that doesn't make him a child …" She couldn't bring herself to complete the sentence. "He bought me coffee nearly every day! There were never any signs."

"There wouldn't be. Self protection would rule everything you'd say and do wouldn't it?"

"I still can't believe it. I'm afraid I think the best of people, not the worst."

"Don't the majority of us?"

*

When Captain Choniburshakanari had settled in the back of the police car, he phoned the most senior doctor attached to the local hospital and got him out of bed. Now they stood over Eugene.

"Cause of death, doctor?"

"Drowning, though there are those bruises and his chest indicates two cracked ribs."

"But he *died* from drowning?"

"In the end, yes, though the assault could have contributed."

"Doctor, how is Wendy?" asked Choni. "She finished school yet?"

"Wendy—my daughter? She's now in second year at university."

"Ahh, they grow up so quickly. Medicine?"

"But naturally."

"Here in Bangkok?"

"No. Melbourne."

Captain Choni turned to the doctor. "Melbourne? That is a long way to go to visit her. I'm sure your wife must miss her."

"Of course, as all mothers miss their children."

Choni took out the packet of money still in the envelope from inside his white slacks. "Go visit her—a surprise visit. You see, there are going to be foreign press here wanting to see your death certificate, wanting to interview you. The Australian Media will be asking questions, picking over our quiet little *Sumbeckarnawan*. Who wants that? Therefore, we need all of those around us to be as calm as possible—until here in Thailand some other poor soul dances upon their stage of sensationalism."

The doctor stared back at the police captain, taking in all he had said.

"I do not want to appear unco-operative in saying 'no' to them, 'no' to their request to interview our esteemed doctor. I don't want to see your face in the newspapers, them doubting your findings. It is better for *me* if there are no loose ends, no dangling questions and better for *you*, if you were in Melbourne having lunch with your daughter, watching that silly football game. So, the cause of death is drowning—simple drowning—water in the lungs—no other complications. Yes?" Captain Choniburshakanari took out the remainder of the money from his other pocket and put it into the envelope.

The doctor sighed, "Yes."

"Excellent. Sign the death certificate."

*

The police car pulled up in front of the white whorehouse down by the pier. The Madam was surprised to see Captain Choni walk in. "I paid the rent only this week!"

192

"It's not that. Official business," Choni said. "You have a woman from the south. I'm not interested in her, rather the Englishman she's with. Where do they live?"

Chapter 29

Captain Choni had managed to get home and find a few hours sleep. Now awake, he'd changed into a fresh police uniform and was standing before the mirror. Today he wished to have every piece of braid in perfect alignment. Today he would reset his world to right.

I will interview those two Australians, listen to what they wish to tell me, suffer their complaints about the incompetency of the Thai police force, smile as they wish to inform me how things are done better in their country and bid them farewell to fly home the body of their friend. All going well, by the end of the day Sumbeckarnawan will once again be a care-free haven for tourists and expats and all those who like to spend and make money.

His wife looked at him. "You are still very handsome, my darling."

He smiled lovingly at her. "And you are as beautiful as the day I first saw you in my father's rice paddy."

Choni was in his office around nine. From home he'd called his Translation Officer. He didn't want a misunderstanding during the interview and, in moments like these, he knew it is best to have a witness at hand.

*

Beatrice and Jack were a few minutes early. She fidgeted while waiting, sitting with Jack in the foyer of the police station. Inside his office, Captain Choni had had enough of waiting. *Let us begin*, he said to the translator, as he pushed back his chair, and walked around his desk to open his office door.

"Come in please." Beatrice and Jack stood. Captain Choni looked at Jack. "You are her husband? Her lover?"

"You know I'm not."

"Then please sit. Wait. She will return in one piece."

"I would never have thought otherwise, Captain."

The two men held each other's eye.

The outside door opened and a large man barged in. Choni was taken by surprise at the sudden bravado of his entrance. Jack recognised him immediately.

"I've been asked by the Australian embassy in Bangkok to speak with a ..." The man consulted a piece of paper he held in his hand. "Police Captain Chon-i-bur-shak-an-ar-i."

"You are; that me," explained Choni in deliberately broken English.

"A tragic event, Captain." The police captain seemed not to comprehend. The large man explained, "On the sand. Last night."

Jack wondered, *How the hell do you know?*

Captain Choni whispered so only Beatrice and Jack could hear. "Miss Young would you mind waiting? My apologies." Then louder to the large man he said, "Sir—please." He indicated his open office door. Choni followed the big man in. The door was shut behind them.

"Jack, how did the police captain know my name was 'Young'?"

*

Captain Choniburshakanari placed a straight backed wooden chair in front of his desk then walked behind it and sat. He spoke to his translator.

"Police Captain Choniburshakanari would like you to sit, please, sir," the translator said, indicating the straight backed wooden chair. He took a second chair and sat to the side of his captain.

After the large man had balanced himself over the chair, audibly bent his knees and sat, Captain Choni leant forward. "How—I—help?"

"I believe a man drowned on your beach, last night?"

Choni glanced at his translator, who said, "That is correct."

"An Australian man, people tell me. I am Australian and I received a phone call from the Australian embassy this morning..."

Choni spoke in Thai.

"Sorry to interrupt," said the translator, "But the captain asks 'who are you'?"

"I am the Australian senator—retired—Brighton St. James," he answered, with weight upon his name as if it were universally known.

"The captain reminds you that you are in the Kingdom of Thailand—Australian titles mean nothing here."

"Yes—but of course—that is understood," agreed Brighton St. James, backing down a little from his blustering opening.

"The captain asks—Australian embassy telephone you—on a Sunday—before 9 am?"

"That is correct," Brighton St. James lied.

Choni opened his arms in a friendly greeting and spoke Thai.

The translator said, "The captain says that it is wonderful to see the wheels of international relations operating so smoothly here in our beloved kingdom. You work for the embassy?"

"No, not as such. But I have friends there. Back in Australia, during my time in office, I made many beneficial ties between my country and yours—trade, international relations. Those ties are still in place today. Let me add that I am often here in your beautiful land as my second wife is Thai and we visit and stay with her brother in a house up in the hills. The embassy knew I was in town and asked me to drop by to see what assistance could be offered—what the current situation is—you know, to offer help with this dead Australian."

Captain Choni leant back in his chair, nodding sagely as the translator took him through what had been said. He spoke in Thai and handed a small file to the translator who read from it.

"The man is Eugene Archibald Parry—63 years of age. A Perth man. The captain says he was a regular visitor to Thailand, here in *Sumbeach.* In particular, Captain Choni asks: Did you know him, senator?"

"No, never met him."

Choni spoke again, the translator informing the Australian, "The body is currently in our hospital here. The captain was going to call the Australian embassy on Monday. He says someone is very efficient at your end. Then again we are a small village here and word spreads quickly."

"Excuse—please." Choni stood suddenly and left the office, shutting the door behind him. He walked to Beatrice and Jack and leant forward putting his head between theirs. He whispered, "Did either of you phone your embassy this morning or last night?"

Jack and Beatrice exchanged glances. "No," they whispered.

"Are there any other Australians staying down at *Sumbar*?"

"No," replied Jack.

196

"Were you the only two Australians at Garry's birthday party last night?"

"Yes."

"Thank you." He turned to go.

"Captain," began Jack, "Beatrice is worried about getting Eugene's body home. Are you able to assist in that? Are you able to notify the relevant authorities?"

Captain Choni didn't reply. Again he held Jack's eye. "Will you be making an official complaint if I fail to act to your standards, Mister Featherstone?"

"No. Why should I? I'm not planning on making any complaints."

"Captain," interrupted Beatrice, "Jack was asking for me. I have no idea what to do next."

Choni studied them both. "What you do next, Miss Young, is sit here and wait. And what you do Mister Featherstone is not ask questions but likewise wait—for the outcome."

Captain Choni returned to his office. He spoke rapidly. The translator straightened in his chair.

"Mister James ..."

"St James," the Australian corrected.

The translator glanced to Captain Choni who nodded that he should continue. "Ah, yes. You said you believed the man has drowned. How do you know that?"

"Rumours, wild chatter. In an expat community tales spread rapidly. I'm told he was found face down in the ocean."

"Yes, that is correct."

"Then obviously, to my way of thinking, that means he drowned."

The translator looked at Choni. Choni glanced at Brighton St James and then spoke rapidly to the translator before indicating to him he should go on.

The translator spoke. "There is a woman outside who feels responsible for flying the body home. She fears that she is completely out of her depth. She has no idea what to do. Now as you are authorised to ..."

"I didn't say 'authorise', Captain." He looked at Choni, then back to the translator. "Please tell him of the distinction."

Choni spoke. The translator said, "The captain is sure she would like the Australian embassy to handle all repatriation etc."

Choni held up his hand to stop the Australian interrupting and spoke to his Translating Officer.

"The captain said—if there are any unforeseen expenses I'm sure that your tightly knit expat community could see their way clear to cover those. Yes?"

"Ah—well—yes," said the Australian ex-senator.

Captain Choni sat back, acting a sense of relief.

"So, it was death by drowning?" the ex-senator confirmed, the interview's tension beginning to dissipate.

Captain Choni spoke. The translator said, "Yes. That is what the death certificate will say."

"That is a relief. You know how it is when a citizen dies in a foreign country, the journalists desperate for a story all fly in—start beating up the most minor of details—getting everyone agitated. Thank goodness they only seem to have a concentration span of twenty-four hours before they rush off to the next hot-spot." He stood. "I thank you for your time, Captain, and the respect you have shown me. I am after all merely a concerned Australian citizen, not some string puller."

Choni looked at the translator, who asked, "String puller?"

"Yes. Someone who pulls the correct strings to get the right result. In English we call such a person, a Puppet Master."

Choni laughed appreciatively when told the Thai translation.

"Captain Choni says that is very insightful of you, sir."

As the large man turned to go, Captain Choni spoke. The translator said, "The lady outside has had a traumatic experience. Captain Choni asked you to talk to your embassy, get this body, when it is officially released, home to Perth."

"Yes, of course, Captain."

Choni spoke again, this time in English, "Mister James, do you know Garry, expat who owns *Sumbar*?"

"*Sumbar*?"

"Yes, a bar and small hotel on beach."

"Oh, with my fair skin I never go anywhere near the beach, Captain."

"Thank you, Mister James."

The Australian ex-senator nodded. "Thank you, Captain." He turned and walked out of the office, and without looking at Jack and Beatrice, out of the station. *The captain suspects nothing, knows nothing,* he reasoned, beginning to smile.

The translator left Choni's office, leaving the police captain to muse, *Puppet Master? A string can be pulled in two directions.*

In the front office, Jack stood looking through the window. Outside the ex-senator climbed into the rear seat of the dark sedan and drove off.

By the time Jack sat again, Captain Choni had joined him and Beatrice. "Good news. The Australian embassy is handling everything. That gentleman will be handling any out of pocket expenses. The matter is completely out of your hands, Madame. Go and enjoy the rest of your holiday."

"You of course know," began Jack, "because you know everything in this town—that, that man—that ex-senator … getting into that car …"

"Mister Featherstone, all through our life we walk a fine line. Here, I may, perhaps, walk one of the finest of them all. Do not push me over it. I will step over it in my own good time." Jack said nothing, not understanding. "Madame, please wait here, I wish to speak to Mr Featherstone alone. Do not worry. He will return in one undamaged piece."

He looked at Jack once more and considered something. "Madame, don't wait. Go enjoy your holiday. Do not worry. Mister Featherstone is free to leave whenever he chooses."

Beatrice stood. "Thank you, Captain." She smiled warily at Jack and left.

Jack followed the captain into his office.

*

Sunny stood in the small shadows generated by the buildings opposite the police station. He didn't want to bump into Werner so he stayed down the far end of the street. He saw the large Australian, Eugene's friend, go in.

Shit! That's the car from last night, he realised. *The one Garry got into.*

After a while he saw the large Australian come out and the sedan drive away. Soon after he was again surprised to see Beatrice emerge and cross directly over and into *Brauhaus Helmut*.

Uncertainty held Sunny back. He'd take a step forward then check himself. Twenty minutes later he was surprised yet again when Jack walked out of the police station. *What is going on?* Overcoming his trepidation, Sunny crossed the street.

"Somsak! Come into my office," said Captain Choni. "I didn't expect you so soon. I want to talk to you about *Sumbar*."

"Later—not now—sir." Sunny could not sit, he paced. "I could not sleep last night." Then he stopped and whispered, "I know who killed Aussie Gene."

"Aussie Gene died from drowning," said Captain Choni.

"Maybe—but I know who beat him up beforehand."

Captain Choni sat back in the chair. "Go on."

"Donny-Three."

"Sunny, you're talking in riddles. 'Aussie Gene'; 'Donny-Three'."

"Donny-Three is the son of an American golfer—Donald Jnr—probably staying at *L'Hotel Majestique*."

"Sunny, the official death certificate will say 'death by drowning'. I cannot tamper with the findings of a highly respected doctor."

Sunny nodded, understanding. "Aussie Gene's ghost needs to be laid to rest. I do not want him, every night when I lock up *Sumbar*, waving to me from the bushes. Donny-Three needs to be punished."

"My hands are tied," explained the captain. "There is no evidence, only your word against his."

Sunny went to go then turned. "That dark car outside, the fat man got into—it took Garry away last night."

Did it? thought Choni, surprised. *Yes,* he mused, slowly nodding, realising. *Garry has made use of his special clients.*

"Captain Choni, Aussie Gene was fucking a boy. I saw. Donny-Three went crazy, smashing into him with his fists."

"Somsak!" reprimanded the police captain. "It was death by drowning. You must let me do my job. Go back to *Sumbar*, become rich and watch your niece grow into a beautiful woman."

Become rich? thought Sunny. *Watch my niece grow up? What does he mean?*

"Somsak, we'll talk about *Sumbar* tomorrow. Today I have other important business at hand."

Does Choni know Garry is not coming back? "Donny-Three just can't get away, can he? He killed." Sunny paused, weighing up whether to tell or not. He blurted out, "Donny-Three's smuggling drugs to the United States."

Choni heard, but made no comment. He escorted Sunny to the door and watched him leave.

Special clients, echoed in Choni's head. *I used to think I knew everything that was going on among the expats. Perhaps it would be best, when Garry returns, he only stays for a month before the British Embassy receives an anonymous phone call as to his true identity.*

Chapter 30

The Orchid Palace Restaurant sits on the top floor of *L'Hotel Majestique*. From outside on its southern balcony, one can see over the giant Buddha at the end of the sweeping bay. From the outside northern balcony, one can almost, on a clear day, see the outskirts of Bangkok. Jack had heard the beer was very cold and the Thai curries were very hot. He was looking forward to lunch.

An immaculately dressed, flawlessly made-up waitress bowed her head. "*Sawadee.*"

Jack bowed in return. He explained that he was expecting someone. She led him to a table for two.

"While you wait—you like beer?" she asked.

"Yes, please. Singha." The vision of Asian beauty moved off.

Jack was prepared to sit and drink for thirty minutes before ordering his lunch. *If she's not here in thirty minutes, then she never will be.* He decided he was a fool to think she'd take up his hurried offer that had morphed into a luncheon invitation courtesy of Olivia. *Ah well, add me to the list of disappointed people who spent this past week at Sumbeach.*

The waitress placed a tall thin frosted glass in front of him. From her tray she took a bottle of beer, and carefully poured it, tilting the glass with the bottle neck and easing it back upright as the final contents flowed and a perfect head formed.

"Wow," said Jack, as he watched, impressed with her control. "Excellent. Thank you so much." The waitress placed the empty bottle back onto her small delivery tray and bowed her head.

He glanced up expectantly, hearing the elevator open. Strangers emerged and were shown to their table. He turned his attention once more to his beer, appreciating its chilled temperature.

At regular intervals during the next five minutes he checked his watch and sipped his beer. Having had enough of nervously sitting there waiting, he left his table, stepped out into the heat of the southern balcony and looked over *Sumbar,* so tiny down below. He couldn't quite believe all that had happened this past week. He knew he'd never forget last night, sitting in the sand next to Eugene, nor this morning's interview with Captain Choni. Standing on the balcony, losing time, the heat warming him, his thoughts drifted back to Amelia.

"Don't throw yourself off. Life is too short to end it halfway."

Jack turned. Amelia was dressed in a brightly patterned full length wrap around sarong, her blonde hair out, the epitome of Eastern adorned Western beauty.

"You came," he said, with surprise and relief.

"It was an offer—rather a set up—too good to refuse."

Jack held the door for her and they stepped back into the air-conditioned restaurant. Amelia ordered a white wine.

"No umbrella drink?" Jack asked, smiling.

"No. I never want to see another ever again." Amelia cleared her throat. "I have to leave at three. There's a car booked to take Olivia and me to Bangkok Airport at four. I still have to finish packing. I've bought too many souvenirs— too many clothes."

The waitress placed Amelia's wine before her.

"Cheers," said Jack. Amelia and he clinked glasses.

"You look worried. Is something the matter? Bad news from home?"

"You haven't heard about last night?"

"No. What happened last night?"

Jack told her about Eugene. "You don't seem too surprised."

"I didn't know the man."

"I meant at learning the news—a drowning."

Amelia leant in. "No, that type of news hardly affects me. I have a confession to make. Both Olivia and I are policewomen from Scotland Yard."

"Right, that explains it. Should I be worried?" smiled Jack.

Amelia smiled back. "Olivia and I were here to find someone from back home hiding here in amongst the expat community."

"And you found him?"

"I can't say. If I told you, I'd have to kill you." She smiled, sipping her wine. "So, you still want to have lunch with a policewoman?"

"Doesn't worry me. I've nothing to hide. Are you really Olivia's stepmother?"

"No, that was a ruse."

"Are you married?"

"No."

"Involved with someone?"

"No."

"What are those insipid Englishmen thinking?"

She laughed. "The only men I find interesting, I tend to arrest." Jack laughed with her. "It didn't take you long to ask your questions. You Australians are forward, aren't you."

"Forward? No—to tell the truth I'm quivering in my sandals. I've no control over my tongue and I'm not responsible for what pours out."

"I try to avoid Australians," admitted Amelia. "Well, men." *Where had that come from?*

"A bad experience with one?"

"No, nothing like that. To be honest, I've no idea why. An optometrist in town here, a few days ago, basically said that I was a racist for believing in and living in fear of cultural cliches. She was most astute. I've never thought of myself as a racist. I was a little confronted by it."

"And this lunch is to prove that you're not adverse to Australian men after all?"

The waitress placed large menus before them. Jack studied his menu in silence, his eyes carefully picking their way over the various Thai curries.

Amelia pretended to read, concerned with how easy it had been to admit her thoughts to this stranger, to admit something as sensitive as prejudice. Her eyes stayed on Jack. The detective liked what she assessed, particularly the way he smiled at the waitress, with no sense of sexist condescension.

"The Massaman Lamb Curry sounds nice," said Jack, eyes on the menu.

"Ah—we'll have two."

"Two?"

"Sorry, I was miles away. You choose for me. Left alone, I'd search the menu for scotch egg and chips."

"Yuk," murmured Jack, his eyes returning to the menu as her eyes remained on him.

Have lunch, she thought, *enjoy it and then fly home to England. Vacation over.*

"Satay chicken?"

"Oh, yes, fine," agreed Amelia, without consideration.

Jack caught the waitress' eye and ordered. She bowed again and moved off.

"I can see why so many of you Western men fall for Thai women. They are exceedingly beautiful."

"Mmm," muttered Jack, *not half as beautiful as you.* He sat back. "Sorry, I've lost my train of thought."

"It'll come back to you."

"Ah, yes I was asking …"

"I *was* married—to the most wonderful man. He was shot, killed in the line of duty. To be honest I've never got over it."

Jack looked at her. "Have you thought about trying?" he asked gently.

"I've come across no reason to try. You know when you're totally in sync with someone—lust, love, respect, friendship, companionship. Well, that's how it was for Mark and me. He died and the next day arrived and the day after that, and before long I'm raising a glass in memory to the first anniversary and then the second and today—I'm not lying—today is the twentieth anniversary." She stopped and stared off to the side. "I just miss him. I don't need him anymore, I just miss him."

Jack passed his unused serviette to her. She took it, dabbing her eyes. "Sorry." She looked at him. "Wow! Where'd that spring from? I should not have unloaded that upon you."

"That's okay. We're a great pair—you and I. Five years ago I lost my wife to cancer and I feel the same way—I just miss her."

The curry and satay arrived. Jack placed two sticks onto Amelia's plate. They ate in silence.

Amelia put down her fork. "What the hell, I'd like another glass of wine."

Jack waved to the waitress and indicated their empty glasses. "What are you doing to me?" Amelia asked. "First you bring me to tears and then you drive me to drink."

"Shh, not so loud. Every woman in the place will want me to do it."

"You hope so," quipped Amelia, laughing.

"You know that birthday party last night?" Jack asked.

"Yes, of course. I wasn't so drunk I'd have forgotten it."

"No, I didn't mean that. It's just that birthday boy Garry has disappeared."

"What?" Amelia asked sitting forward in her chair. "*Disappeared?*"

"It must have been a savage wake-up call Garry experienced."

"Wake-up call? What do you mean?"

"Perhaps he simply couldn't cope with turning forty! Either that or he's simply cleared out. He's not around the bar this morning. Sunny has no idea where he is. Mai, his wife, is in tears. Did you see anything last night that would suggest he'd take off?"

"No, nothing," replied Amelia automatically, wondering if in any way she or Olivia had given Garry any inkling of their recognition of him. She was sure they hadn't. *A tip-off? If so, from whom?* She covered her thoughts, saying, "A drowning, a disappearance—I thought *Sumbeach* was party central."

"I'm afraid there's an underbelly about the place."

"What do you mean?"

"I've no proof of anything and I'm only passing through, but it's a pity you can't investigate."

"*Me?* I'm a foreign cop."

"Yes, I know that. It's just that some things make my skin crawl."

"Jack, you'd better explain."

Leaning in Jack lowered his voice. "One night, in the lot behind *Sumbar*, I saw a young boy get out of a car with money, and run away past me. A priest of all people followed him out of the car."

"A priest? A monk, you mean?"

"No, an English priest, bald with red hair. I also saw him in the playground of an orphanage in town."

Father Aloysius, thought Amelia. "So, this underbelly?" she prompted.

"I suspect there's a paedophile ring operating out of, or around, *Sumbar*. The empty lot at the back is used as a pick-up and drop off area. Wads of cash are passed over the bar to Garry to turn a blind eye."

Amelia thought on that. "Well, Jack, it's best to let the Thai police deal with that," she said, settling back in her chair.

"Yes. Captain Choni had no idea."

"Captain Choni?"

"The police captain. He's not as all-knowing as he thinks he is."

"How'd you meet him?"

"I had an interview with him this morning about the drowned man."

"Oh." Amelia asked no further questions. She ate. *The least I talk about Choni, the better.* She changed the subject. "Jack, I've never said anything like that before—about Mark, about my prejudice—to anyone. I apologise. I've always been the stoic Amelia. Seriously—what have you done to me?"

"Me? Nothing. I was just sitting here conversing, listening."

"Listening," she echoed. *How many men have ever really listened to me?* She smiled and leant in towards him. "Listen, I know you want to see me again, but be realistic. You live in Sydney and I live in London. How's that ever going to work?"

"A couple of weeks back I sold my business. I'm out of Australia—adrift. I'll be in Paris by next Friday. What are you doing next weekend?"

"What?" asked back Amelia, taken by the directness of the question. "Spend the weekend in Paris with a total stranger?"

"Hardly a stranger—I did bring you to tears."

Amelia looked at him and laughed. "Eat your curry before it gets cold."

"And the week after that I'll be on the Riviera," Jack added.

She looked unbelieving at him. He held her gaze and smiling, chewed a satay stick.

"Do you always have that teasing glint in your eye?" Amelia asked with a touch of sly curiosity.

"What glint? From where I'm looking, I can't see it."

"No, of course you can't. Eat your curry."

*

"Three glasses of wine is quite enough," Amelia said, looking at her drained glass.

"Sleep in the car on the way to the airport."

"I'd prefer to sleep on the flight. Oh, it's going to be cold when I get back."

The elevator door opened and Jack looked up.

"That's Olivia, isn't it, come to get me?" Amelia glanced at her watch, "Oh dear. Sorry, Olivia," she said, half turning in her chair. "Sorry, we were just finishing up."

Olivia kept her distance. "Ma'am, it's time we were going," she said with a formality she'd not used since leaving Heathrow.

"Oh, the police are back on duty. Yes, of course." Amelia stood. "Jack, it's been wonderful."

Jack stood and reached for his business card. "My email address is on there if you ever want to write and let me know how you're getting on—or just to say hello."

She looked at it. "You're an architect?"

"I told you that three days ago," whispered Olivia. "I knew you weren't listening." She extended her hand. "Jack, it's been a pleasure meeting you. All the best in Paris and beyond."

"Yes, thank you Olivia. All the best for you as well."

"Goodbye." Amelia shook Jack's hand and walked from the restaurant with Olivia to the elevator. The door opened; they stepped in; the door closed.

Jack sat back in his chair. *Wow. I've met the second woman I'd love to spend the rest of my life with and she's walked out of my life, just like—that.* He clicked his fingers.

The waitress walked towards him.

"No, sorry, I wasn't calling you," apologised Jack "I'd never get your attention like that. Sorry. But, what the hell, you're only young once. Yes, why not, I'll have one for the road—may as well drown my happiness."

She took the empty beer glass and headed towards the bar. Jack stood and walked over to the southern window. He was the only customer in the restaurant now. He hadn't noticed everyone else leave. He recalled the first time he saw Amelia, when he was standing on the footpath with Werner and she got out of the taxi in front of the police station. She'd taken his breath away then. He wished he'd taken a photo of her sitting opposite him at lunch.

A hand touched his shoulder. He turned.

"Next Friday 4pm, in Paris, along from *Gare St Lazare* there is a church—*Estienne* something or other. Over on your right between the main boulevard and the side-street is a cafe. Sit at an outside table."

"What?" A smile covered his face. "That's all? What about the Riviera?"

"Don't push your luck."

Amelia hurried off. Jack called after her, "Pack your swimsuit!"

Chapter 31

The transit van driver lifted Amelia and Olivia's luggage into the back of his vehicle as the two women climbed into the air-conditioned comfort. Olivia hadn't said a word since checking out, giving Amelia time and space to digest her confused thoughts.

Emerging from the revolving door came the Americans, the younger struggling with the bag of golf clubs.

"Hey! Is this the van to the airport?" asked Donald Randalson Jnr.

"Yes, sir," said the driver. "You have voucher?"

"Donny-Three, show the man the booking you made on the internet."

Donny-Three reaching for his mobile allowed the bag of golf clubs to slip from his grip.

"Easy! Easy!" chastised his father. The son showed the driver the screen of his mobile phone and the driver ticked a receipt number he had on a piece of paper.

"All good, thank you, sirs," he said. "Please—go in. Air-con inside."

"Take this will ya, Buddy!" Donald Randalson Jnr passed the driver his over-laden suitcase. "Donny-Three give the man my golf clubs. Make sure he puts them underneath." He climbed in. "Well hello, ladies. We meet again." He tossed his Stetson onto the vacant seat next to him.

"Hello", said Olivia. "Sink a few birdies this week?"

"Sure did—the best kind. What a place—Thailand. I'm gonna sure as hell miss it."

Outside, Donny-Three heard his name called. He turned; it was Maggie.

"I came to say goodbye," she said, approaching hesitantly. "Look—Donny—thank you." She touched the gold necklace. "Safe trip. I just wanted to say—you know—I really like you. I know I was a one-night stand—well, three nights actually—but …"

"Wanna fly to Galveston next year?" Donny-Three asked quietly.

"I can't afford to—there are no cheap charters to Texas."

"Hell, he'll pay."

"I think your father will object to paying for me to fly from England." She kissed and turned abruptly, walking off, not wanting to look back, not wanting him to see she shed a tear. Donny-Three climbed into the van and sat separately to his father.

The transit van bounced over the gutter and onto the street. "Woh there driver," exclaimed Donald Jnr. "This ain't the old wild west and I ain't ridin' shot gun up top." Donald Randalson Jnr laughed.

Amelia hoped it wasn't going to be like this for the three and a half hours to Bangkok Airport. She let her thoughts drift back to Jack. Halfway to Bangkok she leant over to Olivia and whispered, "Jack won't leave me alone. What is it about Australian men?"

Olivia looked at her. "Where would you like me to start?"

*

"Mister Jack—there no food tonight," explained Sunny, as Jack walked into the bar. "Mai upset—sick. Garry still gone!"

"Sunny, did he say where he was going?"

"No, Mister Jack."

"There's no need for food. I've had my fill at lunch."

"Care to join me in the pool?" asked Beatrice, the only other customer in the bar, was sitting down the end, nursing a lemonade, silhouetted by the sea.

"No Werner tonight?" asked Jack.

"Sunday night. I thought I'd have a night off—see if I really miss him."

"And?"

"Sure do. We don't really *know* people, do we?" she asked.

"Eugene?"

"Mmm. I worked with him all that time; had coffee most mornings with him; trusted him enough to come to Thailand with him; and yet I really know nothing about him. I know he's English—only because of his accent—and then I couldn't say if that was real or not. I have no idea where he grew up, where he went to school. I assume he had a university degree." She looked directly into Jack's eyes. "The more I think of it, the more I realise that he never really said anything of importance to me."

"The life he lived needed guarding."

"How can someone do that to a child?"

Jack was unable to answer that. The very thought turned his stomach.

"What a week," Beatrice went on. "I've found a lover; found a friend; and lost a—what? How would I describe him?" She held the thought a moment. "Jack, give me your email address—if it works out with Werner, I'll come back here next year when he has his Uni semester break. I'll let you know how things turn out if you like."

"Yes, I would like that." He took a card from his wallet.

Beatrice glanced at it. "And if you find Amelia, send me an email."

"If I find Amelia, what makes you think I'll be putting my hands anywhere near a computer?"

*

The transit van swung around the long right hand turn into the departure terminal at Bangkok Airport. The bright afternoon's sunshine now well gone. The driver placed all their bags on the busy footpath.

"Ladies, you go here—plane to London. Gentlemen you go down there—plane to USA. *Khob Kuhn Khrup.*"

"Well goodbye, safe flight," said Amelia and Olivia to the Americans as they picked up their bag.

Donald Jnr said pointedly to Olivia, "Anytime you're in the States, honey, you look me up, you hear?"

"Will do!" said Olivia and both women walked off, dragging their suitcases.

Donny-Three looked at his father. "What you invite her for? She's got a dose of the clap!"

"How the hell you know that?"

Donny-Three tossed his father's golf clubs over his shoulder and walked down to the self opening doors. He stopped before them and turned to his father. "You take them. They're getting heavy," he said as he thrust the clubs into his father's arms.

"You gotta build up your muscles, son. You should've played golf, instead of sleeping in that hotel room all day. You sure wasted your time in Thailand."

They walked inside and fronted the departure desk labelled 'First Class'. As Donald Jnr gave their names at the check-in counter, two uniformed Thais

210

approached. "Excuse me gentlemen, do you mind stepping over here for a moment?"

*

Jack knocked on Beatrice's door. "Wanna come up to Werner's for breakfast?"

The door immediately swung open. "I'm ahead of you." She emerged dressed and pulled shut her door.

They walked the beach. "I don't think I'll ever forget this strip of sand. Jack, I've been thinking about Eugene."

"Of course. So have I."

"Oh, I mean, not his death. Rather why he asked me to come."

"And?"

"He'd been here many times before so his reason to have me as a smoke screen to his homosexuality doesn't make sense. So if it hadn't bothered him before, why this time?"

Jack let Beatrice speak.

"We'd become friends. He'd buy me morning coffees, sometimes even lunch. He'd allow me to talk, to dream, to confess. He always listened and I always talked. You know, I think he wanted to simply give me a holiday, get me away from my closeted life and show me a portion of the world. I think it's just that simple. Old fashioned kindness."

They turned towards *Sumbeach* Town. Beatrice added, "I'm never going to forget that funny little sign with its painted arrow."

As they approached *Brauhaus Helmut*, Werner waved.

"I missed you last night!" said Werner as he put his arms around her.

"Me? You missed me?" asked Jack.

"Nein!" declared Werner adamantly.

Beatrice laughed and kissed him.

Jack interrupted their embrace. "Beatrice, order me an orange juice and the fabulous bacon and egg roll. I'm going to buy the paper."

Helmut approached from the kitchen "Werner! You cannot serve the customers with a woman in your arms."

"I know, Papa, but she insisted it was on the menu. Hugs and Kisses—50 baht!"

211

Beatrice kissed his father's cheek. "Helmut, you've got to keep the customer satisfied!"

*

Jack was finishing his coffee when he finally unfolded his paper. He read: *Airport: American Detained.*

Jack called to Beatrice and Werner. "Listen to this! *An American business man, Donald Randalson Jnr, was detained and his luggage searched last night at Bangkok Airport. It is alleged that a large amount of marijuana was found in the base of his golf clubs.* I had drinks with this guy. He was at Garry's party."

"Was he the one who fought over the Thai woman on the beach?" asked Werner.

"That's the one!"

"Read on!" insisted Beatrice.

"*I've been set up! There were two English women travelling with my son and me—those sweet smiling bitches—devils in disguise—have set me up.* There's a quote here, from the son, Donald Randalson III."

"Well, read it," said Beatrice.

"*There's been a big mistake. My father does not do drugs. No one in our family does. It is abhorrent to us. We are leading lights in our church community back home in Galveston. I'll be buying the best lawyer I can find as soon as I get home tonight! My poor mother has had her heart broken! What will she do if her husband is locked up for years in a foreign country? My father is not that young. He could die in prison!*"

Chapter 32

"Cathy! I'm home! Is Amelia still here?"

"Yes! We're in the living room. Pour your own wine."

"Pour my own?" McPherson called back. "Amelia, Cathy's standards are slipping!"

The two women laughed.

"So, Amelia," began McPherson, sitting opposite them in his favourite lounge chair, "a most interesting outcome."

"Yes, the irony is not lost on me."

"I send you out there to find one suspect and you come home with the identity of another."

"Yes; however, Harold Keith Brown, aka Garry Sutherland, has probably by now skipped Thailand. I fear he was long gone by the time I flew out."

"Yes, a pity that has so far proven fruitless. Still, it is commendable you and Olivia managed to find him at all. So, regarding this Father Aloysius from Canterbury—tomorrow we'll start an investigation into him."

"He may only practise his perverted ways over there."

"Yes, perhaps, but a leopard overseas may still be a leopard at home. No matter what, he'll be on our watch-list."

"I'll serve the dinner," said Cathy. "Excuse me."

"Don't worry, Amelia, we'll find Harold Keith Brown. Someday, somewhere. Now we definitely know he's in Thailand we'll make it official and official in the surrounding countries as well. At that level, petty corruption won't protect him. Again, you've done well. And you've managed a suntan and you don't seem to be too alcohol affected."

"Davey, I'd like to go up to Newcastle and see the woman who spotted him in the first place. You know, just to tell her and her sister first hand they were correct and I have identified him. That way they won't think we're entirely useless."

"Yes, of course. So, no trouble with the Thai police?"

"No. Though at first I had reason to believe the local captain was another cliché ridden corrupt cop. Now, I'm not so sure. He didn't openly interfere. He was merely curious about what we were getting up to. Then again I'd have done the same."

"Yes, I'm sure you would have."

"It's a feeling I have, that's all. Maybe not all things are black and white. Thailand …" She left that thought dangle.

"Go on," prompted Davey.

"I've had a reappraisal of things, Davey. I'm too set in my ways—my thoughts, my beliefs, my prejudices. This trip has unsettled me."

"You're not having second thoughts about being a cop, are you?"

"No. Never. It's just …" She shrugged not knowing what to say further.

ACC McPherson let his old friend sit like that for a while, ruminating. He cleared his throat, bringing her back to the present. "I've just come from debriefing Olivia and her statements fully support yours; however, one question remains."

"Really?" asked Amelia, concerned. "One question? What's that?"

"Who is this mystery man?"

Amelia laughed. "There's no mystery man, Davey."

"So, I don't need to check with Interpol for a Jack Featherstone?"

"No! Olivia's got a big mouth."

"She's—we're all …"

"I've made up my mind, the matter is closed. It's personal, after all, is it not?"

"Dinner's ready!" called Cathy.

The two old friends headed to the dining table.

When they were seated and Amelia started to eat, Cathy said, "While you've got your mouth full and can't argue back, I've asked Davey to call person to person the Commissioner of the New South Wales Police."

"What!" exclaimed Amelia trying not to choke.

"Check out this Jack Featherstone for you."

"Cathy!" Amelia swallowed. "Cathy, Davey, sometimes I never know if you two are joking or not. There's no chance. It's realistically impossible. He's a total stranger. No one in their right mind falls for a total stranger and runs off with him."

"I've checked," said Davey. "You've got plenty of leave due."

"Davey! Tomorrow, I've a train to catch to Newcastle."

*

Jack tried to sleep; however, only sporadic dozes came his way. He was six hours from Paris and still his meeting with Police Captain Choniburshakanari wouldn't leave him.

"Come in, sit," the captain had said courteously, sitting behind his desk, Jack in front. "For a man who's not involved with Beatrice Young, you seem to be concerned for her."

"A failing of mine," admitted Jack. "I try to look out for others before myself."

Choni considered that for a moment before responding. "Everyone thinks I know everything there is to know about what goes on in *Sumbeach*. I thought I did, but now I know I do not. I have been played for a blind fool." He paused. "Why do you look at me like that?"

"Well, self realisation—it is a very fine quality to possess and its admittance is very difficult to share with another person."

Choni leant in. "You are philosopher, Mister Featherstone?"

Jack smiled. Choni held his gaze.

"Sometimes, Mister Featherstone, it is best to have a desired result happen elsewhere. You know, do not shoot the duck in my pond because its death makes too many ripples. People see the disturbance. They come to me and ask: *Why did the duck die? Who killed the duck? Aren't you able to find out?* It is therefore much better the duck is shot in the air, miles from the pond."

"Now *I'm* wondering if *you're* the philosopher."

"Outside there, when you wished to tell me something about that large man and the dark car…" He stopped. "I do not need you publicly telling me what I should know. So, what is it you want to tell me, now, in the strictest confidence?"

Jack weighed up what to say.

Choni spoke. "You can trust me, I'm a policeman." He burst out laughing. "Okay—I will tell you what I suspect. That Australian senator—you know him? He is really a senator?"

"Yes, he was. He's an ex-senator."

"This morning he comes out of nowhere wanting to take charge. Why? It was a drowning. I then ask myself *to cover up something?* The man who drowned, what did he do that I should know about? Last night Garry let slip something. 'Special clients' he said to me. I have been asking myself what are 'special clients'? I now have an idea of what they are. Do you have any idea what Garry meant? Could that senator be a special client? He claims he did not know Garry, but I suspect otherwise."

"He knows Garry. I saw him paying Garry a bar bill though I never saw him drink there."

"As I suspected. Go on."

"All I know is, I saw a young boy get out of that car, the car the senator has just driven away in. And I've seen that car being shared with another boy, an English priest from an orphanage, the cigar smoking Senator and Eugene Parry. You will have to make the connections yourself, Captain."

"The priest with the red hair above his ears but not on the top of his head?"

"Yes, that's the one."

Choni raised his eyebrow and then indicated that Jack should refrain from speaking. From inside his desk drawer he took out a black directory. He turned several pages, found a number and picked up the telephone on his desk. He dialled the number, speaking in Thai. The only words Jack understood were *Father Aloysius*. Choni listened then hung up.

"Father Aloysius left *Sumbeach* two days ago. He's gone home to England. Never mind, one day he will return. He regularly comes here and then I will be keeping a closer eye on that orphanage. Yes, since Garry's slip of the tongue I have begun to suspect many things. Oh, do not worry, believe me, I will, one day, act upon these suspicions. One day, the Australian ex-senator will need a very good lawyer, or a very good PR management firm to cover the fall out. Even if he has friends in high places, perhaps we lowly ones can inflict upon him his just deserts. Legal fees, court costs and international embarrassment. That car in which he drove away, the one you needed to point out to me, do you have its registration?"

"No."

"That is why it is best left up to the police—because we do." He let that sink in. "And we also know where he lives when he is here in *Sumbeckarnawan*. Confession time, Mister Featherstone."

"Believe it or not, I'm neither philosopher nor priest."

"And believe it or not," said Choni, "I'm no sinner." Jack began to smile ruefully. "What is it, Mister Featherstone?"

"Nothing."

"No, please, what are you thinking?"

Jack paused then decided to speak. "Captain, everyone hints of the graft you take."

"Me? Where?"

"Well, that white building down by the pier for example, that whorehouse. People say things."

"I own that white building, Mister Featherstone. I am the landlord. They pay rent, not graft. I did not build it, but the original owners went bankrupt. I saw a business opportunity. Do you not have business opportunities in Australia? You see Mister Featherstone, sometimes a little knowledge can be a very dangerous thing. One ends up drawing the wrong conclusions."

He looked at Jack, and Jack at him. Jack nodded, understanding.

"I have a business arrangement with Garry Sutherland—perfectly legitimate. He came to me, six years ago. He wanted to extend *Sumbar*—add rooms upstairs and a swimming pool out the back. I financed that—for a return. I'm sure in Australia people do this all the time."

"Yes," admitted Jack, "They do."

"Until last night and confirmed by the actions of the large Australian this morning and your own observations, I had no idea Garry was aiding paedophiles. That is most abhorrent to me. It completely changes my opinion of him. My greatest asset and my greatest failure is tunnel vision. I see directly ahead. I do not naturally see the movement, nor hear the noise, off to the side. As a policeman it helps me to cut through. But it also holds me back. So now I will try to make myself observe the peri..." He paused.

"Periphery."

"Yes—periphery. It is where I must position myself for I believe that is where a lot of Western people live; from where they hear their sounds; see their sights; hold their desires; and experience their failings."

He stood and opened his filing cabinet. He took out two glasses and a bottle of Thai whiskey.

"It is not too early?" Choni asked.

"I'm on holiday, Captain."

Choni smiled. "Good. I do not like to drink alone, no matter what the time of day." Choni poured the whiskey. "Last night you said to me: *What you arrest me for—compassion?* No one ever question me like that. Oh, they shout at me, they

217

complain to me, they question my parentage, they compare me to female sexual organ, but no one ever touch the nerve—here." He touched his chest above his heart. "In time all this will be solved, made right. Australian ex-senator Brighton St James of Chelmsford Road, Mount Lawley, Perth, Western Australia, will get his come-uppance. From now on there will be no more child abuse based out of *Sumbar*. Live a long and happy life, Mister Jack Featherstone."

Jack raised his glass. "The same to you, Captain Choniburshakanari."

"Ah—you speak Thai."

The two men laughed.

"Salut."

They clinked glasses.

"To 'compassion'," added Choni.

Chapter 33

The following Friday at 3pm, Jack stood facing *Gare St Lazare*, in Paris. People buzzed by him as he checked his map. He looked about, taking in his bearings then headed off to his right. At the next major intersection he came upon a church and its attached park. He checked his map. *Trinte d'Estienne d'Orves.*

So far, so good, he thought, smiling to himself and putting the map into his back pocket. He turned about, his eyes searching in a long pan. The traffic streamed in front along the boulevard he'd been walking down and over to his left he saw a cafe wedged on top of a Metro entranceway and between a side-street.

I hope this is the cafe Amelia said!

He took a step forward and a motorbike almost hit him. The rider screamed at him.

"Sorry!" he shouted back. *Wow! Don't get killed before you find your dream!* he warned himself.

He waited and crossed at the green pedestrian light, sitting at an outside table, one where he hoped he'd be clearly seen among the people emerging from the station below.

"Monsieur?" asked the waiter.

"*Un biere, s'il vous plait.*"

"*Une,*" corrected the waiter as he walked inside.

Jack knew he was an hour early. *What else do I have to do in Paris apart from wait for a beautiful woman?*

The waiter returned with the beer and placed his docket on a little plate in front of him. He stood a few metres away and took out a cigarette.

Jack looked at his watch. He heard his mother's voice from childhood: *A watched pot never boils.*

Twenty-two minutes later, he ordered a second beer. "*Merci.*"

At 3.45, he ordered a third.

At 4.15, Amelia hadn't arrived. Jack stood and stretched.

The waiter asked him, "*Une femme*? You wait for a woman?"

"*Mais oui.*"

"Yes, we all spend our life waiting for a woman."

At 4.30, Jack looked more carefully at the passing faces. He recognised no one. *I'll stay 'til five. What was I thinking anyway? Once she got back home and back to reality, her normal life would have taken over and she'd have realised that I was a hopeless cause and ...*

And she was there in front of him, laughing, waving. "I made it!" she called out.

Jack stood, hugged her, picked her up and spun her around. The waiter caught his eye and gestured with his hand, *Ooh-la-la!*

"Shouldn't we have our first kiss?" asked Amelia.

"I thought Olivia gave me that."

"That was her trying to make me jealous."

He kissed her. She kissed him. They both kissed each other. They finally let go. A crowd of onlookers broke into applause. Jack and Amelia laughed with embarrassment and bowed.

"After all, it is Paris," commented Jack.

They sat. They held hands across the table.

"So, are you here for the weekend—or possibly the week?" asked Jack.

"Let me put it this way: I packed my new swimsuit!"

Made in the USA
Middletown, DE
15 September 2024

60961395R00124